Dear Reader,

It's hard to believe that the Signature Select program is one year old—with seventy-two books already published by top Harlequin and Silhouette authors.

What an exciting and varied lineup we have in the year ahead! In the first quarter of the year, the Signature Spotlight program offers three very different reading experiences. Popular author Marie Ferrarella, well-known for her warm family-centered romances, has gone in quite a different direction to write a story that has been "haunting her" for years. Please check out *Sundays Are for Murder* in January. Hop aboard a Caribbean cruise with Joanne Rock in *The Pleasure Trip* for February, and don't miss a trademark romantic suspense from Debra Webb, *Vows of Silence* in March.

Our collections in the first quarter of the year explore a variety of contemporary themes. Our Valentine's collection—*Write It Up!*—homes in on the trend to online dating in three stories by Elizabeth Bevarly, Tracy Kelleher and Mary Leo. February is awards season, and Barbara Bretton, Isabel Sharpe and Emilie Rose join the fun and glamour in *And the Envelope, Please....* And in March, Leslie Kelly, Heather MacAllister and Cindi Myers have penned novellas about women desperate enough to go to *Bootcamp* to learn how *not* to scare men away!

Three original sagas also come your way in the first quarter of this year. Silhouette author Gina Wilkins spins off her popular FAMILY FOUND miniseries in *Wealth Beyond Riches*. Janice Kay Johnson has written a powerful story of a tortured shared past in *Dead Wrong*, which is connected to her PATTON'S DAUGHTERS Superromance miniseries, and Kathleen O'Brien gives a haunting story of mysterious murder in *Quiet as the Grave*.

And don't forget there is original bonus material in every single Signature Select book to give you the inside scoop on the creative process of your favorite authors! We hope you enjoy all our new offerings!

Enjoy!

Marsha Zinberg

Marsha Zinberg
Executive Editor
The Signature Select Program

Signature Select™
SHOWCASE

BOOTCAMP

Leslie Kelly

Heather MacAllister

Cindi Myers

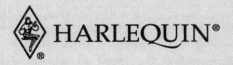

HARLEQUIN®

TORONTO • NEW YORK • LONDON
AMSTERDAM • PARIS • SYDNEY • HAMBURG
STOCKHOLM • ATHENS • TOKYO • MILAN • MADRID
PRAGUE • WARSAW • BUDAPEST • AUCKLAND

ISBN 0-373-83688-0

BOOTCAMP

Copyright © 2006 by Harlequin Books S.A.

The publisher acknowledges the copyright holder of the individual works as follows:

KISS AND MAKE UP
Copyright © 2006 by Leslie Kelly

SUGAR AND SPIKES
Copyright © 2006 by Heather W. MacAllister

FLIRTING WITH AN OLD FLAME
Copyright © 2006 by Cynthia Myers

www.eHarlequin.com

Printed in U.S.A.

CONTENTS

KISS AND MAKE UP

Leslie Kelly

PROLOGUE

ELLEN DEVANE HADN'T been dubbed the "steel-spined lipstick queen of the U.S." for nothing. A *Vanity Fair* reporter had coined the phrase decades ago, at the height of her career, and she'd never shaken it off. In fact, she'd always rather fancied it.

In those days, she'd been the undisputed champion of the cosmetic wars that had escalated during the sexual revolution. Hollywood had taken her advice throughout the fifties, and the *Cosmo* girls had made her an icon of the seventies. Burn your bra and thicken your eyelashes—that had been Ellen's battle cry.

She'd crawled out from behind the Gimbel's makeup counter into her own million-dollar, Manhattan-based company by age thirty. Fresh Face Cosmetics had been her entire life, and she'd never looked back or second-guessed the choices she'd made.

Never.

Not after Rex, the first and only man she'd ever truly loved, had tired of her constant need for more and married someone else. Not after the sad end of her own all-too-brief marriage to another man who'd always known he was her second choice. Not after watching her sons battle each other for control over her empire when she'd retired twenty years ago. Not even after the crushing sense of loss she'd felt when she'd learned

Rex had died at much too young an age. She'd stayed strong and resolute, a powerhouse—the lipstick queen—throughout it all.

So why, goodness, gracious, *why,* had she suddenly gone soft?

"Cassandra's miserably unhappy, you know." She blew on the surface of her steaming tea, taking off a bit of the heat. Bringing the Sevres porcelain cup to her lips, she sipped lightly, then eyed Patricia, her daughter-in-law. Her older son's wife was, as usual, impeccably dressed, but her perfectly made-up face was noticeably pale and tight lines were evident around her lips.

"I know," Patricia replied. "Do you think I don't know my own child?" Lurching to her feet, she swayed on the slender heels of her Italian leather shoes. "I rue the day I encouraged her to fight for CEO when Larry stepped down last year."

"It isn't her *job,*" Ellen snapped with an impatient shake of her head. "It's her...her..."

"Her love life?"

"Her *entire* life," Ellen replied. "Her inability to fall in love with anyone is just a symptom. The girl has changed. She's not the funny, mischievous child who brought light and laughter into this house. She's turned into a corporate drone by day." Her gaze fell upon a pile of tabloid magazines scattered across her dressing table. "And an international playgirl by night."

The images of her sweet grandchild splashed across the trashy magazines wouldn't leave Ellen's mind. Nor would the starkness that had replaced the warmth in Cassandra's eyes.

Empty eyes. Eyes devoid of passion and emotion. Eyes that said she would never let anyone get close enough to hurt her, that she would focus only on all the things Ellen, herself, had once deemed more important than anything. Or anyone.

Funny, at the age of eighty-four, she certainly didn't long for one more product meeting or one more power play in the boardroom. She wished, instead, to feel once again the warmth of a strong hand cupping her cheek with love and tenderness. Or to inhale the familiar, spicy scent of a thoroughly male cologne on the pillow beside hers. Or to hear the laughter of her sons running through the yard.

They were simple things. Gentle things. Things she'd scorned or taken for granted.

Her mood growing darker, she acknowledged one more truth: these were things Cassandra was never going to experience if she didn't chip away the shell she'd allowed to encase her.

"She's capable of loving," Patricia murmured, gazing out the window to the south lawn. "I believe she loved very much once."

Something in her daughter-in-law's voice made Ellen lower her cup and saucer. Staring hard at her son's wife, she asked in her best no-nonsense voice, "What are you talking about?"

And, as if she'd merely been waiting for the opportunity, Patricia told her. The whole sad, sorry truth—a truth Ellen's family had kept hidden from her for eight long years.

It boggled the mind. But the story explained so *very* much. No wonder her little golden girl had grown cold. Wasn't she, after all, following exactly in her grandmother's footsteps?

No. By God, she would *not.* "How long were they married?"

"Less than a year. It was when you were so ill and had your surgery, which was why we thought it best…"

Obviously seeing the tightness in Ellen's jaw, Patricia fell silent.

They'd thought it best to hide the fact that her only granddaughter had run away at the age of twenty to marry a boy she'd met during a vacation in Florida. And had been divorced from him less than twelve months later.

Lord in heaven, everything made sense now. Why Cassandra had changed from a sweetly thoughtful, smiling young woman, who'd loved books, the sea and black jelly beans, to the tabloids' second-favorite flavor of the month after that Hilton child. She'd thought it was simply wild college life that had brought about the change. Now she knew it was much more serious.

Ellen couldn't bear it. "Leave me," she barked, hoping Patricia hadn't heard the shakiness in her voice.

Once alone, she reached for her telephone. Ellen's body might have given up on her, but her brain was every bit as sharp today as it had been when she'd argued with Alberto de Rossi over Elizabeth Taylor's skin tone during the filming of *Cleopatra*.

Dialing the number of a private investigator she'd used on more than one occasion, she related the details Patricia had revealed. The P.I. would find out everything he could about the man Cassandra had loved, this Wyatt Reston. Where he was, what he'd done with his life. If he was as heartbroken as her granddaughter.

But it still wasn't enough. Finding the former husband wasn't the real issue. Even if she was correct in thinking that Cassandra had been nursing a broken heart for eight years, it would mean nothing if her granddaughter allowed no one access to that heart.

She had to open up—spiritually, emotionally. Had to chip away the shell and rediscover the girl she'd once been. Then and only then would she allow herself to lay her heart on the line for anyone, be it her first love or a new one.

Fortunately, Ellen knew exactly where Cassandra had to go to do it. As if fate had planned this, she'd just yesterday been speaking to Maxine Warfield, someone very dear to her, about Max's new business venture, a so-called "boot camp" for women.

The idea had sounded ludicrous when Maxine had proposed it. She'd been seeking Ellen's financial assistance for the project, and Ellen had been able to think of nothing more ridiculous than turning a Texas ranch into a camp for wealthy women to learn to get back in touch with their emotional sides, find out exactly what had gone wrong in their lives and learn how to fix it.

Of course, those doubts hadn't stopped Ellen from investing. She cared much too deeply for Maxine Warfield to refuse.

Besides…she owed it to Max's father.

"My dear," she mumbled to herself as she dialed the number, "if you can bring the light back into my granddaughter's eyes, I'll consider that investment the best one I've ever made."

"Warfield Retreat."

Her heart lurched as she heard Maxine's voice. How strange that a woman could sound so much like her father. And how appropriate, really, to seek help for her grandchild from the woman who could have been Ellen's daughter.

Maxine was Rex's only child…by someone else. She was also the one person who could help Ellen ensure that her granddaughter did not repeat the mistakes that had haunted Ellen all her life.

"Max, I need you to help me get my granddaughter back."

She only hoped that when Cassandra did get her eyes opened up, she'd grab any chance she could to change her life. And that she wouldn't follow in Ellen's lonely footsteps.

CHAPTER ONE

CASSANDRA DEVANE fully expected to hate Texas.

When her plane touched down in the big, loud state, she mentally equated it to landing in hell. The limo ride through miles of pretty woodlands from Houston to the Warfield Retreat improved things a *little*. She hadn't expected much more than dust. Still, trees and forest were almost as bad as desert. Mainly because they weren't the city, which was where she needed to be right now, running her cosmetics company.

She couldn't believe her grandmother had guilted her into attending this two-week program. Cassandra had been tempted to chalk up the silly idea to an old lady's whim, but something about the intensity in Nana's shaky voice had made her understand just how important this was to the elderly woman. Which was why Cassandra was en route to a place where wealthy, successful businesswomen could regain their softer sides and come out ready to cook like Betty Crocker, fall in love like a romance-novel heroine and live happily ever after like Snow White. Yawn.

Snow White was a twit. Cassandra sure wouldn't have hooked up with some horny prince who went around kissing dead chicks in the woods. The necrophilia rumors alone would have been bad enough to live down, not to mention the shacking-up-with-seven-men thing.

How funny that *Snow White and the Seven Dwarfs* had been her favorite story as a kid. "But you grew up," she whispered as the stretch limo pulled through the gates of the ranch.

Yes. She had definitely grown up. Fairy-tale fantasies had been left far behind. Along with a lot of other things, like romantic dreams and expectations. Even, perhaps, a bit of her optimism.

Shrugging off the flash of sadness, she forced her thoughts to the present. Craning closer to the window, she hoped for at least a glimpse of a sexy cowboy, the only thing she'd figured she'd like in Texas. But there wasn't a single one in sight. Just rows of neat, tidy cottages and nicely manicured grounds.

The hedges lining the mulch-covered walkways were covered with an unusual pink flower that seemed at odds in such a rustic setting. When she saw the doors of each cottage, she realized the flowers weren't the *only* things that were pink. "Good heavens," she said, wondering what she was getting herself into. Pink and lavender doors on cabins that had once housed ranch hands?

It was only the thought of Nana Ellen's disappointment that made her refrain from telling the driver to take her back to the airport. Because Cassandra was in no way ready to see the dismay on the old woman's face when she learned her only granddaughter *hadn't* miraculously transformed from a socialite cosmetics executive to a softer, gentler female who wanted to get married and have babies—the girl she'd been years ago before life had toughened her up.

Sucking it up and staying here seemed preferable to crushing her nana's hopes. Of course, a root canal did, too, so that wasn't saying much.

Arriving at the main building, Cassandra accepted

the limo driver's hand as he helped her out, then waited on the porch as he removed her matching Louis Vuitton bags from the trunk. After tipping him, she looked for a bellboy, but spied no one. Finally, she made her way inside, searched around the empty foyer, then entered a large office. A well-dressed, middle-aged woman with graying dark hair sat behind a desk, filling out some paperwork. Cassandra cleared her throat.

The woman looked up. "Ms. Devane."

Used to being recognized, Cassandra nodded.

"I recognize you from the photo that accompanied your application," the hostess smoothly explained, coming out from behind the desk to extend her hand. "I'm Maxine Warfield."

Ahh, the entrepreneur herself. The genius who somehow managed to get wealthy females to cough up ten thousand dollars to come here and find out why they were deficient as women. Good trick.

"You should know I'm only here to make an old woman happy."

"Yes, yes," the woman said as she turned and walked out of the office, not even bothering to see if Cassandra followed.

She did, of course, both amused and perplexed by the other woman's all-business, no-nonsense attitude. Usually anyone who recognized Cassandra at least asked about the Brad Pitt rumors.

Lie. And sort of true.

"You'll be sharing a cabin with two roommates who I feel will be a good fit in terms of interests and personality," the camp owner said as they walked onto the plank board porch.

Sharing? Five thousand dollars a week to *share?* She was about to comment when she realized Maxine was waiting for Cassandra to pick up her suitcases and follow her down the steps to the path.

"This retreat is about getting back to the basics," Maxine said, obviously seeing her surprise. "Being self-reliant."

With a flush of embarrassment, Cassandra picked up the two largest bags, wishing like crazy she hadn't had to tuck those salmon-colored Ferragamo shoes in at the last minute. Or the black ones. Or the Chanel suit. By the time they arrived at her cottage, she was even cursing her favorite Jimmy Choos because she was going to have blisters by the end of this day. Not that she'd let Maxine Warfield see her discomfort for one second.

"Here you are," Maxine said, leading her inside.

Quickly looking around, Cassandra breathed a small sigh of relief. The cabin was large, with three nicely appointed bedrooms and nary a spot of pink, other than the front door. With rust-colored carpeting and a brilliant shine on the rough-hewn pine floors in the kitchen area, the place felt almost like a ski lodge.

She could deal with this, no matter what Miss Maxine might think. At least, she could now that she'd managed to discreetly tug one of her high-heeled shoes off an aching foot.

"I'll see you tomorrow morning at ten," Maxine said. "We'll all meet to go over the program. In the meantime, please look over the list of courses. Pay attention to the ones I've noted. I think, given your history, they would be most appropriate."

Then the woman breezed out, leaving Cassandra with a shoe in one hand and a lavender-and-pink brochure in the other.

She thought her day was already bad. But when she read the brochure, she realized she'd been way off

base. The absence of cowboys and being in Texas and
pink doors and tight shoes were minor irritations
compared to classes with names like "Crock Pots:
They're Not Such A Crock," and "Cattiness Is For Fe-
lines," and, her personal favorite, "If He Likes to Fish,
Bait the Hook!"

"I'm going to be sick," she muttered, dropping her
shoe to the floor. Groaning, she added, "Nana, if you
weren't so old and I didn't love you so much, I'd get you
for this, I swear."

Of course, she wouldn't do a thing in the world to hurt
her grandmother, but over the days that followed, she had
to admit to a few fantasies about hurting Maxine Warfield.

Her first week at the camp was painful, but she
wasn't a quitter. Cassandra attended every course, took
anything they threw at her, including a social graces
course that made her want to ask if they thought she routinely wiped her mouth on her sleeve when she dined
at The Rainbow Room. The dancing course had left her
with a genuine hatred of whomever had invented the
polka, but she'd kept her mouth shut. She'd even
managed to smile though she'd failed miserably at the
"your egg is your baby, keep it safe" experiment. Her
baby might as well have been a western omelet an hour
after it was put into Cassandra's hands.

Despite that she liked her two roommates, Rebecca
Ironwood and Barbara Powers, Cassandra still felt out
of place at Warfield. She seemed to be the only person
who hadn't come here by choice, the only one who
didn't think she needed to change.

Until the moment she realized maybe she *did* need
to change.

It happened during a group exercise on trust, one of
those corporate retreat type things where one person fell

back into the arms of a partner. She'd marched up there...and frozen.

She couldn't do it. It was the first exercise or challenge she'd refused to accept since the moment she'd arrived. Despite telling herself that she knew—just *knew*—that Rebecca would never let her fall and hurt herself, she'd simply been unable to let herself go. To give herself over...to *anyone*.

"You shouldn't keep tearing yourself up," a voice said, interrupting her musings late that night in her room.

Looking up from her bed, she saw Rebecca, whose youthful, unlined face belied her prematurely silver hair. Behind her was red-haired, plainspoken Barbara. "About what?"

They came in and sat down. "About not wanting to split your head open," Barbara said, matter-of-fact as always.

"Or not wanting to get dirt on that gorgeous skirt you were wearing," Rebecca offered.

She blinked. The women were *worried* about her. They were, in fact, *comforting* her. It was just so surprising, so unexpected, that she simply didn't know what to say.

"But just in case it was something other than that," Barbara added, her voice quiet, "I want you to know something."

Cassandra paused, still turning over the thought that these people—strangers to her a week ago—were worried about her. So it took her a second before she tuned in to the rest of Barbara's comment. "Whoever it was who let you fall in the past? Well, that person *wasn't* the one standing behind you today in class."

Whoever it was who let you fall in the past...

Something roared in Cassandra's head, spinning, shouting, screaming for attention. A voice she'd thought she'd extinguished.

As a dark-haired image filled her brain, she blinked against hot, completely unexpected tears. Because after eight years and lots of money and a great job and tons of travel, she realized the truth: she hadn't extinguished a thing. She'd merely buried it. Buried it alive without ever trying to heal from the wounds her brief marriage had carved into her heart.

And suddenly she got it. Why she was here. What she was supposed to learn. What she had to do. She understood everything.

It was all about *him*. Wyatt Reston.

The time had come for Cassandra to deal with her past.

"I'M NOT the person I was when I arrived here two weeks ago," she told Maxine Warfield, whom she and her roommates had fondly dubbed Mad Max due to the woman's bossiness.

It was her last day at camp, and she was sitting across the desk from the camp owner as she had her exit interview. Trying to find a way to voice her self-realization, she looked around the office. Behind Max's desk, amid the photographs of former graduates covering the nauseating pink rosette wallpaper, was a hand-stitched sampler with the camp's motto: "Leveling the Playing Field with the Womanly Art of Romance." *Gag.*

Romance wasn't what she'd be seeking after she left this place. Reality was. Reality. Answers. Closure.

Cassie cleared her throat. "I never anticipated waking up one morning and realizing I've deliberately sabotaged myself in so many relationships in my life. With my family, my staff…"

"Men?" Maxine asked with a knowing look.

Yes, she supposed she had. God, it galled her to admit, if only in her own mind, that Nana had been right. Cassandra had been making horrid choices when it came to her rather turbulent love life. Not that love life was the correct term—love hadn't had anything to do with her life in a long time. *Eight years.*

"Someone let me down once and I let that single incident knock me off the course I'd been on right up until then. I took over the family business when what I'd always wanted to do was teach."

"You regret that?"

Max's raised brow told Cassandra she already knew the answer, so Cassandra didn't even try to fool her. "No," she said with a rueful laugh. "I love my job. But I regret that I've allowed myself to become someone I'm not, all because I let a guy make me feel as though I wasn't worth loving."

"Not worth loving?"

Well, she had to admit the truth, if only to herself: Wyatt *had* loved her. She knew he had. But not enough. "Not worth fighting for," she clarified. "Because when the going got tough, well, as the expression goes, he got going."

She didn't go into any details. Max didn't know that it was Cassandra's own insecurity that had made their marriage blow up in their faces. After eight years, Cassandra was ready to admit her own culpability in the divorce. She had, after all, been the one who'd gone to her parents for financial help, knowing it was the last thing her husband wanted her to do. But Wyatt had been the one who'd walked out without even trying to understand.

"So, you have acknowledged the problem. All that remains now is to determine what to do about it," Maxine said.

"You *knew* all along what my problem was, didn't you?" she asked. Somehow Mad Max had already figured her out, something Cassandra, herself, hadn't been able to do until very recently.

"The way you talked about him in the group sessions was a dead giveaway," the older woman replied, not unkindly. "You may laugh off your whirlwind romance, but it's clear to me that you've never truly moved on from that relationship."

Hadn't moved on? "Sorry to disappoint you," Cassandra said, not ready to admit defeat. She had moved on, just not in the way she should have. "I've dated men on three continents since then."

Mad Max's knowing expression never broke. "Correct. Which merely proves my point. No man has broken through the exterior you show to the world." Her voice lowered. "You've been running away from your past. Instead of dealing with it, you've been seeking out any distraction you could find. None of which changed a thing."

"No, they didn't," Cassandra said, picturing all the ways she'd tried to prove she wasn't still hurting. Mainly by dating lots of men, trying to find one who made her feel—even for a moment—what she'd felt with Wyatt.

As Max's eyes finally revealed a glint of emotion— God, hopefully not pity—she added, "You have to deal with him."

Cassandra knew it was no use pretending anymore. "You're right. I suppose I never did say the things I wanted to say that would have given me some sense of finality with Wyatt."

"And until you have that finality, do you think you will ever really be able to move on?"

In many ways, she had. She was a far cry from the bookish college sophomore who'd lost her heart and her virginity during a passionate spring break in Florida. The foolish, naïve girl who'd run off to live on love and had wound up alone and heartbroken before her senior year. That girl was gone.

But was that a good thing…or a bad one? She wasn't so sure anymore.

"I think you know what you have to do," Max said, finally offering what might have been a comforting smile. It disappeared so quickly Cassandra wasn't sure she'd seen it at all.

"Yes, I guess I do," she said with a heavy sigh. "I have to take a *journey*." They stressed journeys here—the journey from childhood to adulthood, from girl to woman, from isolation to commitment, from past to future. "I wish you could've just told me what was wrong with me when you figured it out."

Maxine tsked. "You had to learn it for yourself."

"Right. Like Dorothy and the no-place-like-home thing," Cassandra muttered. The other woman didn't smile or even seem to understand the *Wizard of Oz* reference. Maybe Cassandra's years as jaded socialite had dulled her ability to make people laugh. But she'd get it back. Damned if she wouldn't.

Looking at the photos again, Cassandra wondered if she'd ever find that kind of happiness, if she'd send a picture of her happy future self for Max to add to her collection. *Doubtful.* Maybe she'd send her some face cream samplers instead. The woman could use some help with those frown lines.

"Well, Ms. Devane, I think we're finished here. Why don't you return to your cabin and enjoy your final evening with your roommates?" Maxine said, rising and effectively dismissing her.

Feeling very much like a schoolgirl, Cassandra stood

and turned to the door. But before her hand could turn the knob, Max walked out from behind her desk. "Enjoy your trip to Massachusetts."

Confused, she raised a brow. "Massachusetts?"

Maxine's head tipped forward in a small nod as she handed Cassandra a manila envelope. "Yes. You're going to Boston. And here's something for you to read along the way."

Cassandra looked at the bulging envelope, somehow knowing it contained information on Wyatt. She had no idea how Maxine had tracked down Cassandra's ex-husband, but she knew she held in her hand specific details about Wyatt's current life. The thought left her a little breathless. Was she really ready for this?

After leaving the office, she headed back toward her room, not quite having the courage to open the file and read whatever secrets Mad Max's sources had uncovered about the man Cassandra had once loved with every ounce of her being. Later. She'd open it later. After she'd had a glass of the French Chablis she had stashed in the kitchen of her bungalow.

Tucking the file under her arm, she went inside and greeted her roommates. "Okay, I'm all finished."

"How'd it go?" Barbara sounded anxious, probably because her outgoing appointment with Max was the next day.

"It was okay," Cassandra murmured. "I'm okay."

Rebecca came out of her room, her hair newly blond—apparently her "journey" involved a makeover. "Did she give you a mission?"

Barbara's worried green eyes now twinkled. "You don't have to hog-tie a cow to get your ticket home, do you?"

Cassandra had received a lot of good-natured "city-girl" ribbing from her two Texas-born roomies, even though they were now city-dwelling businesswomen, too. "Hog-tie a cow? Are cows hog-tied? And if so, wouldn't it be called *cow*-tying?"

"I bet they'd prefer tying to cow-tipping," Barbara said.

They all grinned. The three of them brought out the silly sides of one another, a silly side Cassandra had almost forgotten had once been an intrinsic part of her. To think she'd been considered a prankster as a kid. She'd almost forgotten what real laughter was until this past week.

"To answer your question, Barbara, no, I won't have to rope any living creatures," she explained. "Unless you want to count Wyatt. Who did, I must say, have some bull-like attributes."

Rebecca and Barbara shared a knowing look, then began laughing. Cassandra grinned, not a bit repentant. "I meant he was as stubborn as a bull…not that he was, well, hung like one."

Though, when she thought about it… *Enough, Cassandra, you're going to confront the man, not jump on him.*

This wasn't about sex appeal. Or, um, size. It was about shutting the door on the past. That was all.

Barbara shook her head, as Rebecca did a good job looking scandalized. "That kind of talk isn't going to get you reelected to the board of the Junior League of Manhattan."

"I'm not going to Manhattan," Cassandra murmured, looking at the dossier Max had given her. "I'm going to Boston."

"Boston?" Barbara asked. "What's in Boston?"

Cassandra slowly tore open the flap of the envelope, suspecting the support of her friends would be better than a glass of Chablis. "Not what," she murmured, "but who."

Sliding the papers into her hand, Cassandra focused on the large black-and-white photograph Max had provided of Wyatt's still incredibly handsome face. The dark, deep-set, heavily-lashed eyes. The strong nose. The firm jaw and the mouth she remembered kissing for hours on end.

Time stopped. For a moment, the rest of the world seemed separate, distinct, and very far away as Cassandra existed only with the photograph of him. Wyatt Reston. The man she'd once vowed to love until the day she died.

And suddenly she couldn't help wondering…was she *really* flying to Boston to finish things with Wyatt once and for all?

Or to start them all over again?

CHAPTER TWO

IF WYATT RESTON HAD walked into his office overlooking the Newmarket business district in Boston and found a goat napping on his desk, he couldn't have been more surprised than he was right now. In fact, the goat would probably have been better for his sanity. Because this couldn't be happening. The blond woman standing at the window, looking down toward the bustling street eight stories below, couldn't be…couldn't *possibly* be…

"Hello, Wyatt."

Damn. It *was* happening. It was her, the person he'd hoped never to see again, even though his heart lurched every time he spotted her picture in a society column or a magazine.

Cassandra Devane Reston—now just Devane again—stood framed in the brilliant afternoon sunlight pouring through his office windows. Her full lips were curved into a very small, demure smile and her expression was calm, as if she visited him every day instead of only in his deepest, darkest, most torturous dreams. Or his deepest, darkest, most dangerous fantasies.

Dressed in a yellow blouse and a pair of silky pants, she looked cool and springy, perfectly at ease. Like she'd stepped out of one of those magazines that always seemed to have her on display, setting fashion trends and causing eyebrows to raise.

"I imagine you're surprised to see me," she said.

He closed his eyes, instinctive protection against that soft, lyrical voice. Cassandra's sweet voice had reduced him to a six-foot-tall pile of want the first time he'd heard it on a sunny Florida beach. When he'd seen the bright smile and blue eyes that accompanied the voice, he'd been halfway in love already. Her red bikini had added to the steam. He'd never wanted anyone else the way he'd wanted her. Before or since.

"Surprise. That's one word for it," he finally managed to say in the charged air, ripe with tension only he seemed to feel.

Surprise. Yeah. That was the only reason his blood was rushing through his veins so loudly it could surely be heard above the chatter of voices outside the office and the city traffic far below them. Just surprise.

Bull. He was an ad man, and he couldn't even sell that garbage to himself.

Adrenaline was fueling his response. And excitement. A response he'd always had around this particular female.

"You look almost the same," she said as she stepped away from the window, her high heels sinking into the plush carpet of his office. She approached him, but stopped several feet away, as if she suddenly felt the charged expectation in the room and didn't quite know what to do about it.

He had a few suggestions. *Back away. Disappear. Leave me with my sanity and my comfortable life and kindly remove yourself from my memories.*

"Really, other than that glower on your face and the shorter hair, you could be the same guy I met outside the Blue Dolphin nine years ago," she said.

Wyatt kept his teeth clenched, determined to get

through this unexpected meeting with his dignity—and his heart—intact. Not to mention with his pants firmly zipped, despite how uncomfortably tight they'd begun to feel the minute he'd set eyes on her. He forced an impersonal smile. "You look older."

She stiffened, taking his words as a criticism, then said, "Isn't the standard response 'some things get better with age'?"

Oh, yeah. Definitely. He could think of lots of things that would probably be better now. He imagined that with a little more experience on each of them, they could be absolutely combustible together. They'd already been an inferno when they'd been a couple of young, inexperienced kids.

"It wasn't an insult," he managed to mutter, trying to keep his mind out of the corner of his brain filled with his more erotic memories of their short-lived marriage. "You look great."

As a coed, Cassie had been a pretty girl. Her long hair had been a thick mass of golds and browns, every day on the beach adding more streaks of sunshine. Her stunning eyes had caught and reflected any shade of blue within a hundred-yard radius. She'd had a delicate face and full lips that tasted like sin against his own.

But now…well, now she looked simply amazing. Softer. More womanly. Mature and sultry rather than simply young and lovely.

He tried not to react to her, tried again to stomp the memories out of his brain. He should have known that wouldn't work. It certainly hadn't over the past eight years.

Funny, right now, he couldn't muster up any of the bad images. Just the good ones. Images of the crazy, sexy, wonderful way they'd been in the beginning.

He'd been a twenty-two-year-old kid, struggling to

finish college before his scholarship money ran out.
Hitching a ride with a buddy to Florida for spring break
had been an impulsive idea inspired by a bitch of a
chemistry midterm.

Sure, like every college guy heading south on I-95
in April, he'd had his mind on girls. He'd never,
however, expected to fall in love with one. Certainly
he'd never dreamed he'd be married ten days later. But
he *had* fallen in love, and he *had* married the girl with
the sultry voice, the sapphire eyes, and the red bikini.
The one who'd always had her nose buried in a book,
as if completely unaware of the raucous party going on
around her.

Some people had tried to stereotype her as a rich
bitch, interpreting her reserve as arrogance. On the
contrary, Cassie was one of the nicest, most intelligent,
unpretentious girls he'd ever met. And she'd had a
wicked sense of humor that seemed to come out of
nowhere and take people completely by surprise. It had
delighted him. *Everything* about her had delighted him.

"You're more beautiful than you were," he admitted.

Most of Cassie's long, straight golden hair was gone,
and it was now almost platinum-colored, framing her
face in short curls. Though sun-kissed, her skin lacked
the deep tan of a Florida spring, and he'd bet there were
no tiny freckles dotting her nose like there had been that
first day they'd met near the pier.

He didn't intend to find out. Self-preservation
demanded that he remain five feet away from this
woman at all times. This was as close as he ever wanted
to get—and it was much closer than he'd ever expected
to be considering they hadn't set eyes on each other
since the day they'd signed the divorce papers.

So why couldn't he tear his eyes away from the soft

neckline of her blouse and stop remembering the way the skin just below her collarbone had tasted?

Swallowing hard, he muttered, "What do you want, Cassie?"

She frowned. "Nobody ever calls me Cassie."

Like he *needed* a formal reminder of the difference in their social stature? That she'd been the rich blue-blooded golden child and he'd been the dirt-poor blue-collar kid from Indiana? The jab stung. It didn't bother Wyatt personally—he'd never given a damn about the society set, beyond landing the accounts of companies that sold them their Rolexes. But he hated that Cassie could have changed so much. She might have been rich, but she'd never been a snob.

Still, he supposed the way their marriage had ended should have burned the truth into him forever: she cared a lot more about money than he'd ever have expected.

Careful to maintain his five-foot distance, he moved around to the other side of his desk and sat down. "What is it you want, *Ms. Devane?*"

She frowned slightly, looking confused. "I didn't mean that. I meant...call me Cassandra," she said.

He'd rather call her *gone,* but said nothing. Still, he relaxed a little, glad his warm beach angel hadn't turned into a total corporate ice queen. "Fine." Leaning forward, he dropped his forearms onto his desk. "So why are you here, *Cassandra?*"

Years of dealing with people had taught him how to figure out what it was someone wanted by the way they moved, the clench of a hand, the shift of the eyes, the tightening of a mouth. Right now, Cassie was doing all of the above, meaning she was bothered about something. It could be that she was as disturbed about seeing him as he was her, but he doubted it.

Cassie took a seat on one of the chairs across from him, leaning slightly forward, with her knees together and her ankles crossed. Ladylike. Prim. Well-bred. "Great view," she commented, gazing at the window. She quirked a brow. "I'm surprised your window actually opens. In New York, you never see that because of the leapers."

He had to chuckle. "This is Boston. Much more genteel."

"Right. Red Sox fans were the height of gentility in '04."

He and Cassie used to have regular weekend dates in front of their tiny TV—which had had lousy reception barely boosted by rabbit ears—whenever the Red Sox or the Yankees were playing. Smirking, Wyatt hit her where he knew it would hurt. "At least they had something to celebrate."

Funny, since the divorce, he hadn't been able to sit down and watch an entire baseball game.

"I suppose you're entitled to *one* win every millennium."

Unable to defend himself against her smile or her laughter, Wyatt shook his head. "So are we done talking about my window?"

"Nope. I wasn't finished. With this view, I imagine this is some pricey real estate. Business must be good."

Business *was* phenomenal, not that he planned to get into that with her. After all, hadn't his lack of financial prospects been a big part of what had destroyed the remnants of their marriage? A marriage that had already been incredibly shaky near the end of their first year.

At age twenty-three, a young husband, a recent graduate, he'd been confident about his prospects and his financial future. He'd known from age six that he was a natural-born salesman. Advertising had been his career goal from the first time he'd heard everyone he knew humming that Bubble Yum jingle and had realized its power.

He'd thought Cassie had understood and supported that. He'd been wrong. Cassie had gone behind his back to her rich parents, who had been so disapproving of their marriage that they'd refused even to meet him.

He could have predicted what would happen if she'd told him what she'd planned to do. Once she'd proved to them that they had her back where they wanted her— under their financial thumb—her parents had told her Wyatt should give up his dreams and come work for them, live on their money. They'd tried to *buy* him.

Wyatt had been shocked, first that Cassie would have gone to her parents so furtively. He'd also been dismayed that she hadn't had enough faith in him to know he could make it without anyone's help. She'd made it clear that the differences in their financial backgrounds really *did* matter.

Her decision had done one more thing: it had proved that, despite what she said, his wife had not been able to break herself of her need to have her parents' approval and to allow herself to be under their control. So Wyatt had walked out.

"Can we cut to the chase?" he asked, glancing at his watch, wishing he had an appointment.

"Wyatt," she said with a sigh, "can't I even comment on your company? Your business is doing really well, isn't it?"

Cassie's expression told him she was glad of that. Happy for him. And for the first time since he'd walked into his office and found her there, he relaxed—just a bit. "Yeah, I guess so. I'm sure Reston Promotions isn't quite as big as Fresh Face Cosmetics, but we're doing okay."

"You really did it," she murmured with a smile.

"I really did it," he said. He wasn't surprised by her visible happiness for him, because he knew—if he'd never known anything else about the real Cassandra Devane—that she'd truly wanted him to succeed. That had been part of the problem, after all. Her wanting him to succeed, no matter what it cost.

Like his pride and independence.

Their eyes met and held for a heavy moment, during which a number of questions were silently asked, questions neither one of them would ever voice aloud. *How are you, really? Are you happy? Is there someone else?*

Most importantly, *Why did we let things fall apart?*

But the time for asking questions was long past. Maybe if he'd been more mature rather than just a dumb twenty-three-year-old newlywed, he would have handled things differently all those years ago. He might have stuck around to talk things out, to try to make her understand how deeply her actions had wounded him. To let her know that he really *was* worried about the differences in their backgrounds, wondering if he'd ever be able to afford to keep up with her family.

It was too late, though. Much too late. Whether she'd moved on or not, *he* had.

If only he could make himself really believe that.

"Okay, Cassandra," he said, forcing the thought away and sitting straighter in his chair, "what is it you want?"

WHAT WAS IT she wanted? Well, that was the question of the hour, wasn't it? Maybe even the question of her life.

When she'd walked in here a while ago, Cassandra had been sure she knew what she wanted. Closure. Finality. A chance to tell him off for breaking her heart and then walk out the door, ready to march into her new, bright and shiny future. She'd even admitted—at least to herself—that she was also looking for reassurance that whatever feelings she'd had for Wyatt had been fully extinguished by time and maturity.

But they hadn't. As soon as she'd turned around and seen him, Cassandra had known she was in trouble. Deep trouble. Because her heart sang at the sight of him.

It was a silly expression, one she'd normally scoff at, but it was true. Seeing Wyatt was like seeing her very best friend again, after a long separation, which seemed to fall away the minute their eyes met. Every memory of every moment they'd spent together leapt to the forefront of her mind.

Good memories, great moments. Like the way they'd slept wrapped around one another, wanting, even in their sleep, to be touching from head to toe. The trips to the beach where they'd glide through the waves for hours. Going through every aisle of the grocery store creating imaginary menus for the dinner parties they'd host when they were rich and successful. The time they'd painted their tiny kitchen yellow, panicking as they realized they couldn't leave the windows open to air out the smell of paint for fear the landlord would find out what they'd done, so they'd tried to dry the walls with a hair dryer.

Stupid stuff. Young kid stuff. *Wonderful stuff.*

The year they'd been together had been the happiest of her entire life. She'd been madly, deeply, irrevocably in love with him. Right up until the day he'd broken her heart.

"You must have come here for a reason," he prodded.

She tried to stall for time, wondering if her face betrayed her jumbled feelings. "I was in Boston."

"On business?"

Somehow remaining calm, she replied, "Sure. Yes. Business."

She didn't know what else to say, how to go on. Lord, she hadn't expected this mix of emotions that made it difficult to know what to say. Emotions, yes, she would have expected that. But if she'd been a betting woman, she would have wagered on anger or indignation. Not this strange, anxious sort of longing. Not tenderness. Yet that's exactly what she was feeling, just looking at his still-so-handsome face, his sexy mouth and his dark, stormy eyes. Eyes which were narrowed now, as if he was trying to figure out her thoughts.

"I just got back from a ranch in Texas," she said quickly. "And I had to come here before going home to New York."

His mouth quirked up in a tiny grin. "A Texas ranch, huh? I thought you were scared of horses."

Her jaw dropped. "I am *not*."

"Cass, you were terrified of my roommate's dog," he pointed out, daring her to deny it.

"Horses don't drool as much as Great Danes," she replied with a lofty lift of her chin.

His grin widened into a broad smile. "True. And I don't suppose while you were horseback riding in Texas you wore a pretty white dress that attracts animal hair like a magnet."

Remembering the day when she'd first gone to his Virginia apartment and met his roommate—and the infamous dog—she had to laugh. "I wonder what the Elvis impersonator thought about me vowing to make a fur coat out of a Great Dane as I plucked black dog hair off my wedding dress."

Wedding dress. Oh, she shouldn't have mentioned that. Shouldn't have let her thoughts travel down that road—or invited him to take that trip with her. Because they were both picturing it. The whirlwind romance in Florida. The drive back to Virginia, where they attended different colleges. The visit to her place for a white dress, and to his for a suit, and then the quick flight to Vegas for their secret elopement. The discussion over whether they'd wanted to be married by the fat Elvis in the white jumpsuit or the thin one in the tight black pants and Hawaiian shirt.

It was as fresh in her mind as if it had happened days ago, instead of eight years ago. Which was funny considering she hadn't allowed herself to think about Wyatt or her marriage for a long time.

Wyatt's smile had faded. Not wanting to give him a chance to go all dark and morose on her again, Cassandra quickly brought them back to the subject at hand. "Well, I didn't ride any horses in Texas, but it wasn't because I'm afraid of them. I was just there…for some training." *In how to find happiness.*

He looked relieved that she'd steered them away from dangerous topics, like their wedding day. Which could only lead to thoughts of their brief—but intensely passionate—marriage. And their sad, angry divorce.

He grabbed a pen and started tapping it on the wooden surface of his desk. "I can't picture you in a cowboy hat."

"Well, I never pictured you with your hair so short."

He grinned, that breath-stealing grin that had always turned her legs into jelly. "I have my barber on speed-dial."

Wyatt as a young man had been lean and wiry, with a thick head of jet-black hair that defied any attempts to tame it, particularly after a day of sand and saltwater at the beach. Time hadn't thinned out those sinfully dark locks. They were now, however, short and smoothed down, no longer curling wildly at the back of his neck. Cassandra's fingers itched to tunnel through the professional style and see the windswept guy she'd known.

His hair wasn't the only thing that had changed. Wyatt's body was also different. He was thicker, filling out his suit exactly the way a perfectly formed man *should* full out a well-cut suit. Broad-shouldered, lean-hipped, exuding strength and power.

Oh, yes, the cute college guy had turned into one amazingly sexy man. And all her softest parts couldn't help but noticing.

"So, you're here on business and you stopped in to see me…for old times' sake?"

Old times' sake? Or *new* times'? Was she here to lay to rest the past? Or perhaps to open a door to the future? Or maybe just grab one more wild, hot memory for posterity.

That sounded like a halfway decent idea right about now.

She just didn't know. Particularly because in the few minutes they'd been sitting here talking and laughing together, she'd remembered there was so much more than his amazing looks, brains and charm that had attracted her to this man.

They'd had a lot in common, and they'd had conversations that had gone on for hours. Wyatt had somehow understood her the way no one else ever had in Cassandra's life. He'd encouraged both her quiet, brainy side—and her wickedly naughty one.

"This is just hard to explain," she said. Not to mention complicated. She'd come in here with one goal, and now she had no idea what to do. Slap him or embrace him. Tell him off or strip and drop to the floor. Leave him…or *take* him.

One thing was certain, she needed time to determine how she felt and what she wanted and where Wyatt fit into that picture.

"I'm not here for a social visit," she finally said, looking around the office to stall for time. Her training at the Warfield had kicked in. She could hear Max's advice to always have a plan of attack. But she needed time to formulate that plan.

"Well, what do you want?"

She blinked. "What do I want?"

"Yes," he said, his eyes narrowing as he stared at her, obviously trying to figure out why she was parroting his words like some kind of trained bird.

Good luck with that. Cassandra couldn't even figure herself out! One thing she did know, however: she wasn't ready to deal with this right now. All her carefully prepared words, her well-thought-out speech and her righteous indignation had sailed out the window and she had no idea what she wanted to say.

Luckily, before she had to say anything, the door to his office flew open and a woman burst in on a wave of energy that was almost palpable. "Wyatt, I have a marvelous idea..."

The tall, dark-haired young woman's words trailed off as she saw Cassandra sitting across from Wyatt at the desk. She looked back and forth between the two of them, visibly curious. "I didn't see an appointment on your calendar," she said.

Cassandra couldn't help wondering who the girl was. Her first thought was coworker, but the jeans and funky tie-dyed halter top suited a social call, not a business meeting.

This slender, very attractive brunette—who looked no more than twenty—was visiting Wyatt socially.

She had absolutely no right to be jealous. The man was no longer her husband. But, oh, it hurt to think he had some young, fresh-faced girl sharing his life. A girl like *she'd* once been.

As if sensing the charged atmosphere, the girl tried to back out. "I'll come back later."

Wyatt stood abruptly. "No. Don't leave. It's okay, honey."

Honey. Ouch.

The girl's brow shot up, but she stayed. "You're sure I'm not interrupting? Is this a business meeting or something?"

Wyatt's expression was wary. "I'm not sure."

A business meeting. She seized on the explanation. Because no way did Cassandra want to launch into a you-broke-my-heart speech right now when the man she'd once been wildly in love with was looking at a younger, adorably perky girl with such affection and warmth.

Formulate a battle plan, she reminded herself, thinking again of how Max would handle this. The most important element in an emotional battle—per Max's training—was to be close to the enemy. Business would ensure close proximity, and proximity would give her time to figure out these wildly erratic feelings she'd been having since seeing Wyatt again.

Because, frankly, telling him off and walking out the door just didn't seem the right move. Diving across the desk and leaping into his arms suddenly seemed more appropriate. Even if he had broken her heart all those years ago by being so angry—so hateful and cold—when she'd admitted to having a crisis of faith and going to her parents for help.

He'd walked out without even *trying* to see her side of it. Her side had been the scared, lonely college girl who missed her parents and hated to see her young husband put in fourteen-hour days, once even nearly cutting his hand off in the lumberyard where he worked. All when she knew her family would help.

Sure, it'd been a mistake, she knew that now. But at twenty-one, surely she was entitled to make a slip-up or two.

Huh-uh. Wyatt Reston allowed no slip-ups, he'd made that brutally clear with the loud slamming of the door.

So why, oh why, did she still want him so much?

"I've come on business," she finally murmured, looking around the office at the variety of framed poster-sized print ads, many of which she recognized.

Wyatt remained standing behind the desk. "Sorry, Cass, I'm not in the market for eyeliner or skin cream." Though he wasn't laughing, Wyatt's dark eyes twinkled. "So whatever you're selling, maybe you ought to find another customer."

Slowly rising to her feet, Cassandra gave a quick thanks that she'd worn the heels with her blue slacks. Staring up at Wyatt was bad enough. At least the shoes put her on eye level with the other person in the room. The dark-haired girl.

"I'm not selling," she said pleasantly. "I'm buying."

Wyatt's mouth tightened.

"I need some fresh ideas for our latest cosmetics line," she added. "I'm here to hire you. I want to see what you can come up with for a new ad campaign."

He said nothing for a long moment. Cassie willed herself to meet his even stare, not intending to give him the tiniest hint that she was bluffing, that her reasons for coming here today had nothing to do with business and everything to do with the past. *Their* past.

"Excellent! Wyatt is the best," the dark-haired girl

said, breaking the silence. Then she started babbling. "I just figured out who you are—you're much prettier in person. I always thought your hair must be fake, but it looks so natural. What was Tom Cruise like? I saw that picture of you with him at Sundance."

Cassandra's head spun as the girl prattled on, but she was aware enough to note Wyatt's expression. His unsmiling face had pulled into a frown and his eyes were flinty.

When the young woman finally paused to take a breath, Wyatt finally spoke. "Forget it."

As if his words weren't answer enough, he shook his head and strode toward the door. Not even looking back, he added, "There's absolutely nothing on this earth that would *ever* induce me to work for your family, Cassandra Devane."

Then he strode out, slamming the door behind him.

CHAPTER THREE

WYATT REELED over Cassie's unexpected reappearance in his life throughout the rest of the day, and the following day, too. He was still so stressed about it the next evening that he decided to pound out his frustrations at the gym. The office building had a well-equipped fitness center on the third floor. It was rarely used, so since moving his company's office here, he'd become accustomed to visiting the gym a couple of times a week. He usually had it to himself, and most times ran on the treadmill or pressed a few weights.

Tonight, however, he was beating on a punching bag.

Trying to land a major campaign with a Japanese automotive company had cost him a lot of energy and a lot of sleepless nights over the past few weeks. But now…he'd have to say the stress he was feeling this evening was personal, not professional. And the sleepless nights in his immediate future were not going to be caused by a tough foreign executive but by a sexy blond American one.

He still couldn't get over Cassie showing up in his life again. Or what she wanted—for him to work for her family. It would have been laughable if it weren't so infuriating. Because her trying to get him to work for her family had been the match that had lit the fuse on their troubled marriage eight years ago and made it explode to pieces.

When he'd graduated college a month after they'd married, he'd been a young kid with big dreams of advertising success in his head. His bank account...well, that hadn't been so big. He'd refused to think it was a major problem, even though deep inside, he'd suspected it was. Still, love and canned ravioli had been just fine for the first six or seven months of his marriage to Cassie.

Those had been the best of times. He'd fallen more in love with her as every day had gone by—in love with her spirit and her intelligence, her sense of humor and her kindness. He'd realized how fortunate he was to have actually found the love of his life. There had been some nights when he'd lain awake in their small bed, simply watching her, listening to the sounds of the breath passing her lips. Wondering what he'd ever done in his life to be so damn lucky.

But as the months had come and gone and he'd still been working at the lumberyard, trying to break into advertising—his *real* dream—she'd gotten nervous. Concerns about money had turned into arguments, which was why she'd gone to her controlling, disapproving parents for help.

That'd been the match. His reaction to her utter lack of faith in him had been the fuse. Their resulting fight had been the TNT. *Goodbye marriage.*

Now she was back in his life. *Hello, heartache.*

"Go back to Texas, little girl, because I am not going down this road with you again," he muttered as he used his arm to wipe off the sweat dripping from his brow.

"Texas wasn't exactly my cup of tea."

He froze, recognizing the voice, not to mention the amused tone. Closing his eyes and willing her to be a figment of his overactive imagination, he slowly turned around. But he didn't have to open his eyes to know he hadn't imagined Cassie's presence. A sweet, feminine scent that made him think of wildflowers blooming under the hot summer sun filled his head. Evidence enough of Cassie's very real presence in the room.

"Hi again," she whispered, sounding nervous.

That made his eyes open, because Cassie and nervous were two words that didn't go together. Cassie and sweet. Cassie and quiet. Cassie and sexy. Cassie and smart. *Cassie and insanity.* Yeah, they went together. But nervousness had no connection to the woman he knew.

"What are you doing here?" He looked at her, standing wide-eyed and openmouthed a few feet away.

She didn't respond at first. It wasn't until he saw a flush of pink color rise up her throat and into her cheeks that he realized why. She was staring at him. Hard. Looking at his body as if she'd never seen a sweaty, shirtless guy dressed in just a pair of nylon gym shorts working out.

When he realized he was seeing feminine appreciation in her stare, he took about two seconds to savor it. A visceral, completely instinctive sensation of warmth flooded his veins, making his pulse roar even harder than it had during his workout. Because the bedroom was one place where they'd never had any trouble. They'd had an incredibly erotic relationship, one that hadn't been matched with anyone else in the ensuing years—not even close.

Wyatt had to forcibly shake off the memories that instantly filled his head. Vivid, evocative memories of long, sultry nights and hot, steamy days. Both before their wedding and after.

To this day he couldn't smell the ocean without remembering what it had been like to lie on the sand with her, kissing, tasting and stroking every inch of her body. Or how erotic it had been one day to stand in the waves, the windblown whitecaps hiding the fact that beneath the surface, his hand was inside her bathing suit as he stroked her to an absolute frenzy.

God, he wanted to touch her, *ached* to touch her. But that was the very last thing he could afford to do. Because one touch would never be enough.

Finally, he managed to mutter through a very tight throat, "I said, why are you here?"

She swallowed deeply before answering. "You left so soon yesterday, we didn't get a chance to finish our conversation."

"I was finished," he said as he unlaced a boxing glove with his teeth, not having the strength to look at her anymore. He'd sooner go ten rounds with a heavyweight than spend ten minutes looking at Cassie, being tormented by what had, for Wyatt, been the biggest failure of his life.

"Well, I wasn't finished with you," she said. "Fortunately, your sister is a good listener and she heard me out. She thinks you could do remarkable things to bring Fresh Face Cosmetics to the average woman. Up until now we've been focused on the upscale department-store market, but we have to diversify."

His sister. Damn. He should have known better than to leave his office when those two were together. Jackie—his baby sister—had probably spilled every detail about Wyatt's personal life to Cassie in exchange for a single tidbit about Brad Pitt. "Yeah, well, Jackie doesn't work for me. She's a student."

"It was nice to meet her," Cassie said. She stepped closer, bringing that intoxicating cloud of woman-scent with her to mess with his head some more. "You should have introduced us."

"When, yesterday? Or eight years ago?" he muttered as he removed the second glove. Tossing them into a bin in the corner, he walked over to a stack of towels and used one to dry the sweat off his face and neck.

She followed, so he moved again. And so did she. It was like being in a human chess game, with her countering his every move, until they stood only a foot apart.

Wyatt tried to ignore her, tried not to notice the warmth of her breath on his shoulder, so sensual against the cool air-conditioning in the room. Focusing on the faint sound of the terry-cloth towel scraping against his skin, he tried to tune out her low, steady inhalations that seemed to deepen with every passing moment. Unfortunately, he didn't think anything could muffle the raging beat of his heart, which had been on overdrive since he'd found her in his office yesterday.

Too bad the fitness center didn't have a pool because he could use a few bracing laps right about now. Though, honestly, he knew that wouldn't help. With Cassie watching his every move, every Y chromosome in Wyatt's body was at full attention. No swimming pool, no cold shower, not even a dip off a glacier in the Arctic would do a thing to cool him down.

Not when Cassie was wearing that aware, hungry look.

It was the same one she'd had on her face the day they'd met on the beach. She'd never been able to hide her emotions behind those big blue eyes or that expressive face. When Cassie was interested in something— be it a book or a male body—she could never disguise that interest. Just one of the things he'd found so utterly fascinating about her, since no girl he'd ever known had been so open.

Right now, the physical desire was dripping off her in buckets. Palpable. Intoxicating. And Wyatt was unable to prevent himself from sharing it. As if their marriage and the ensuing years weren't hanging there between them, he allowed himself a few luxurious moments to study her through a lover's eyes—not an angry ex's, as he had in his office.

She looked different than she had yesterday, no longer the cool professional woman. She now wore a pair of tight white jeans and a sleeveless red top. The color contrasted brightly against her blond hair. Her time in Texas had given her skin a healthy glow, and she wore almost no makeup. Damned if there weren't a few freckles on her nose.

Wyatt's jaw tightened, because Cassie looked like a coed again. The beach angel he'd found utterly irresistible.

She wasn't, however, *exactly* the same. Her casual, tight clothes did sinful things to her body, reminding him that Cassie was no longer a lean, willowy, college girl. She was a curvaceous, soft, desirable woman. And she was looking at him like she wanted to gobble him up.

Which, he realized, was probably the *last* thing she'd want him to see. Knowing for sure how to get her to back off, he decided to call her on her interest. Curving up one side of his mouth, he gestured toward the weight area. "There are no beds in here, but some of the weight benches are padded."

She sucked in a quick, surprised breath.

"What?" he pressed. "You gonna deny you're eating me up with your eyes?"

Her chin shot up and for a split second he thought he had her.

He should have known better. Because he recalled a moment too late that she had never been the quiet, demure girl some people had thought her to be. She'd always had a danger-loving streak. And now, she was every inch a sexy, confident woman. No way would she be embarrassed into backing down.

"How could I not when you're standing there half-naked? Could you please either put a shirt *on* or take your shorts *off?*"

Whoa. Wyatt's jaw dropped and his fingers clenched reflexively as though to reach for his waistband and do as she asked. Then he saw the glint of amusement on her face.

The woman was good. Too good. "Okay, you win," he said with a rueful chuckle, snatching up his T-shirt, which was draped across a bench press machine.

She pursed her lips. "That wasn't your only option."

"Stop trying to seduce me."

"Who said anything about seduction? I just wouldn't mind seeing you naked again."

"Tell you what," he said with a drawl as he pulled his shirt on, "you first."

That wicked glint appeared again and Wyatt immediately threw his hand up, palm out, to stop her. "Forget it, I did not mean that. What happened to the Cassie who was voted 'nicest girl' in your snobby, high-brow high school?"

She licked her lips. "I thought you figured that out a long time ago. She secretly knew that being naughty is a lot more fun."

He grinned, liking the way she raised a suggestive eyebrow. This playfully wicked Cassie appealed to the man Wyatt was now even more than the supposedly "nice girl" had appealed to the kid he'd been when they'd met.

Which was bad news all around.

Stiffening, he said, "Okay, tell me what you really want. And just what did you tell my sister?"

The distraction worked, as he'd expected it would. "She had no idea who I was."

"She recognized you from *People* magazine."

She crossed her arms tightly over her chest. "I mean, she has no idea you and I have a history. It's strange to realize we never met each other's families. Jackie... I didn't even recognize her from her pictures."

"She was only twelve when we met. And it wasn't like we were together long enough to take that trip home to Indiana for you to meet my folks."

That had been the plan. Since his parents hadn't had the money to come to Virginia for Wyatt's college graduation, he and Cassie had talked about getting into his beat-up old truck and driving out to Fort Wayne to visit and spring the news of their elopement on them. The marriage, however, hadn't lasted long enough for them to do it. He'd eventually told his parents about Cassie, but they'd never talked about her after the divorce.

As if she could read his mind, she asked, "Does Jackie even know you were once...married?"

He shook his head. "No. My parents didn't tell her when they found out, because I wanted to surprise her. Then came the divorce and, well, there was no point anymore."

When her lashes lowered a bit over hurt-looking eyes, he almost regretted admitting that to her. It made her seem like an insignificant part of his life, when, in fact, she'd been anything but. "She wouldn't have understood," he admitted grudgingly. "She was just a kid."

Her expression softened. "Of course." Then a grin tugged at her mouth. "Your sister's definitely grown up. I don't think I've ever met anyone who can talk quite as much as she can."

He groaned. "You have no idea. Ever since she moved here to go to college, I've been considering investing in earplugs, or a hearing aid, because I know if she sticks around for a few decades, I'm going to go deaf."

She chuckled. Then, growing serious again, she said, "Jackie thinks you won't take me on as a client for personal reasons and she pumped me to find out what they were."

"Jackie is going to be dead meat for shooting off her mouth, so you really shouldn't listen to what she has to say," he replied, matter-of-factly.

"Is it true?"

"No, but only because there are laws against murdering your sister."

"Wyatt!"

Rolling his eyes, he finally answered her question. "Okay, maybe it's true. Maybe I'm still angry at you."

She stared into his eyes, as if determining how to respond. Finally, she murmured, "Maybe I'm still angry at you, too. And maybe that's why we *need* to work together."

Twisted logic. Made about as much sense as eating a big burger two days after you'd gotten food poisoning from another burger. Some wounds were just better left alone, covered deep under an emotional Band-Aid, rather than exposed to the light of day. "I don't think so, Cass," he finally said. "It happened a long time ago. We should leave it in the past."

Her sigh of frustration was audible, and the accompanying roll of her eyes almost made him laugh. Cassie didn't like being told no. She never had.

He should have known better than to think she'd given up, however. Because before he could say *sayonara* and invite her to have a good life, she offered him a sunny smile. "Well, I think you're wrong. And I guess I have to convince you of that over dinner."

Immediately wary, he simply stared.

"That's why I'm here. Jackie said it would be easier for me to just ride home with you, and your secretary—what a nice lady she is—you know, she's fifty-four and doesn't look a day over forty-five, which means she must use Fresh Face skin-care products. Anyway, she's the one who told me you were in here, uh...working out."

She was babbling, another sign of the nervousness he'd never seen in Cassie before. Meaning somewhere in that incoherent string of sentences was a piece of information she knew he wasn't going to like. And when he thought about it, he zeroed in on exactly what it was. "Ride with *me*? To *dinner*?"

She nodded so hard her hair flopped over her brow. He had an insane urge to reach out and brush it away. Probably would be safer to stick his hand into a deep fryer; he'd have less chance of getting burned.

"Yes, we figured it'd be easier that way. My hotel is close to here, but I'd probably get lost if I tried to drive over to your place by myself in my rental car."

Jackie, you are so *in for it.* "You're not serious...."

"Oh, yes, I am. Didn't I tell you?" she asked, her voice holding a suspicious hint of laughter. Her mischievous streak had apparently won out over her nervousness, which was too darned cute for his peace of mind.

"Tell me what?" he asked, already knowing the answer.

Cassie flashed that bright smile which, in the old days, could get him to agree to absolutely anything. "Your sister invited me over to your place for dinner tonight."

CASSANDRA REALLY LIKED her former sister-in-law. And not only because Jackie had provided her with the perfect opportunity to be close to Wyatt for a while longer—so she could work on him about taking her on as a client. The young woman was also witty and exuberant, friendly and flamboyant. And the very minute her brother had stormed out of the office the previous day, she'd apparently decided to become Cassandra's ally.

Why, Cassandra had no idea. But seeing the spark of excitement and mischief in Wyatt's sister's face, she'd had the feeling Jackie was doing it as much to entertain herself as to help Cassandra. Hence the dinner invitation to Wyatt's place. The idea had doubly angered him because, as he kept muttering, Jackie didn't even live with him.

"You couldn't have spared us both this agony and just said no to my sister?" he asked, not for the first time as the two of them drove through the busy streets of downtown Boston, heading toward his apartment.

Agony? Oh, it was more agonizing than she'd ever imagined. If she'd realized how darned uncomfortable this drive was going to be, she might have rethought her acceptance of Jackie's invitation. Because Wyatt drove a sleek, tiny little sports car, which currently cocooned them both in a dark, intimate bubble of intensity. Awareness. Heat.

But she knew that wasn't what Wyatt meant about the agony. So maybe she was the only one feeling the tension between them in the car. "Is spending a couple of hours with me really such agony? We used to enjoy spending time together, remember?"

He glanced over, then focused straight ahead again. "Yeah, I think that was around the time when I also used to enjoy cold pizza and warm beer for breakfast, too."

"I had you on fruit and yogurt smoothies pretty fast," she said with a smile, remembering the way she'd gotten Wyatt to start taking better care of himself.

"I hated fruit and yogurt smoothies."

She frowned in indignation. "You absolutely did not."

Wyatt's lips quirked in a tiny grin. "I just didn't want to make you feel bad. I'm lactose intolerant."

This time, Cassie's jaw dropped open completely. "Get out! You are not. How did you eat pizza then?"

"Pizza was worth suffering for. Yogurt was not."

"But you still drank them for breakfast all the time…."

His eyes shifted a tiny bit and she suddenly understood. He'd done it for *her.*

She fell silent, not knowing what to say to that. God, they'd been such babies. Her playing housewife, trying to get him to eat healthily, and him making himself sick so she'd feel like she'd succeeded. "What business did two infants like us have getting married, anyway?" she mumbled, thinking out loud.

Wyatt tensed, his hands tightening so hard around the steering wheel they turned white. Probably because she'd used the *m* word. But there was no getting around it. Their marriage was a huge, vibrant presence between them, taking up every bit of air in the car, like the proverbial nine-hundred-pound gorilla in the room.

She wanted to talk about it…and yet, she didn't. Not now. Not until they were out of this car and she didn't smell the sultry aroma of warm man, didn't hear his low breaths, didn't feel the warmth of his arm just a few inches away from her own.

Didn't keep picturing him in those flimsy gym shorts and nothing else.

Okay, girl, get a grip. She thrust the images out of her head, but knew better than to think they wouldn't be taunting her later. Probably late tonight when she was lying alone in her hotel bed. *Wondering.*

Shifting in her seat because of her suddenly uncomfortably tight jeans, she crossed her arms and glanced out the window, wondering what they could talk about that would make her heart stop its flippity-flopping. Not sex, that was for sure. Because just thinking about it had her wondering just how much they could manage in a car this size.

Her jeans got even tighter.

They couldn't talk about their marriage, either. She needed to make sure she wasn't too close to him when they had that conversation because she'd already realized she was still susceptible to Wyatt. Not just physically, either. Every minute she spent with him was reminding her why she'd fallen for him so hard in the first place.

So they'd need to be in less confined quarters, when she told him he'd been a fat-headed, stubborn, proud fool to throw their marriage away because she'd been scared and stupid.

"So tell me about this automotive firm you're trying to land," she said, finally coming up with a topic of conversation that might leave her breathing normally and keep her panties from getting any more moist from her overheated imaginings. "Why'd they shoot down your first presentation? I liked the concept of various men in different models of cars all stopped at the same intersection at different times."

Wyatt's jaw dropped.

"Jackie," she explained, almost feeling sorry for him. Couldn't be easy to have such a chatterbox sister. Then again, any sister would be nice, as far as Cassandra was concerned. Being the only child in her family, she'd often wished for a sibling to share in the attention. And the pressure.

"The bigmouth," he said, shaking his head in disgust.

"Okay, right, but get past that. What was the problem with the campaign? Sounds pretty cute to me. Playing on the whole 'you can tell a man by what he drives' thing, but keeping it sexy and light."

He looked over again, though he should have had his eyes on the road. Wyatt's gaze narrowed and he tilted his head in confusion. "How'd you grasp that so quickly?"

"Grasp what?"

"The playful boys-and-their-toys image we were going for."

She shrugged. "I don't know. It's just what I visualized when Jackie mentioned it."

A horn beeped, startling them both. Wyatt quickly returned his attention to the road, giving an apologetic wave to the driver in the next lane who he'd nearly swerved in front of.

"Well, you visualized it exactly the way *I* visualized it," he admitted, his words slow, as though he was surprised by the realization. "They just didn't get it."

"It's pretty American," she said.

"They're selling to an American audience," he said, his tone dry. As if he'd made the argument before.

Apparently, however, that hadn't helped him land the difficult account. "So did you scrap it and go back to the drawing board entirely?"

Wyatt shook his head. "Not entirely. We all liked it, but I know something didn't click. I just haven't figured out what yet, or how we can salvage some of the overall concept."

She tapped her index finger on her cheek, thinking about it. "How about a line of women at a stoplight, all putting on eye shadow?" she asked, not trying to hide the mischief in her voice.

"To sell imported cars?"

"Nope. Cosmetics."

"Forget it. I'm not working for you."

"Or," she said, as if he hadn't spoken, "wind blowing wildly through an open car window, but never messing up her foundation."

"Cassie…"

"A couple lying on the hood of a sexy convertible, kissing passionately without smearing her lipstick?" That certainly put *her* imagination into overdrive….

"Cassandra!"

She clapped her hands together. "I've got it! A well-dressed woman crying to the cop who pulled her over to give her a ticket, without getting all raccoon-eyed from runny mascara."

He groaned, deeply, helplessly. But then, as if unable to help it, Wyatt began to chuckle and shake his head. "When did you get to be such a pain in the ass?"

"When did *you* get to be so stubborn?"

Wyatt stopped at a stop sign and looked over at her, the soft reflection from the dashboard casting lines of light and shadow across his handsome face. His amusement gradually faded until he was staring at her, looking both intense and also perhaps a bit concerned. "Why is it so important that I work for your company? Are you in some kind of trouble, Cass?"

Trouble? Well, not the kind he meant. He was asking if Fresh Face Cosmetics was in trouble. And while they did need to diversify and open up their company with an expansion into lower-priced markets, things weren't dire or anything.

No, Cassandra's only dire problem was her personal life. Her confused emotions. Her lack of ability to get over what had been the most important relationship in her life. Her lack of ability to get over *him*.

CHAPTER FOUR

DINNER WAS shaping up to be a complete disaster. Despite having issued the invitation, Wyatt's sister obviously had no idea how to cook. Cassandra quickly discovered that when she walked into the large, fully equipped kitchen of Wyatt's spacious apartment near Beacon Hill. Wyatt was getting cleaned up so Cassie had asked Jackie if she could help.

"Is there an easy way to get this stuff out of the bottom of the jar?" Jackie was shaking an open container of premade alfredo sauce into a much-too-small saucepan. "I was going to put water in it to get the last little clumps out, like I do with tomato soup, but I was afraid it might get runny."

Cassandra sucked her bottom lip in her mouth so Jackie wouldn't see her amusement. The girl looked thoroughly confused, with globs of whitish-gray sauce splattered on the stove, the counter and Jackie's face. The scene, and Jackie's woebegone expression, emphasized her youth. Wyatt's sister was probably only twenty or twenty-one, and in way over her head. She looked a lot like Cassandra probably had during her brief marriage.

The realization made her heart twist.

"Is Wyatt really lactose intolerant?" she asked, to see if he'd been messing with her head earlier, and to make sure his sister wasn't about to make him sick. As his wife used to do.

"Oh, cripes, I forgot," Jackie said, her eyes widening into big circles. "Is this stuff dairy?"

Wincing as she read the label, Cassandra nodded. "I'd expect so. Cheese, cream…"

The girl muttered a four-letter word, then gave Cassandra an apologetic smile. "Sorry."

"Don't worry about it. I did my share of cursing when I was first learning to cook. Especially when I first made soufflé."

"Are you a good cook?" The hope in Jackie's face and voice told her just how overwhelmed the girl felt.

Thinking of the hours she'd spent with her family's cook growing up—because the woman was the only person on the estate who'd ever made her feel welcome, rather than underfoot—Cassandra nodded. "Cooking is the one thing I'm very good at."

"What about selling makeup?"

Cassandra winked. "I'm pretty good at that, too. But it helps to have an awesome product line."

"Which you do," Jackie said with an earnest nod. "I never thought your company's cosmetics were worth the outrageous prices, but that thickening mascara makes my eyes look incredible." Her face instantly reddened. "I'm sorry. I was trying to pay you a compliment."

Grinning, Cassandra said, "Don't worry about it. The overpriced perception is one of the reasons I need your brother's help." Striding to Wyatt's pantry, she took stock. Then she scoped out the fridge, noting the fruits and veggies. She was already picturing pasta with marinara sauce and a big salad. "He sure eats healthier than he did in the old days," she murmured.

It was only when Jackie cleared her throat that she

realized what she'd said. Whirling around, she stammered, "Your brother and I have known each other for a while."

Jackie stared at her, but didn't answer at first. Instead, she walked to the kitchen door and pushed it open, peering into the living area of the apartment. Then she pulled her head back in, closing the door again. "I know," she said in an exaggerated whisper. Her wide, sparkling eyes and the way she bobbed her head up and down in several jerky nods added to the melodrama.

Cassandra was almost afraid to ask what the girl meant. Because judging by the way she'd scoped things out to make sure Wyatt wasn't going to overhear, Jackie knew a lot. And she didn't want her brother to know she knew.

"I lived here with Wyatt for a couple of months last summer after sophomore year, instead of going home to Indiana," Jackie said, still sotto voce. "I wanted to be helpful, so I was doing some cleaning and I found a box of stuff in the closet."

"Stuff?"

"It was a bunch of pictures. Of him…and you."

Oh, boy. She didn't know whether she was touched that Wyatt had kept pictures of them—as she had, though she'd never admit it to him—or if she worried about which pictures Jackie was referring to. Hopefully they didn't have a skinny Elvis in them.

"They were of your wedding."

So much for that hope. Cassandra lowered her eyes, not quite knowing how to face the young woman, who could have been her sister-in-law all these years. "I see."

"He had your divorce papers in there, too, but it was the pictures that really made me sad."

Jackie crossed the room before Cassandra even realized she was moving. Throwing her arms around Cassandra's shoulders, she gave her a big hug. "You and

my brother were perfect together—I can tell by the
pictures. So what on earth happened? How did you two
screw it up? Are you here to get him back?"

Since Jackie's hair was going up Cassandra's nose
and in her mouth, and she could barely breathe because
of the bear hug, she couldn't reply at first. Finally, Jackie
let go and stepped back. It was then Cassandra noticed
the tears on the girl's cheeks. "Oh, honey, I'm so sorry,"
Cassandra said. "Wyatt knew you'd be hurt by it, that's
why he never told you."

Jackie shook her head, her brown eyes—so like her
brother's—wide and miserable. "I'm not sad for me,"
she said. "I'm so sad for you two, that you let it slip
away. Because, Cassie, honest to God, judging by the
things he wrote to you in the letters he never sent, my
brother loved you more than life itself."

To WYATT'S GREAT SURPRISE, his sister had pulled off a
really nice dinner Tuesday night. Considering Jackie
had set off his fire alarm every time she'd tried to cook
something last summer when she'd lived with him,
Wyatt had been very impressed.

For her part, Cassie had been vivacious and funny,
amusing both him and Jackie with her stories about her
travels and some of the people she'd met. Somehow, it
hadn't hurt, thinking of that lifestyle she lived, because
it had seemed from her words and her expressions that
she considered that side of her life—the famous, rich,
socialite side—a source of amusement more than
anything else. The way she'd laughed about one movie
star's bad breath and a tycoon's floppy toupee had made
him suspect there was still a bit of that same down-to-
earth girl he'd known. She was just in a very sexy,
mature, confident package.

The one thing he'd found incredibly amusing was the way Jackie had kept pointing out all of Cassie's accomplishments to Wyatt. It had eventually dawned on him that his little sister was trying to set him up with his own ex-wife!

He'd glanced at Cassie, expecting to see her amber eyes sparkling with laughter. Instead, he'd realized she was focused on shuffling all the cucumbers to the side of her salad.

She had never liked cucumbers. Just like he'd never liked olives. The two of them had always done an automatic salad dance whenever they'd gone out to dinner, dumping anything they wouldn't eat onto each other's plates. Glancing down, Wyatt hadn't been able to prevent a sharp stab of sadness when he'd seen the lonely black olives in his bowl…and the cukes on hers.

That moment had killed the pleasure of the evening for him. Because it had been so startlingly clear that they'd lost so much more than just their marriage, just their passion.

They'd also lost their friendship.

It had been almost too much to stand, the intense sense of loss that had overwhelmed him. Which was why he'd abruptly risen from the dinner table, announcing that he had to drive Cassie back to her hotel because of an early-morning meeting the next day. With Jackie crammed into the small back seat of his car, he and Cassie had been unable to exchange anything more than the most minor pleasantries before saying good-night.

Which was exactly what he'd wanted.

So why was he now, not even twenty-four hours later, pulling into the parking lot of her hotel, having agreed to meet her for a drink Wednesday night? "Because you're a masochist," he said aloud as he got out of the car and pocketed his keys.

Something had forced him to accept her invitation when Cassie had called him earlier today. Wyatt had been prepared to refuse when he'd suddenly realized a Pandora's box had opened up inside him. So many crazy, tangled memories had come soaring out last night, he now felt he *had* to see her again, if only to figure out what she was really doing in Boston. Because the whole excuse of her wanting to hire him had been bull. She had another reason for being in town. And he needed to find out what it was.

Entering the pricey hotel, he glanced around and immediately saw Cassie sitting on an overstuffed couch. She spied him and rose, smiling as she approached. "Hi. I'm glad you came. A drink is the least I owe you for last night's dinner."

"Honestly, I have *no* idea why I agreed to this." The words had left his mouth before he'd even considered them. He couldn't regret the statement, though. It was, after all, only the truth.

Taking her arm, he led her through the lobby toward a nearby lounge, noting the attention she received from the hotel staff. She'd obviously made her presence felt already, because everyone—from the concierge to the bellhop, to the waitress—greeted her with a genuine smile.

Once inside the bar, they sat at a quiet table in the corner. Only a few other people were around. A bored-looking middle-aged man sat at the piano. His fingers danced lightly over the keys as he plucked out quiet standards—inoffensive background music that covered all other conversation in the place, leaving them cocooned in their own private bubble.

"So when are you going back to New York?" he asked after they sat down and ordered their drinks.

"Not sure." She shifted in her seat—which was beside his, not across from it—and crossed her legs. He was so tuned in to Cassie that he could hear the scrape of the fabric of her jeans. Even, he believed, her slow, deep breaths.

Their eyes met and held for a long, electric moment. It was as if both of them had suddenly realized they were completely alone in a hotel bar. At night. With only the clink of glasses and some quiet music to disturb them.

The waitress returned with their order, breaking the silent connection, and then disappeared again behind the bar.

"Tell me why you're really here."

Her reply was just as challenging. "Tell me why you want me to leave."

Maybe because your jeans are so tight and my will-power is down to zero?

"I'd think that would be obvious."

"Not to me. So say it, Wyatt." As if she knew exactly what he was thinking, and was determined to increase the pressure, she leaned close and dropped her hand onto his thigh.

Her touch burned. Fried him until he had to drop his hand to cover hers on his leg. "What do you want from me, Cassie?"

She laughed softly, a sultry sound that rolled over him the same way her subtle scent was flowing over his whole body. "I thought I wanted closure. To see you again and see that the past is over and that I can go on with my life."

God, it felt like she'd put a knife in him, even though he'd been telling himself exactly the same thing. It was over. He'd known that for eight years. So why in hell did it wound him to hear the words coming off her gorgeous lips?

She swallowed, her hand tightening almost reflexively on his leg, until he had to close his eyes in self-protection. "But I don't know, Wyatt. I'm here now and I see you and all I can think about is the way you tasted like rum punch the first time you kissed me at that beach party."

Groaning, he gave himself over to the memory. That night, the flicker of the bonfire had turned Cassie's hair into a long, living flame and had made her sapphire eyes glow. He'd just met her that day, but he'd already known he was experiencing his first real adult desire. Not young guy lust, but true, genuine desire to explore every erotic, sensual delight with a woman…and wake up with her the next morning.

He leaned forward a bit. "You tasted like cotton candy."

She licked her lips. "And the Celine Dion song from *Titanic* was playing on Joy Miller's boom box. She loved that soundtrack."

He laughed softly, leaning in a little more. A little closer to her scent. A little closer to her smile. A little closer to madness. "I hated that movie."

"I know you did." She shifted in her seat, until their thighs brushed together. "I loved it."

He watched the way her soft, moist lips parted with her exhalations. "I know you did."

Then there was no more conversation; there were no more words or platitudes or excuses. They simply came together, cheeks brushing, then lips meeting in a sweet, languorous kiss of reunion and apology. Admission and anticipation.

Wyatt gave himself one second to regret it, then a full minute to savor it. Tasting her mouth and sharing her breaths, he slipped his tongue between her lips to tangle with hers in a lazy exploration. No tension, no frenzy, no desperation. This was just a lazy greeting, a hello after a long time apart. It was saying *I missed you. I want you.*

It was like coming home.

"Ahem."

The waitress's presence beside their table was enough to shock them both to the present. Almost stunned at how overwhelming it had been to kiss Cassie again, Wyatt pulled back and drew in a deep breath. He shifted away. Space was necessary for propriety. And for sanity.

Once they were alone again, they each sipped deeply from their glasses, though, of course, alcohol would do nothing to cool either of them down. And they both knew it.

But he needed to stop this in its tracks. In the calm aftermath of a wildly unexpected kiss, Wyatt acknowledged the mistake he'd just made. He'd kissed her and opened up the floodgates. He'd let her start crawling back inside him, allowed her to dig into his heart by way of his libido, a mistake of monumental proportions.

A mistake he needed to correct immediately.

So, forcing himself to remain calm and aloof, he leaned back in his seat and eyed her impassively. "Aren't you worried about things going wrong with your business while you're gone?"

He couldn't believe how normal he sounded. How calm. How focused. Especially when every brain cell he had was telling him to breathe deeper of her scent, to lose himself in her eyes. And reminding him that Cassie had a bed somewhere very close by.

"I'm not as worried about the business as I am about things continuing to go wrong in my life."

Her words were soft, whispered, but they rang in Wyatt's head. And kept ringing, as more ominous possibilities filled his imagination. "What's wrong, Cass? You never really answered my question last night. Are you in trouble? Has something happened?" He wondered if she could hear the genuine concern he couldn't hide, and what she made of it. Hell, *he* didn't know what to make of it. All he knew was that the thought of Cassie being sick, or in trouble, filled him with tension. Dread. *Fear.*

Just as the thought of her kiss filled him with hunger.

"Nothing's happened," she said. "Except I took a little time-out from my normal life. My grandmother helped me realize I needed a break from everything. Work, friends…family."

Wyatt couldn't help it, his hand tightened reflexively on his glass as he brought his neat Scotch to his lips. "Your grandmother and parents still trying to run your life?"

Cassie's voice shook with emotion as she replied, "Don't say that. They never controlled me. My family loves me."

"Sure they do." Wyatt sipped again, then put his drink down. "But they also manipulate you into doing whatever they want you to do. They always did, by disappearing whenever you needed them most, or silently disapproving whenever they didn't like something you'd done." *Like getting married.* "They had you jumping through hoops, trying to make them proud of you. Not to mention trying to make them see you as something other than a pretty blonde."

Cassie was watching him with wide eyes and an open mouth. She looked stunned and confused. And, judging by the way her jaw was clenching, angry. "You don't know what you're talking about. You never even *met* my family."

"I didn't need to," he replied, feeling weary. "I knew everything there was to know about them whenever you mentioned your childhood. There wasn't much you wouldn't do to get their approval."

Their eyes locked in a long stare. He knew she was mentally denying his accusations, but she wasn't doing it verbally. Because she couldn't. He had said nothing but the truth, whether she wanted to admit it or not.

From the day they'd met until the day they'd split up, he'd known Cassie was forced to walk a fine line with her family. Many of her relatives, particularly her grandmother, were downright cutthroat. Her parents were, to put it mildly, aloof…more interested in each other than their daughter. Which was why Cassie had been so eager for love, to love and be loved in return. And oh, she'd been so *easy* to love.

Cassie hadn't even touched her drink, but she stood, anyway. "Good night, Wyatt. Thanks for the drink." Her lips tightened. "Not to mention the psychological evaluation."

She turned around and strode through the bar before he could respond. For several long moments, he sat at the table, wondering if he should go and find her, apologize to her, try to dry the tears he suspected were spilling down her cheeks.

He'd made Cassie cry. *Again.* God, he felt like a scumbag.

But maybe it was for the best. Whatever had driven Cassandra Devane to Boston to look him up, maybe the reality of what he thought of her family would be enough to make her leave again. Which—especially after that kiss—was the best thing for Wyatt's sanity, and probably Cassie's, too.

As for his heart? Well…he wasn't even going to consider what his heart wanted. It was much too dangerous.

And *much* too late.

CHAPTER FIVE

CASSANDRA PACKED her bags that night, deciding to leave the following morning. It was time to get back to New York, to her real life. This trip, this "journey" as Mad Max would have called it, had proved to be a complete waste of time. She hadn't gotten her closure, but there was still a chance to cut her losses.

Alone in the hotel room, she muttered and fumed, crying a bit while talking to herself. She opened the minibar and poured herself what was probably a twenty-dollar ounce of alcohol. It didn't help. Nothing would get Wyatt's words out of her head.

So much for Jackie's assurances that her brother had "loved her more than life." He obviously hadn't if he had such a low opinion of her. Not that she knew the content of Wyatt's letters, nor did she want to. She'd scolded Jackie for invading her brother's privacy and had absolutely refused to hear any details.

That didn't, however, mean she hadn't been thinking about them—wondering, imagining—ever since Jackie had opened her mouth. She'd even been playing the "what if" game. As in, "what if" he'd sent her those letters, and "what if" she'd had the guts to answer them.

But it was too late. Because even if he had felt those things once, he didn't anymore. Whatever his opinion of her had been back then, he sure didn't think much of her now. His words proved it, and it hurt. *She* was hurt. Not to mention depressed.

Mostly, though, she was mad.

Wyatt was wrong. *Wrong.* She wasn't who she was because of whatever her family wanted. She'd worked her ass off to become the woman she was today. If he was mistaking her for the girl she'd once been, well, he hadn't really been paying attention to who she was now.

The girl she'd once been... The words bounced around in her brain, as did Wyatt's assessment of their marriage. Despite her certainty that he was way off-base, she couldn't help questioning herself, just a tiny bit.

What if he was at least partially right? What if she had been seeking a lot more than just her parents' money? What if she'd *always* cared more about her family's opinions than she had about her own happiness?

No. Wyatt was wrong. She knew herself, didn't she? Dammit, she better know herself after spending two weeks—not to mention thousands of dollars—at Warfield Boot Camp.

Glancing at her watch and seeing it was after 11:00 p.m., she figured it was still only eight or nine in Texas. She never could remember whether Houston was two or three hours behind.

Without giving it much thought, she picked up her cell phone and flipped through her electronic address book. Mad Max had told her to call anytime. And right now, Cassandra wanted to call. She had a few things to tell the camp owner. First, that the woman needed to stop meddling in people's lives.

She also wanted to tell Maxine Warfield to add a new mantra to her list of life's lessons: *You* can't *go back.*

"Warfield Retreat, this is Maxine," a smooth, emotionless voice said.

Cassie wasn't feeling exactly emotionless. "This journey stuff you shove down people's throats is a load of bull."

"Well, well, Ms. Devane, isn't it? And how is Boston?"

Cassie plopped onto the bed, sitting cross-legged on the plush comforter. "Boston is beautiful but I am out of here."

"But you only just arrived, didn't you?"

Some papers shuffled in the background. Maxine was probably working on some other plan to torture another poor client who'd made the mistake of paying the exorbitant fee to attend Warfield. "Wyatt accused me of always doing only what my family wanted. Making choices only to please them."

"Hmm…"

Cassie waited but the reserved woman didn't say another word. "Well? What do you think? I thought we agreed that the problem was I needed closure in my relationship with *Wyatt.* Not that I needed to look at my relatives' involvement in my life, and how I react to it."

Another pregnant pause. Cassie almost groaned, picturing the frown lines on the older woman's forehead growing ever deeper. Max would be way beyond any anti-wrinkle cream if Cassie kept harassing the woman, but she just couldn't help it. "Do you think he's right? Is it possible my relationship with my family, my need to please them, was the heart of the reason for my breakup with Wyatt? That it was *my* fault all along?"

Papers ruffled again. And Max made a sighing sound.

Cassandra barely noticed. Because her own words were echoing in her head, suddenly sounding plausible.

No, she absolutely did not live her life for her family anymore. She'd decided to go to Warfield Boot Camp because Nana Ellen had asked her to as a personal favor—not because she'd demanded it.

But this was *now*. And that—Wyatt, her marriage—was *then*. Maybe the Cassandra of eight years ago hadn't been quite as confident and independent as she'd thought.

"He's onto something, isn't he?" she whispered. "Maybe I wasn't just asking for my parents' financial help to set Wyatt up in business. What if I was seeking their approval, knowing how angry they were that I'd married him? Perhaps I was trying to make my parents happy by showing I still needed them, instead of waiting for them to acknowledge my right to make my own choices."

This time Max had the courtesy to grunt a little.

"And when I got their money but *not* their blessing," she continued, still almost thinking out loud, "maybe I… Is it possible I subconsciously sabotaged my marriage? Punished Wyatt for it, even? Maybe not even realizing it made him think I was giving him an ultimatum—to take their job or else?"

"Mmm."

"Not intentionally!"

"Mmm."

Cassie began to wearily rub the corners of her eyes. "Damn," she whispered, finally forcing herself to admit the truth. Maxine might be right. More importantly, Wyatt might be right. Maybe the problems she and Wyatt had had really weren't because of money or financial worries. Or because of her need for security and his lack of patience. Maybe they'd simply been about Cassandra making a subconscious choice. The *wrong* choice. The choice to seek her parents' approval, rather than have faith in her young husband.

The realization stunned her into silence for a moment. She stared sightlessly at the wall, the cell phone still up to her ear, and let a montage of images sweep through her mind.

Images of herself as a young girl. Needy. Lonely.

Images of herself as a young wife. Scared. Uncertain.

Images of herself today. A very different person. One who sure wasn't the type to run when the going got tough.

She immediately sat straighter on the bed and swung her legs around to dangle off the side of it. "Thank you, Max," she said, meaning it. "I can't tell you how much this has helped. You really talked me off a ledge."

Maxine started to laugh, her amusement taking Cassandra by surprise. Then she said something completely unexpected, something that made Cassie reevaluate everything she'd thought about the woman. "Well, Ms. Devane, you are most very welcome for my complete silence. I hope now that you've found the ruby slippers, you and Toto can make your way back home."

Cassandra's mouth fell open, but the call was disconnected before she could say a word. Remembering their conversation the other day in Max's office, she began to look at the camp owner in a new light. Maybe Maxine Warfield wasn't quite the hard-nosed drill sergeant she appeared to be. And maybe Cassie had, like Dorothy from the *Wizard of Oz,* needed to learn for *herself* how to get her heart's true desire.

Funny, she almost missed Maxine. Her time at Warfield suddenly seemed so long ago, even though it had only been a few days since she'd left Texas. Things had certainly changed in those few days. Deep things, intrinsic things, like her view of herself and her world and her marriage. What she wanted for her future. Many things.

She was about to make another call or two, wanting to talk to Rebecca or Barbara, her former roommates. It would be interesting to see how their "journeys" were going, and if their lives had twisted and turned like hers had. Since she wasn't entirely sure where the women were, however, she didn't do it. Mad Max might have "assigned" them visits to the French Riviera for all she knew, which meant the time difference could be a real issue.

Smiling as she pictured pretty, silver-haired Rebecca with a hunky Frenchman, she finished the watery remnants of her drink, then looked at her stacked luggage. Putting her friends out of her mind, she focused on what she had to do. Like unpacking.

Because Cassandra Devane wasn't going anywhere. Not until she'd had a chance to see if the no-place-like-home she'd been seeking had been in the arms of the man she'd let slip away.

This was no longer about closure, or letting go of the past. No. She was going on a different type of journey.

A journey into her future.

OVER THE NEXT FEW DAYS, Wyatt came to a realization: Cassandra Devane was not going to give up and slip quietly back out of his life.

He should never have gone along with Jackie's stupid dinner scheme, or have met Cassie for drinks Wednesday night. Because both of those events had given them a reminder of how good they'd once been together...as social friends during dinner. And as intensely compatible lovers during their crazy kiss at the bar.

Wyatt couldn't think about that kiss at the bar. Nor could he allow himself to picture the hurt expression on Cassie's face after he'd said those cruel things to her. He'd been so certain that driving her away had been the right thing to do. He'd almost been able to ignore his own pain at having done it.

In the end, though, neither had been true. He couldn't ignore the pain, and he hadn't driven her away. Cassie was still here. And she was driving him absolutely nuts by insinuating herself into every part of his life. Not only did he have to hear his sister chattering nonstop about Cassie, but he got the same spiel from his own secretary.

Worst of all, he had to deal with his ex-wife in the flesh. Very, *very* tempting flesh.

God, she'd practically taken up residence in his office. She was constantly coming by, stopping his heart whenever she appeared in the doorway, with that sunny smile and that warm laugh. She always came in on a wave of excitement. Like now, late Friday morning, when she emerged from the elevator, carrying an enormous box. Wyatt's jaw dropped. "What the hell is this?"

"Lunch," she said brightly. "A giant submarine sandwich. Everyone's been working so hard on this automotive campaign, I figured you could use a break."

Sylvia, his secretary, came hurrying out from behind her desk and hoisted one end of the six-foot-long box Cassie was maneuvering around the corner to the break room.

"Thanks so much, Cassie, everyone will really appreciate this," Sylvia said.

As if the box contained an elixir of the gods, every one of Wyatt's employees poked their heads out of offices or over the tops of cubicles. Sniffing, they followed her like she was the Pied Piper of Hamlin.

Lunch that day was practically a party, with Cassie serving up slices of turkey sandwich to his staff. She charmed them, praised them and pretty soon had all of the men ready to kiss her feet and all the women lining up to take makeup advice.

The afternoon wasn't much better. She came back around three, loaded for bear with a case full of face creams and makeup for his staff. With Sylvia's help, she gave makeovers to any woman who wanted one. It wasn't until he heard her chatting up each and every product to his design team that he realized she was working on them—to work for *her!*

"We're not doing this campaign," he told Stu Wiley, one of his top guys, who'd come to work for Wyatt fresh out of Georgetown University last year.

Stu was peering into the break room, where half a dozen women sat reading product labels while waiting for green slime to harden into some kind of rocky paste on their faces. "They really do make good products," the younger man said. Wearing a reminiscent smile, he added, "My girlfriend has this Fresh Face raspberry body lotion that absolutely drives me insane."

He didn't want to think about that because he couldn't imagine raspberries without remembering the way he and Cassie had once devoured a small container of them while lying naked in bed. They'd bounced and fallen and rolled into some very interesting places—places he'd been happy to explore with his mouth.

Thinking about raspberries would soon get him thinking about the vanilla ice cream he'd insisted went so well with fruit. And which he'd smeared all over Cassie's belly and thighs, laughing while she shivered. He'd warmed her up by licking off every drop.

Dangerous memories.

"My sister raves about the vanilla lotion," said Jerry, his in-house graphic designer.

Closing his eyes, Wyatt groaned softly. He simply couldn't escape his thoughts. Or Cassie. The woman was utterly relentless.

He hadn't even realized *how* relentless until he found out that afternoon that Cassie had already made appointments with his art director and his on-staff photographer. She was getting input for the cosmetics campaign he was so not going to design for her.

When she wasn't winning everyone over with bribes, she was asking him for directions to a good Thai restaurant or bursting into his office with a bunch of touristy guide maps. Like the one for the Olde Towne Boston Tour, which she'd begged him to take her on over the weekend.

He'd refused, of course. He had more common sense than that. But it hadn't deterred her. She was in his face, in his world, in his life.

And now, in his dreams.

That Friday and Saturday night, he endured long, restless hours full of intense, erotic dreams. Waking up sweating and aroused Sunday, he had to get up and take a cold shower at 5:00 a.m., though it didn't help to cool him off. Neither did the five-mile predawn run, or the *second* shower he'd taken after his workout. He had a feeling he'd be wanting another cold shower at some point in the afternoon.

Because he was going to be spending the day with the most frustrating, desirable woman he'd ever known.

He was taking Cassie on the stupid tour. Somehow, he'd let himself be talked into it by Sylvia and Jackie, both of whom guilted him about Cassie being a stranger in town, alone for a whole weekend in a cold, impersonal hotel.

Ha. Cassie was little Miss Sunshine these days. She probably could have had the hotel manager give her a private tour with a quirk of her finger.

Arriving to pick her up at 10:00 a.m., he couldn't help wondering once again why she simply had to do the most touristy thing there was to do in this town. Revolutionary War era sightseeing. He'd rather watch the women in his office getting another makeover.

"I am so excited," she said as she hopped into the passenger seat of his car. He hadn't even had to go into the lobby; she'd been waiting right outside, giving the doormen a cheery wave as she flagged Wyatt down. Her eyes sparkled, and she practically bounced on her seat with anticipation.

Which was when he realized why he'd given in to her. The woman was absolutely irresistible. If "dazzling" was a product, he could market it with one shot of Cassie's brilliant smile.

"Yeah, I can barely contain my enthusiasm myself," he said, determined to keep his defenses in place.

She rolled her eyes. "Stop being such a grouch. I can't believe you live in Boston and you've never been to the Old North Church or the Minutemen National Park."

"And I can't believe you got my sister *and* my secretary to work on me until I agreed to take you."

She leaned back and made herself comfortable. Damn, he wished she'd worn jeans again today. Instead, she was dressed in a cute, flowery skirt that wisped around those fine, creamy thighs. "Believe me, Wyatt, when I set my mind on something I want, there's not much I won't do to get it."

He met her stare for one long moment, wondering exactly what she meant. But Cassie didn't say another word, just opened up the guide maps and began mumbling under her breath about all the exciting historical stuff they were going to do today.

Exciting and historical seemed a contradiction in terms to him. But somehow, seeing the excitement on Cassie's face made him think the day might not be such a waste of time, after all.

CASSANDRA LOVED HISTORY. But her enjoyment of the proud old city of Boston couldn't compare to the thrill she got out of spending a whole day with Wyatt.

After his initial reluctance—and grumpiness—he'd relaxed and become the fun and entertaining guy she knew. He'd laughed with her, humored her and teased her. At one point when they were walking over a rocky area in the park, he'd even taken her hand to steady her. Cassie had laced her fingers through his and held on tight, not letting him pull away.

Oh, yes, she definitely knew how to get what she wanted. As she'd warned him in the car, she could be relentless about that.

And after her call to Maxine the other night, she knew what she wanted. *Him.* Wyatt Reston.

She wanted him in her life and in her future. Most of all, right now, she wanted him in her bed. Which was why she took every opportunity Sunday to brush against him, to lean close enough for him to smell her skin or feel her hair caress his cheek.

But the darn man resisted. Oh, sure, he was fun and sweet, playful and entertaining. Despite her best efforts, however, he had not found the nearest bed, thrown her on it and had his wicked way with her.

"Probably ought to stop reading racy novels," she muttered under her breath as they drove to Landsdowne Street, where they planned to stop for dinner.

"Sorry? What did you say?"

She shook her head. "Nothing. Just thinking about how great today has been. You were so sweet to take me sightseeing, Wyatt. You should come to New York sometime and let me repay the favor."

He stiffened, just a bit, but said nothing. Cassie

realized she'd made a tactical error, bringing up the whole dual-city lifestyle thing. She hadn't quite figured out how to handle that. At this point, though, getting Wyatt to admit there was still something strong and unbreakable between them seemed much more important than geography.

"You really liked all that stuff, didn't you?" he asked as he parked the car near Fenway Park. Trendy restaurants and clubs surrounded them, and the street was full of residents enjoying the late-afternoon sunshine.

"I did," she murmured. Then, knowing she had to grab whatever chances she could, she leaned toward him. Cupping his cheek with her hand and not giving him any warning, she added, "Thanks again, Wyatt." Without another word, she pressed her lips to his, gently, softly. A simple kiss of thanks.

She should have known better. Simple couldn't begin to describe what was between them. As Wyatt groaned a little and parted his lips to hungrily taste her mouth, Cassie found herself wishing she'd just gone ahead and kissed him sooner. Like first thing this morning. Because she'd inspired such a delightfully strong reaction.

The deep, hot kiss soon had her quivering with the need for more, and Cassie crawled across the seat into Wyatt's lap. He dropped a hand on her leg, his other arm curling around her shoulders to hold her tight. The kiss went on and on, sweet and wet, his lips and tongue soft and delightfully familiar against her own.

God, she loved kissing this man. Almost enough to forget where they were. But *not* enough to drown out the sound of some teenagers hooting and yelling from a passing car. Cassie regretfully pulled away, looking into Wyatt's eyes, seeing the longing he couldn't possibly disguise.

After a long moment, he shook his head as if to clear it, then gently disentangled his arm and helped her over to her own seat. "Cassie…"

She waved an airy hand, determined not to let him get all regretful and pessimistic. Not when she was still reeling over how right—how perfect—they still were together. "Forget it. It was a thank-you kiss. No big deal."

His doubtful look told her she hadn't fooled him. They both knew that kiss had been a lot more than one of gratitude. Since neither of them was quite ready to say exactly what it had been, however, they both simply let it go.

"Okay," he murmured. "Let's leave it at that."

CHAPTER SIX

WYATT WAS IN TROUBLE. Big, enormous trouble. It was all because of the day they'd spent together. And that brain-zapping kiss.

He'd been doing okay, telling himself he could handle having her in town, hearing her voice, seeing her face. He'd even allowed himself to indulge in the fantasy that they could somehow be friends—could go out and spend a day together with no problems, no repercussions, no longing.

But no. Uh-uh. Because he'd made the monumental mistake of letting his guard down and truly enjoying being with her. Not to mention the whole kissing thing.

He'd had her in his arms and he'd tasted the mouth that he'd dreamed about for eight long years, and it was as if time had completely fallen away. No one had ever felt as perfect in his arms. No one, he feared, ever would.

And now, nothing was going to help get Cassie out of his mind, his dreams, his fantasies. Not until she left.

Or not until he *had* her again.

"Did you want me?" a familiar voice asked, startling him as he stood at a table in his office, looking at some head shots.

Her words stunned him for a second. Did he want her? Only more than he wanted to keep breathing. He closed his eyes briefly against the thought, then stiffened his shoulders.

"Hi, Cass," he said, slowly turning on his heel as she walked into his office.

She was all springy and sunshiny again, dressed in bright colors and soft fabrics that draped across her curves and emphasized her femininity. She didn't look nearly tough enough to run a major international cosmetics firm. Yet from the research he'd done about her on the Internet over the past week, she was about as tough as they came. Ambitious and bright. Charming when she needed to be, and ruthless if the occasion warranted it.

Right now she looked about as ruthless as the Easter bunny.

"Sylvia said you wanted to see me," she said, her smile indicating she was pleased at that. "I was on my way to a meeting with your graphics guy, but thought I'd stop in on my way."

"Thanks, I did want to talk," he admitted as he crossed his arms and leaned back against the table. "I've been thinking about your company, the new campaign— and I think I could maybe squeeze you in as a client."

He'd rather squeeze her into his bed. But this was the *sane* option.

She clapped her hands together. "Wonderful. You have no idea how happy that makes me. I don't think I realized how stale our previous campaigns have been until I came here and started talking to your people, seeing some of the innovative stuff you've done." She moistened her lips with a flick of her pink tongue, nearly making him forget to breathe. "I never knew you were behind that sexy Gleam Detergent commercial. The whole 'go ahead, get a little dirty' thing was incredibly hot and suggestive."

It *had* been, but he didn't want to think about it.

The last thing he needed was anything causing more hot, suggestive thoughts about the woman standing a few feet away.

Suddenly looking more serious, she stepped closer and said, "You're really good, you know. You deserve to be where you are."

He held her stare for a moment, hearing what she wasn't saying. She was proud of him, happy for him. Cassie was pleased to see that his drive and ambition and dreaming had paid off and things had worked out so well.

They had…in every way but one. And that one way was standing here, staring at him with honest admiration shining in her big baby blues.

Wyatt cleared his throat, more certain than ever that he had to make Cassie go away. Because after only a week back in his life, she was already making him feel things he didn't want to feel. Not for her. Not again.

"Thanks. Now that we've settled things, you're free to go on back to New York and have your marketing staff get in touch. We'll need to see what you've done in the past, as well as product samples and descriptions."

Her jaw stiffened. Steeling himself against the flash of disappointment that took a bit of the sparkle from her eyes, he continued. "There's really no point in you sticking around anymore. You were here to convince me and you have. So it's probably time for you to get back to your real life. I don't imagine your company is running itself."

She didn't say anything for a moment, instead walking silently closer, until she stood only a foot away from him. Close enough for him to smell the sweet, delicate scent of her hair. Close enough for him to feel the warmth of her breath. Close enough for him to see the moistness of her pink lips.

Close enough for him to lose his mind.

"You're trying to get rid of me," she murmured.

His jaw clenched and he tightened his arms across his chest. "That's ridiculous. You're getting what you want. Now we can proceed just like I do with any other client. I don't need you here for this."

"What if I say that I *want* to be deeply involved? That I want to stay here for the initial planning sessions?"

Then I say so long to a good night's sleep ever again.

"There's no need," he said from between gritted teeth. "If you want me to take the account, you must let me do it my way."

She raised one fine brow. "Meaning, you insult the client and kick her out of your town?"

Out of his memory would be better. But his town would do for now. "Do you want me to do this job or not?"

She simply stared, her blue eyes wide and assessing, as if she was trying to peer into his mind, to read his thoughts.

If she knew exactly what he was thinking—that he'd very much like to know what she had on under that silky, sleeveless blouse of hers—he'd be in deep, deep trouble. And she'd probably slap his face. Or take off her blouse.

He'd be better off being slapped.

"You want me…"

He waited, figuring she wasn't finished her sentence. But she didn't say another word. She just kept watching, waiting. Her mouth curved into a tiny smile and she took another step closer, until her bare arm lightly touched his. He wished he hadn't rolled up the sleeves of his dress shirt because the delicate brush of her warm skin against his took the tension and awareness and thrust it up exponentially.

Then he realized that there *was* no more to her sentence. She'd said all she was going to say, accusing him of wanting her. That he *did* want her didn't make the accusation any easier to deal with. Because he knew, he'd known for years, that he couldn't *have* her. Their short-lived marriage had proved that.

They were opposites, from completely different backgrounds, going in completely different directions. The media stories he'd seen about her over the years had hammered that reality into his brain. Sure, she laughed about her wild, exotic lifestyle, but she still lived it. She hadn't made any effort to change it.

She was still the rich golden girl and he was, deep down, still the simple, hardworking blue-collar guy he'd always been.

Besides that, she still went out of her way to please her family. Hadn't she admitted the other day that she'd gone to a Texas ranch at the request of her grandmother? Cassie on a Texas ranch made about as much sense as Wyatt at a Tupperware party. So she obviously hadn't lost that need to get her family's approval.

What it came down to was that they'd only ever hurt each other. Going down that road again with Cassie would be not only self-destructive but damn near suicidal.

Wyatt was a strong man and he wasn't afraid of much. But letting himself love her again, only to have his heart skewered when she returned to her flamboyant, jet-setting lifestyle among the rich and jaded...well, he wasn't strong enough for that.

"You can't even deny it, can you?" she said, that sultry half smile still playing about her lips.

He stiffened. "I don't know what you're talking about."

"Liar." She moved until her bare legs, gloriously emphasized by her short skirt, brushed against his pants.

"You're trying to get rid of me to keep yourself from doing what you really want to do."

What he really wanted to do was grab her, spin her around, lift her onto the conference table and devour every inch of her. But he didn't figure her imagination had taken things quite that far. "What I really want to do?"

She nodded.

"Maybe what I want to do is get you out of my hair so I can get back to work without you underfoot," he said, straightening up so she had to tilt her head back to meet his eyes.

"Double liar." She raised up on tiptoe, lifting her face to his until he felt her slow exhalations on his chin. Their breaths mingled. "What you really want to do is kiss me again."

Kissing was definitely part of the devouring-her-on-the-table thing. So he didn't try to deny it.

"But you won't do it," she whispered. "You have this invisible wall around yourself and you're not going to let it drop." She stretched up just a bit more and placed her hand flat on his chest, right above the heart she'd once mangled and left in tiny chunks. "So," she added, "maybe I'll just have to climb over it again, just like I did yesterday in your car."

She moved another centimeter, another breath closer, until there was nothing but a sliver of air separating their lips.

And Wyatt gave up all resistance.

With a helpless groan, he lowered his mouth to hers, tasting the sweetness of her lips. That same immediate sense of pulse-pounding pleasure and *rightness* rushed through him. It was a feeling he'd forced himself to forget until yesterday when she'd shocked him with her "thank-you" kiss. Just like then, he was overwhelmed with the memory of all the kisses, the passion, the desire, the emotion they'd shared from the day they'd met.

Hearing her moan of pleasure, he gave up any last hint of doubt, deepening the kiss into a hungry mating. She parted her lips and their tongues met and tangled, wet and hot and carnal.

Cassie slid her arms around his neck, pulling him tighter against her body. Almost shaking with want for her, he wrapped his arm around her waist, one hand pressed possessively on the small of her back. He teased the gentle indentation above her sexy backside with his fingertips. With his other hand, he cupped her head, letting his fingers slip into her soft, curly hair.

The kiss went on and on, lethargic, then frenzied. Sweet, then sultry. A dance of give and take that soon had them both breathing hard, with pulses pounding.

Cassie writhed in his arms, pressing against him. The pebbled tips of her breasts scraped with agonizing delight against his shirt and Wyatt hungered to taste them, remembering how very sensitive she was there.

When she tilted her hips closer and rubbed against the erection barely contained in his trousers, they both groaned at the delicious torment. Because they knew how good it could be, how good it had *always* been. There was no wondering. They *knew*.

Never taking his mouth from hers, Wyatt leaned down until he was again half sitting on the table. And it was so easy, so damn easy, to lower his hands to her hips and lift her higher, until he bore all her weight. She whimpered and tightened her hold around his neck, even as she lifted her legs and wrapped them around his hips, sitting completely on his lap.

The position was incredibly intimate. Incredibly intense. Even through his clothes, he could feel her heat, feel the welcoming, hot place where he'd once found ultimate satisfaction. More than anything, Wyatt wanted to tear away whatever sexy little panties she wore beneath her skirt—which had risen to pulse-pounding heights—and plunge into her.

"Please, Wyatt, touch me," she whimpered against his lips. "Touch me. I want your hands on me."

Unable to resist, he reached for one long, smooth, silky thigh and ran his palm over it. Caressing the delicate skin, he moved higher and higher, under her skirt, until his fingertips brushed the elastic edge of her panties. She jerked in reaction. Needing, wanting, silently pleading for more.

And oh, how he wanted to give it to her. Even while somewhere in the back of his mind he knew this was utterly crazy. The two of them had no business doing this at all, and they absolutely shouldn't be doing it *here*. His office door wasn't locked and his secretary was right outside.

Somehow, though, Wyatt couldn't bring himself to care. He had to touch her, drench himself in her. See if she still felt as soft and wet and tight as she always had.

Moving his mouth from her lips, he kissed his way down her neck. Cassie dropped her head back, throatily whispering, "Yes."

With another quick movement of his hand, he discovered just how tiny her panties were. Because he'd easily pushed them aside and now there was now nothing separating them. As he tangled his fingers into the warm thatch between her thighs, he sighed deeply, knowing this had been inevitable. Making love to Cassie again was something that had been destined to happen, ever since last week when he'd first walked into his office and found her here.

She began to shake, arching toward his touch, visibly

and audibly aroused. As was he. So he gave her what she needed, let his thumb drop to that sweet, sensitive spot, and ever so delicately stroked her.

"Wyatt!" She grabbed his hair and tugged his mouth to hers for another mind-numbing kiss as he continued to caress her, bringing her higher and higher with every flick of his thumb.

She was gasping against his mouth, and he recognized the signs. Close. She was very, *very* close. He pulled away a little, wanting to see her reach that peak of pleasure, to see the way her eyes would close and her face grow flushed.

Instead, to his shock, he saw something else.

The door to the office...slowly opening.

ONE SECOND, Cassandra was feeling the waves of her climax rolling through her body and was preparing to ride them to full fruition. The next, Wyatt was hoisting her off his lap and hopping down to stand beside her, shifting in his pants. When she saw his secretary standing in the doorway, with a dark-haired man looking over her shoulder, Cassandra understood why.

"Brazen it out," she muttered, knowing that to act guilty would make the situation worse. Without knowing just how much had been seen, there was no use acting all penitent about it.

Wishing her panties had snapped back into place more comfortably, she patted her hair. "Hi, Sylvia."

The older woman's eyes were wide, but her lips quivered with suppressed laughter. "Hi, Cassie. I didn't realize you were still here." Everyone was apparently following Wyatt's lead and calling her by the nickname only he had ever used. Somehow, Cassandra—*Cassie*—couldn't bring herself to mind so much.

The man standing silently behind Sylvia was a conservatively dressed man of Japanese descent. Cassie realized she and Wyatt had been caught doing some serious making out by an important potential client. Damage control was definitely in order. "Oh, you caught us trying things out," she said with a breezy smile.

Sylvia backed out of the office, and the businessman stepped in. "Trying things out?" he said, his voice frosty.

Wyatt strode across the room. "Mr. Katowa, how nice to see you again. I wasn't expecting you until later this afternoon."

"If you'd prefer, I will come back later…."

"Oh, no, don't be silly," Cassie said, taking the man by the arm and putting on her best charming, nobody-says-no-to-me pout. "We were just talking about the revised campaign for your company. I was being naughty and insisting on demonstrating my idea to Wyatt." Then, figuring Wyatt couldn't kill her until after the automobile executive had left, she added, "I'm Cassie Devane, by the way. Wyatt's…fiancée."

Wyatt coughed into his fist, but with a quick kick at his ankle, he quickly backed her up. "Right. Yes. Cassie, this is Mr. Katowa, a visitor from Japan."

The man bowed slightly, and Cassie responded with a bow of her own. Quickly recalling the little bit of Japanese she'd grasped during a business trip to that country last year, she greeted him in his own language.

The man's rigid expression finally relaxed, and he offered her a smile. "Congratulations on your engagement." Looking at Wyatt, he said, "I was not aware of your happy news."

Afraid Wyatt was about to mumble, "Me, neither,"

Cassie quickly said, "Wyatt and I were sweethearts in our college days," she said. "We've only recently, um…rediscovered each other."

Oh, yes, they'd definitely rediscovered each other. And they'd been on the verge of doing a whole lot more rediscovering a few moments ago on his conference table. She was still hot and moist just thinking about it.

"Right. Cassie whirled through my door again one day, as if she'd been here all the time."

She didn't know how she was sounding so calm and normal when she felt anything but. Her lips had to look thoroughly kissed and her throat probably had a few reddish marks.

It was still shocking, what had just happened between them, and she hadn't had time to evaluate it yet. One thing was sure, she hadn't been spending every waking minute putting herself in front of him all week for a few stolen kisses on his office table.

She hadn't come here to initiate anything physical. She just wanted to be near him, to spend time with him. She needed to understand why he'd been her first thought every morning and her last dream every night since their paths had collided again.

Coming to Boston was supposed to be about closure, putting an end to her feelings for Wyatt and saying the things she never got to say before. After her phone call with Maxine the other night, and some serious self-evaluation, however, she knew she no longer wanted closure and that her feelings were far from over.

They still needed to talk about what happened—how they went so wrong—and she still needed to let him know he had probably been right about what had driven her to make the choices she'd made. But she also wanted…*needed*…to find out what was in his heart.

Maybe even what had been in those letters Jackie had mentioned the other night.

Mr. Katowa cleared his throat, interrupting Cassie's musings. "So you were saying you were, uh, conducting a *demonstration* of an idea for my commercial?"

Wyatt opened his mouth, but Cassie spoke first. "Yes, absolutely." This account was important to Wyatt and she knew it. Too important to have it slip away because Cassie had laid a kiss on the man right in his office where anyone could—and did—wander in. So she had to do something to salvage the situation. "The idea of showing men at varying stages of their lives stopped at a stoplight in different cars was clever. But it was missing that one thing, that little spark that would make it truly stand out."

She was babbling, pulling ideas out of the air. Beside her, Wyatt watched, one brow up, laughter dancing in his eyes as he probably wondered how she was going to talk her way out of this.

"Cars are very important to Americans, and a lot of life's most important moments take place around them. Private moments. Joyful moments." Giving Wyatt a wickedly suggestive smile, she said, "Sometimes very intimate moments."

Thinking of the teasing suggestion she'd made the other night when they were driving to his place, about women having various things happen to them while in, or near their cars, she continued. "It isn't enough just to have the men sitting there at an intersection. What about showing the *same* street corner, with different cars, a succession of men in various scenes, a continuing series of commercial spots that would be like snapshots of important moments in the men's lives."

Mr. Katowa had his head back, and was looking at

the ceiling. With his hands clasped behind his back, he appeared to be deep in thought.

Cassie didn't wait for him to disagree, quickly adding, "They'd convey the same message, but there could be more chance for variety. More opportunities to hammer home the message that your automobiles can take a man through his whole life."

"Interesting," Wyatt murmured, his amused expression fading as he narrowed his eyes in thought.

Though it had started as a joke, she was warming up to the idea. She could see it. "There'd be a young man opening the door to one of your less expensive models for his date. A bride and groom smiling out the window as they drive off in a midsize."

She gave Wyatt a quick glance and saw him watching her with interest and speculation. He was catching the vision. "Parents buckling their kids into the seats of the SUV," he said. "All at the *same* corner, but at different times, alternating seasons, varying points in people's lives. The connection is the place and the *brand* of car. The vehicle gives the viewer an immediate hint of what moment in someone's life they're going to see, and the street corner is the window through which they watch it."

Moments in people's lives. For some reason, Cassie suddenly began to think in terms of more than cars. Much more.

Relationships were just as changeable at different moments, weren't they? Who didn't dream of going back to an important point in their life to see if things might have turned out differently? To determine if they could make it work out better the second time around?

She and Wyatt were embarking on just such a risky endeavor. Only there was a lot more on the line than the sale of an expensive automobile. Cassandra's future happiness was at stake, and she knew it.

Forcing the worrisome thoughts out of her mind, she focused on the task at hand. Mr. Katowa was stroking his chin with the tips of his fingers. He said nothing for a long moment. Cassie almost held her breath, wondering if Wyatt always felt this sense of anticipation and excitement when pitching a new concept. It was intense. Dramatic. No wonder the man got off on it. For someone as creative yet grounded as Wyatt, it was the perfect career.

Finally, when she thought for sure they'd blown it, Mr. Katowa spoke. "It couldn't be a very busy corner. Not too many people around."

She didn't follow, but wasn't about to argue with the man.

"Because," he continued, "a couple having a *passionate* moment on the hood of our 340L convertible would need a little privacy." He straightened and looked at them both, his eyes twinkling. "The consumer wouldn't want to think just anyone could walk up and interrupt them."

Cassie sucked her bottom lip into her mouth, realizing the man had seen more than they'd hoped. But the amused smile on his face told her it was okay.

His words confirmed it. "I like this idea. Now, let's get to work."

CHAPTER SEVEN

WYATT SPENT the rest of the afternoon with Mr. Katowa. After two hours, he had Sylvia order some takeout, and got the rest of his staff in on the creative meeting. It was high-energy, high-voltage and intensely creative. And the client *loved* it.

He felt positively high with the thrill of it all by the time they wrapped up the session and bid Mr. Katowa good-night. As he drove away from the office that evening at eight o'clock, he realized there was someone he wanted to share that dizzying excitement with. *Cassie.*

It was probably both stupid and crazy but she was the one he most wanted to see right now. And not just because a lot of today's success was entirely due to her quick thinking in his office earlier. Frankly, whether she'd been involved or not, he'd want to celebrate with her. To laugh and plan, to have a drink and to enjoy the thrill.

"Why?" he wondered aloud as he pulled out of the parking garage. Why her? Why now? Why *again?*

He didn't have the answers. He only had the desire. So without giving it too much more thought, he turned up Lexington Street and headed toward Cassie's hotel.

He was in the lobby within a few minutes. The friendly clerk at the desk wouldn't give him her room number, but did offer to connect him. She answered on the third ring. "Hello?"

"It's me. You want to come down and meet me for a drink?"

He heard the audible breath she sucked in. "Did you get it?"

Smiling, he replied, "We got it."

"Yes!"

"So whaddya say? Still drink cheap Asti Spumante?"

"I prefer expensive champagne," she said with a dry laugh.

"You're on. Tonight, I can afford it. Come downstairs."

She hesitated for a second, then murmured, "I've got a better idea. This place has great room service."

Room service. In her room.

Don't do this. He heard the voice of caution whispering in his subconscious, but somehow Wyatt didn't want to listen to it anymore. He'd known when he decided to come over here tonight that this could happen. Hell, the condom burning a hole in his pocket told him he'd known it could happen since the day she walked back into his life.

Though he knew they might both regret it later, he said, "You're sure, Cass?"

She said nothing for a moment. They were both thinking about what would take place if he went up to her room. Given what they'd shared today in his office, Wyatt knew making love to Cassie again was going to be amazing.

He also knew he *should* be getting out of here to save his heart.

But tonight, his body was calling the shots. He just wondered if Cassie's was.

"Come up, Wyatt," she murmured, giving him his answer.

After getting her room number, he hung up the phone

and strode to the elevator. His whole body was wound tight in pure anticipation. There were no second thoughts, no recriminations, just adrenaline and desire.

Riding up to her floor in the elevator, he closed his eyes for a second, picturing the way she'd looked earlier in his office. He could see her beautiful mouth, open as she panted desperate little breaths. Her lids had been heavy over her eyes, her lips pink and moist. Cassie had been utterly glorious. She still aroused him in a way no other woman had.

Maybe tonight had been inevitable. Somehow in the past several days he and Cassie had rediscovered something he'd thought was lost forever: a closeness, a friendship. So maybe the culmination of that was just meant to be in bed. They could put away the sad memories of their marriage and leave something good and honest in their place.

That was for tomorrow, all the tomorrows. Now, though…now Wyatt was only going to live for tonight.

CASSIE HAD BEEN in the hotel for a week, so she knew how long it took to get from the lobby to her room. She had only a few minutes to get ready for Wyatt's arrival. Not just his arrival in her hotel room, but his arrival in her arms. In her body.

Because there was no question in her mind that's where he was going to be very soon.

The moment she hung up the phone, she dashed into the bathroom. She'd showered an hour ago and her hair was still damp, so she quickly ran a brush through it. Without a dot of makeup on her face, and clothed only in the thick terry-cloth hotel bathrobe, she looked completely unseductive. Not at all a sexy come-and-get-me vixen.

She'd known Wyatt would contact her tonight,

though she'd figured he'd call and ask her to meet him. After what had happened in his office today, they had to talk. And have sex. Frankly, she hoped the sex would come first, because she was dying for it and had been dying for it for days.

She'd figured she had plenty of time to get ready for him this afternoon, but then her office had called with a little problem. Her father had called while she was on the phone with the office, leaving an impatient message.

Cassie had been reaching for the phone to call him back when it had rung. Rebecca Ironwood, one of her Warfield roomies, was calling for dating advice, just as she had a couple of days ago. *Ha.* As if Cassie had any to give! She was completely winging it romantically these days. Still, it was good to talk to Rebecca, and to Barbara, whom Becky had conferenced in again.

But it had taken a lot of time, which was why she was unprepared for the arrival of the sexiest man she'd ever known. Blowing a frustrated breath out of the side of her mouth, she thought about the mountains of luscious, sexy lingerie she had back home. "Next time," she told her reflection, "pack more."

One very important item she *had* packed, however, and she quickly took care of the birth control issue.

Somehow, as she glanced in the mirror, seeing the excited sparkle in her eyes and the flush on her cheeks, she didn't think Wyatt was going to care what she was wearing. Frankly, neither did she. She didn't need to race for the cute little pajamas she'd brought with her or throw on a tight pair of jeans. Because it would take too much time to get those things back *off*.

She wanted Wyatt with almost desperate hunger. She needed him to walk in the room and just *take* her. Her whole body was soft and ready and she could feel the dampness between her legs growing hotter just at the thought of it.

God, she hoped he wanted her as much, so much that he wouldn't care whether they made it to the bed or not. There was no time for words, no need for small talk. She didn't want stilted conversation, or any discussion about whether it was a good idea.

Just sex. Hot, raw, hungry and intense.

Smiling as she pictured the perfect way to welcome her ex-husband back, she quickly moved to the door of the room and unlocked it. Opening it the tiniest bit, she looked around for something she could wedge in there to keep it from closing again. She quickly found something.

Her robe.

Figuring he had to be on the elevator by now, she dashed to the king-size bed and pulled the covers down. Wyatt was going to walk through that door, see her lying naked on the bed and lose every bit of his control.

Or else a maid was going to walk through that door, see her lying naked on the bed, and send Cassie scurrying into the bathroom out of sheer embarrassment.

"Hurry up, Wyatt," she mumbled, praying nobody else decided to investigate the propped door. She could see the news story now: "Cosmetics heiress found naked in hotel bed without even a spot of makeup on."

Her nerve wavered for just a second, but before it compelled her to yank the covers up, she heard his voice. "Cassie?"

"Come in." Her words were soft, barely making it out of her dry mouth. She cleared her throat. "Come in, Wyatt," she repeated. "And shut the door behind you."

He did. Wyatt must have suspected how he'd find her, because he maneuvered through the door very carefully, keeping it angled to block the view from the hall.

He was being thoughtful, considerate, as always. But once that door closed, she didn't want the thoughtful, considerate Wyatt. She wanted the crazy-with-want lover who'd once ripped her clothes right off her back in a moment of unbridled lust.

She heard the click of the lock, the slide of the bolt, and his slow steps across the carpet. The intensity built, the want increased as she waited for the moment he'd spot her. Cassie stretched, liking the soft friction of the sheets against her skin, knowing it would soon be replaced by the friction of his hands.

When he saw her on the bed—naked, wanton, with one knee bent, and one hand lying on her stomach—his eyes flared. Cassie offered him a sultry smile and slid her hand up her body, until her fingers brushed the bottom curve of her breast. "Hi."

His jaw tightened, but he didn't lose control. He definitely didn't rip his clothes off and leap on her, as she'd sort of hoped he would. Instead, he gave her a seductive look of his own. "I guess it's a good thing you didn't meet me downstairs for that drink. You're a little underdressed."

"And you're a little overdressed," she said, her voice nearly a purr.

He didn't respond, merely reaching up to slowly loosen his tie. Was there a sexier sight on earth than a gorgeous man with desire in his eyes taking off his clothes? If so, Cassie had never seen it. Her mouth went dry as she watched him, his every move controlled and deliberate, building the tension and the hunger.

"Hurry, please," she whispered, shifting her legs impatiently on the bed. She wanted his lean hips between her thighs and his heavy chest pressed against hers. Wanted his mouth and his hands and his tongue and his...everything.

Wyatt ignored her demand, continuing to lazily unbutton his shirt, revealing his broad chest. Cassie stared at his body, noting again the width of his shoulders and the stripes of muscle across his taut abdomen. He was even more masculine now than he'd been as a young guy, with a whorl of sexy dark hair on his chest, trailing down in a thin line until it disappeared into his trousers. Trousers that were much too slow in coming off, particularly given the powerful bulge she was dying to see freed from behind his zipper.

"You know you're killing me, don't you?" she said with a groan.

"Uh-huh."

"When did you get to be such a tease?"

"When did you get to be so impatient?" he countered.

"I've *always* been impatient for this."

He smiled, looking wicked. "I've learned that anything really worth having is worth waiting for."

Cassie squirmed on the covers, certain she wouldn't be able to take it. But she couldn't help watching him, letting the intensity build until it was thick enough to taste.

Umm, taste. She wanted to taste him. To lick the salty sweat from his skin and drive him crazy with her mouth, as she used to when the man had had a whole lot less self-control.

He continued his torture, unfastening his belt with that same deliberate, agonizing restraint. The slow hiss of his zipper sounded loud in the otherwise silent room and Cassie's heart skipped a couple of beats. But before he let his trousers fall, he reached into his pocket. After grabbing something, he tossed it to the table.

Seeing the condom packet, Cassie smiled, glad she wasn't the only one who'd been hungering for an intimate connection. "You won't need that," she said. "It's already taken care of."

His dark eyes glittered. "Good. Because I really didn't want anything wrapped tight around me except *you.*"

"Oh," she said on a moan, arching her back as his words rolled over her like a caress. He hadn't even touched her, but just watching him, listening to the promise in his words, was arousing her nearly to the breaking point. Her hips thrust up a little, and she clenched the muscles of her thighs. The need to be touched by him—filled by him— was almost overwhelming.

Wyatt finally dropped his trousers and kicked them, along with his shoes and socks, out of the way. Clad only in a pair of white boxer briefs that did almost nothing to disguise the strength of his erection, he knelt on the bed and moved toward her.

"You're not done," she said, almost choking on the words as she glanced at his briefs.

He ignored her and came closer until he was kneeling beside her calf. She lifted her arms, reaching for him. Wyatt instead lowered his mouth to her leg and pressed a warm, openmouthed kiss to the inside of her thigh, just above her knee.

"Wyatt," she said on a deep moan.

A throaty chuckle was his only response and he continued to nibble and kiss her shaking limb, his slightly stubbled cheek scraping deliciously across her skin. His warm mouth burned a trail higher, slowing as he neared her hip. A soft kiss in the hollow just inside her hipbone had her ready to howl. "Wyatt!"

"I've missed this," he said, his mouth moving into more dangerous territory, until she felt the brush of his breath on her curls.

Unable to help it, she arched up to him, offering, demanding, knowing that she'd lose her mind if he tasted her and she'd just die if he didn't. As if knowing that, he dipped down and delicately licked her, dead on target, sending every nerve ending she possessed into overdrive. A powerful orgasm came out of nowhere and rocked her body hard.

When she could pull herself together enough to look at him, she saw the smile on his face and knew he was nowhere near through playing with her. The man had the patience of Job. And he expended every bit of it as he kissed and licked and nibbled his way across her belly, her midriff, to the bottom curve of her breast.

"Beautiful," he murmured as he drew up enough to look his fill.

"Taste me."

He licked his lips. "I can still taste you on my tongue and, damn, you taste good."

Oh, Lord, she was dying and dancing and spinning and floating. Unable to stand it, she grabbed him by the hair, tangling her fingers in those thick, dark locks, and pulled him closer. He took mercy and allowed it, covering her sensitive nipple with his warm mouth. Cassie cried out as he sucked hard. When she felt him move his hand between her legs to begin making slow love to her with his fingers, she flew apart all over again.

She was still shaking when she shimmied down to meet his mouth with her own, moaning with want and need. She licked hungrily at his lips. With a low groan, Wyatt kissed her back, his tongue catching hers in a deep, heady mating.

He somehow managed to continue the kiss while pushing off his briefs. Feeling his thick, rock-hard heat against her hip, Cassie's heart sped even faster. "Now, please, Wyatt," she said with a whimper, tangling her legs in his and twisting restlessly beneath him. He hissed when she rubbed against him, her drenched body sliding effortlessly against his erection. His hiss was followed by a helpless groan and she knew, finally, that she *had* him. He would no longer be able to resist.

Giving himself over to her, he began to ease into her body, as if coming home after a long time away. But Cassie was done with the slow torture. She thrust up, taking him in one deep, hard stroke, crying out as he filled her to her core.

Nobody had ever filled her this way. Her body. Her heart. Her soul. *Nobody.*

"How can you still feel so perfect, like you were made for me?" he asked throatily as he rocked into her, delighting her with deep, steady strokes.

"Maybe because I was."

He stilled, looking down at her, his dark eyes questioning.

Cassie didn't question it anymore. She wrapped her arms around his neck and pulled him toward her mouth, whispering, "I love you, Wyatt," just before their lips met.

He kissed her sweetly, hungrily, forcing her to let him slow down and taunt her with short, teasing thrusts, followed by deep, mind-blowing ones. Until even Wyatt couldn't resist it anymore and gave over to raw passion.

The tempo increased, frenzy took over, and soon they were both breathless and slick with sweat. As yet another orgasm rolled over Cassie's body, she finally heard Wyatt cry out his own release.

And in those last moments of coherence, she also heard something else. Wyatt whispered faintly, as if he wasn't even aware he was speaking, "I love you, too, Cassandra."

WYATT WOKE UP the next morning to the sound of the shower. Glancing at the clock beside the bed, he realized it was after ten. He hadn't slept this late in years.

Rolling onto his back, he looked up at the ceiling and slowly smiled. Because oh, wow, did he have good reason for sleeping so late. So many good reasons, he honestly didn't know if he was gonna be able to walk this morning.

He and Cassie certainly couldn't make up for eight years of lost time in one night, but they'd sure as hell given it a shot. And he knew, without a doubt, that he loved her. Still. Always had, always would.

He just wondered if he had been wise to admit it to her. *But she feels it, too,* he acknowledged. Cassie had revealed her feelings and the emotion shining in her blue eyes had shown without a doubt that she spoke the truth.

So, he loved her and she loved him. But what would happen now, he had absolutely no idea. Because love hadn't been enough the last time, not when real life had set in.

Rolling to the side of the bed, he decided to put off thinking about anything outside this hotel room and just go climb into the shower with the woman he loved. The thought of getting wet and soapy with her suddenly made him feel a lot more wide awake. But before he'd taken a step, someone knocked on the door to the room.

He considered ignoring it, since he was certain he'd put the Do Not Disturb sign on the knob last night. But whoever was knocking wasn't giving up. The intrusive sound grew louder, more insistent.

"Dammit," he muttered, looking around the room for something to put on. When he spied his trousers on the floor, he grabbed them and yanked them up, zipping them as he stalked to the door.

Figuring he was about to see a maid who wanted to get the room done, Wyatt yanked the door open. Instead of a maid, he saw a sixtyish, gray-haired man, with an attractive middle-aged blond woman by his side.

The woman's eyes widened and the man's jaw dropped.

"Yes?" Wyatt said, wishing he'd grabbed his shirt, too.

"Is this Cassandra Devane's room?" the man asked.

He nodded, wondering who these people were. But his question was quickly answered. Because from behind him, he heard Cassie's voice. "Dad? Mother?"

Her parents? Holy shit, her parents were at the door and he was standing here in only an unbuttoned pair of pants! And right behind him was a hotel bed that looked like a herd of kindergarteners had been jumping on it all night.

The older man—Cassie's father—pushed into the room. "I've been trying to reach you," he said to Cassie, his jaw as stiff as stone.

Cassie's mother remained in the hallway, her face coloring. "Larry, maybe we should come back later."

Mr. Devane was, by now, glaring at Wyatt. Wyatt merely crossed his arms and leaned against the wall, raising an expectant brow. If Cassie's father was going to berate him, Wyatt was going to come back at the man with exactly what he thought of his parenting skills.

Cassie stepped between them. "What are you doing here?"

"We came to bring you home," Devane snapped. "Your grandmother confessed that she sent you off on some ridiculous quest to find yourself and you've been ignoring your responsibilities. You need to return to New York. The company doesn't run itself, you know." He cast a derisive look at Wyatt. "This isn't like you to forget everything you're *supposed* to be doing."

Cassie didn't say anything for a second, looking as

stunned as Wyatt felt about the intrusion into their sensual cocoon. At least Cassie had some clothes on, but she still looked vulnerable, with bare feet and her hair wrapped in a towel.

She also looked more beautiful to him than any other woman in the world.

Wyatt waited, wondering what she was going to say, though he suspected he already knew. Damn, he wished the moment of truth hadn't come quite so soon. He'd have liked to spend a little more time with her—being with her, *loving* her—before having to watch her choose to be the eager-to-please daughter rather than the passionate woman. *His* woman. His wife.

Money wasn't the issue this time—he no longer mistakenly believed Cassie needed the cash that came with her family's lifestyle. Besides, he certainly was no longer the poor kid he'd once been. Of course, he was nowhere in the Devane family league either. But he didn't believe that mattered to Cassie.

What he wasn't at all sure about was whether or not Cassie had ever lost that need to keep her parents happy, to have their approval. As she had all those years ago, she was standing between her parents and Wyatt, and her parents were trying to pull her away.

He couldn't bear to see her make the choice and he loved her too much to stand here and pressure her into it. Something in him couldn't stand to watch it in person. "You know what?" he said, his throat tight. "I'm going to give you some time alone."

After grabbing his shirt off the edge of a chair and his shoes from the floor, he walked past Cassandra's father toward the door. He needed to get away from the Devanes before he exploded with the resentment he'd carried toward them for the past eight years—a resentment rooted in the knowledge that their coldness had been at least partly responsible for the divorce. They'd given their daughter money and demands when what she'd wanted was their love and support. Then Wyatt had tossed that hated money into her face and allowed it to tear them apart.

But before he could get out with his emotions still somewhat in check, Cassie grabbed his arm. "Wyatt…"

He touched her hand lightly, then shook his head. He didn't want to have this conversation here, in front of her parents. One thing he would not be able to bear were any excuses, apologies or explanations. He didn't want to hear Cassie tell him she had to go back to her real life, her family. Without him.

So he didn't wait around to hear it. Instead, he met her steady stare and spoke what was in his heart. There was, really, nothing else to say.

"I love you, Cassie. I always have. You know where to find me." Shaking off her hand, he took one step to the door. Then he paused, adding, "I hope the next time I see you at my door it's to hear you say you never want to leave."

Then he walked out of the room, leaving the Devane family staring after him.

CHAPTER EIGHT

CASSIE WAS SO MAD at Wyatt she could scream. She couldn't believe he'd walked out of her room a moment ago, visibly wounded and angry. He'd acted as if he just knew she was going to do something stupid…like throw away the incredible connection they'd found again.

She had absolutely no intention of doing that. Zero. She might have come to Boston questioning her life and the road she was on—the "journey"—but now her questions were answered. Her future was set and it was all wrapped up in Wyatt Reston—the man she was going to smack for walking out on her, right before she was going to throw herself into his arms and ask him to marry her.

But first, there were her parents to deal with. "What are you doing in Boston?" she asked as she reached into her suitcase and grabbed some socks and shoes. If she was going to be running after Wyatt, she ought to have her sneakers on.

"We were worried. You practically disappeared off the face of the earth for three weeks. First to Texas, then we found out you were in Boston. Only your grandmother had any idea what you were doing."

A brush. Where was her hairbrush? "My office knew where I was and how to reach me at all times," she said absently, wondering if Wyatt had made it out of the building yet.

"You hardly ever called the house!"

"I hardly ever call you when I'm home," she said in her own defense. "Because *you're* almost never home."

"Well, we've been home for the past three weeks, and *you* were not," her father said. "Cassandra, are you even listening to me?"

She looked up from tying her shoes. "Not particularly, Dad. Were you saying anything important?"

His face grew red and suddenly her mother took his arm. "Larry, I think it's time for us to go. Cassandra's obviously got something pretty serious going on in her life right now."

Shooting her mother a grateful look, Cassie grabbed her purse and dug out her tiny brush. It wouldn't make much headway on her tangled curls, but it was better than her fingers.

"I can tell how serious," he father said, with a disdainful look at the rumpled bed.

The old Cassie—the girl she'd once been—might have been ashamed or embarrassed by her father's obvious derision. This Cassie—the ball-breaking executive—might have been outraged and told him where to go.

But she'd changed. She wasn't either of those women anymore. Nor was she an immature, hungry-to-please daughter trying to find anyone to blame for the mistakes she'd made.

She and Wyatt had been responsible for what had happened in their past. She had decided what her parents would think and how they would react all those years ago—never really giving them the chance to prove, one way or another, how they felt about her husband. God, they'd never even met the man!

That was another fault to lay at her feet. She'd wronged

her parents, too, in some ways. But she wouldn't make the same mistake. *Any* of the same mistakes!

It was Cassie the mature, independent woman—Wyatt's woman—who answered. "Dad, I'm going to say this once and only once. That man who just walked out of here was, is and always will be the love of my life. I will be with him until the day I die. I denied you the chance to get to know him on honest, open terms the last time. Now, I'm hoping you'll give *all* of us a chance to come together the right way."

Her mother sucked in a quick, shocked breath. "Was that…"

She nodded. "That was Wyatt Reston, my ex-husband."

Even her father's frown began to ease. "I didn't realize you were even still in touch with him. Are you…all right?"

Her parents were watching her closely, probably looking for signs of the completely dejected, heartbroken girl who'd sobbed in their arms after her divorce. Cassie gave them a reassuring smile. "I'm fine. I'm better than fine—I'm going to be absolutely terrific. I just need to go make sure my ex-husband knows he is also my *future* husband. I don't know whether I'm going to move my job here, or commute for a while or what, but I am not letting him get away." Narrowing her eyes, she added, "And I will never let anyone or anything come between us ever again. Not even my own self-doubts."

Her parents stared at her for a long moment, but Cassie barely noticed as she closed her purse and stood. She was too busy wondering if Wyatt was already out of the parking garage. Probably.

Heading for the door, she glanced over her shoulder at her parents. "Well?"

They looked at one another and she'd swear they

smiled a little. "Well," her father said, "whenever you two get around to getting married again, don't forget to drop us an invitation this time, all right?"

Her mother's smile was slightly more secretive. "And I'd bet your grandmother would like one, too."

Giving them an appreciative smile, she blew her parents a kiss and walked out.

WYATT REALLY THOUGHT about going directly to the office after he left Cassie's hotel, but he knew there was no point. He wouldn't be able to get any work done because he couldn't focus on anything except the look in her eyes when he'd left her there with her parents. But he'd had to do it. Cassie needed to decide what she wanted.

He only hoped and prayed it was him.

As he drove back to his apartment, he also acknowledged the other reason he couldn't go to work. Considering he was wearing the same shirt and trousers he'd had on yesterday—with nothing underneath—a trip home to change was definitely in order.

Once he'd reached his apartment, he went into his bedroom and stripped off his clothes. He'd just turned the water on for a hot, steamy shower when he heard a loud knocking on his front door. He was instantly reminded of that moment, just about an hour ago, when a knock on Cassie's hotel door had interrupted everything good in his life.

Was it really only an hour ago? It seemed like an eternity.

He at first intended to ignore the knocking, but some residual spark of optimism demanded that he at least see who it was. After turning off the shower and wrapping

a towel around his waist, he went to look out the
peephole, almost holding his breath.

Seeing her familiar blond curls, Wyatt began to
smile. Then to laugh. Because she'd chosen him. She'd
chosen *them*. He knew it the way he'd known he would
love her forever the day he met her on the beach in
Florida so many years ago.

He yanked open the door and reached for her, only
to have her whack him in the chest with her small fist.

"Hey!" he exclaimed.

"You jerk. I can't believe you walked out on me."

His lips twitched.

"Don't laugh at me unless you want me to hit you
again."

"Oh, I'm shakin' in my shoes."

Her gaze dropped to his bare feet, then slowly
traveled back up. Her pretty cheeks pinkened as she
realized he was wearing nothing but a towel.

Wyatt reached around her and pushed the door shut.
Giving Cassie his full attention, he smiled at her and
reached out again. This time she came into his arms with
a gentle sigh. "Don't ever leave me again."

"I won't. I love you, wife," he whispered into her hair
as he held her tightly in his arms, pressing soft kisses
on her temple and her forehead.

"I love you, too, husband." She leaned away and
tilted her head back to look up at him. "And I want
you."

Wyatt reached down and dropped the towel.

Cassie's eyes flared in excitement. She wiggled against
him, but she also chuckled. "I meant, I want you forever."

"Not now?"

Her eyelids lowered and her smile turned sultry. "Oh,

yes, I definitely want you now." She slid her arms around his neck. "But forever, too."

He began to stroke lazy circles around the small of her back. "You've got me forever."

"I want us to get married again." Her voice sounded breathy now as that familiar, wild spark of desire danced between them.

"We will." He pulled her shirt free of her waistband, tugging it off so he could feel her smooth skin against his.

She shook and moaned, whispering, "I want your children."

He tossed the shirt away, then her bra. "Three at least."

Cassie arched toward his hand, rubbing her breast against his palm. "I will never let anyone or anything—not money, not a job, not family—come between us again. I'll always put you first, Wyatt. I'll always put *us*—our relationship—ahead of everything."

His hands grew still. "I'll do the same thing, Cassie. I'm not the impatient hothead I was and I'm sorry that I reacted so badly in the past." He kissed her temple, breathing in the sweet smell of her skin. "I won't doubt you again," he whispered, before lowering his mouth to hers, kissing her deeply until their hearts beat in unison and they shared every breath of air.

Wanting her again, desperately, Wyatt bent down to lift Cassie into his arms. "I'd do anything for you," he said as he carried her into his bedroom.

She nodded, tucking her head in the curve of his neck, tasting his skin with delicate little nips. "Will you pose for a picture with me? I have someone I want to send it to."

He shrugged, a little curious but unwilling to deny her a thing. "Absolutely. Anything else I can do, other than making love to you until neither of us can move?"

She touched his chest, tangling her fingers in the hair

there, teasing and stroking him. "Yes. Will you read me the letters you wrote to me?" she asked.

He lowered her to his bed and followed her down. "How do you know about those?" Then he shook his head. "Never mind. Jackie?"

She nodded. "Will you read them to me?"

"I don't have to read them," he said as he gently removed the rest of her clothes. He began to stroke her, the long delicate lines of her thigh, the curve of her hip, the sweet indentation of her belly, where he hoped to soon feel one of those babies she wanted. "I know them all by heart."

Cassie sighed and caressed him in return, her hands gliding over his body as if she wanted to memorize him. "Prove it."

So impatient. Always so impatient.

"I will. *Later.* When I can think of something besides how much I'm going to enjoy loving you every day for the rest of my life."

She stared up at him, emotion shining in her blue eyes. "Starting now?"

He nodded and lowered his mouth to hers, whispering, "Yeah, Cassie. Starting right now."

EPILOGUE

IT WAS OFFICIAL. Ellen Devane was dying.

She didn't mind that so much. Dying seemed pretty fair after eighty-four years of a good, strong, secure and wealthy life.

Others would say she'd been completely blessed, spoiled even. While she might disagree with that, she couldn't deny she'd been fortunate.

Maybe her life could have been happier. Perhaps she could have had a little less money and a little more love.

Or maybe not. Maybe things happened for a reason and things had happened exactly as they were supposed to.

It wasn't for her to decide. She could only look back on all the things she'd done, the choices she'd made, and accept the results of those choices.

But that wasn't her concern right now. Not today. This death the doctors had warned her about wasn't at the top of her to-do list, at least not for the rest of this year. She had a while yet—time to get things in order. To see her sweet Cassandra happily settled with the man she'd loved through her entire adult life. A man Ellen liked very much.

There was a wedding planned for the fall, and Ellen fully intended to be there, wearing rust silk because the autumn colors really had always favored her.

There were flowers to choose and jelly beans to tie

into tiny net bags for favors. There were photographs to look over and toasts to make.

Mostly there were words to be said. Words like *I love you.* And *I'm so very thankful I had you in my life.*

Yes, there was time. Time for all those things. Maybe a short amount of time…but time enough.

Then it would be over. Ellen could go on to whatever was waiting for her around the next corner. Hoping— always hoping—that somewhere along the way that unknown future would include Rex.

And maybe even one more adventure.

SUGAR AND SPIKES

Heather MacAllister

CHAPTER ONE

REBECCA IRONWOOD DIDN'T handle humiliation at all well. It made her do things like fire her personal assistant and plunk down ten thousand dollars to attend the Warfield Retreat north of Houston, Texas, in hopes of making herself better able to make a good impression—on people in general and men in particular. Actually, one man in particular. Cy Benedict.

Yes, Cy Benedict's rejection had driven Rebecca to the Warfield Retreat. With its motto, "Leveling the Playing Field with the Womanly Art of Romance" Warfield Retreat. The pink brochure with purple ink Warfield Retreat.

Rebecca sat in her car in the pine-needle-covered parking lot and stared at the rustic building with the— oh, God, yes—pink door.

What had she been thinking? Rebecca thunked her head on the steering wheel of her BMW SUV, and then quickly checked the parking lot to see if any other women were in their cars banging their heads on their steering wheels. Or if anyone had seen her. This was so embarrassing.

The lot was filled with BMWs, Mercedes, Cadillac Escalades and pretty much any luxury car imaginable, but they were unoccupied, their drivers presumably already behind the pink door.

It should have made Rebecca feel better that other clearly successful women were here, but it didn't.

Focus. Rebecca picked up the glossy newsletter and read the headline once again: Lonely at the Top: Houston Female Business Owner of the Year Goes Solo to Awards Banquet.

Well, so what? was Rebecca's first thought when she'd seen the headline. She'd been interviewed by a couple of college interns for this article in the *Future Business Women's Journal.* She'd been encouraging, witty, charming and generous in her advice—in other words, fabulous as usual.

But had these two little chippies quoted any of her generous advice? No, they'd quoted the whining of her assistant, Adrienne. Make that former assistant.

Rebecca had hired that whiner right out of college four years ago, mentored her, given her a job that enabled her to learn firsthand from the best—that would be Rebecca—and how had Adrienne repaid her? By smearing Rebecca's carefully established reputation.

There, in print for everyone—friend, foe or male— to read were the details of Adrienne's unsuccessful attempt to find Rebecca an escort for the awards banquet.

Frankly, Rebecca vaguely remembered suggesting names and having Adrienne make the phone calls, but she hadn't kept track of just how many names. Adrienne clearly had.

"Eight," the article quoted her as saying. Rebecca imagined her whiny little voice. "And those were only the men she suggested. I came up with a couple on my own. They all turned me down. Some weren't even nice about it. I wasn't surprised. If there's one thing I've learned

working for Ms. Ironwood, it's that you can be successful or you can have a man in your life—but not both."

That was just wrong on so many levels.

Rebecca gripped the steering wheel and stared at the
pink door. The problem was that if a man was intimidated by her, she didn't want him, and if he wasn't, she
didn't like him. That left a very shallow pool of candidates so, no, she currently didn't have a man in her life.
She had a broken marriage in her past, so it wasn't as
though she'd never had a man, but equating success
with loneliness in print for the next generation of professional women to read was hideous. What were these
future business leaders going to think?

And the worst of it was that not having an escort at
the banquet actually bothered Rebecca. As she'd given
her acceptance speech and soaked up the applause, the
entire time Rebecca had been aware of a radiant Patricia
Eggelston, sitting at the first group of tables just below
the dais, cooing into the ear of her new husband.

It was sickening. Last year, Patricia had owned the top-
ranked female-owned company and she'd sold it—which
was why Rebecca was number one this year. Now Patricia
kept telling everyone how blissfully happy she was.
Adrienne had helpfully pointed that out in the article, too.

But bad as it was, that wasn't what had ultimately
cost Adrienne her job or sent Rebecca heading to the
Warfield Retreat. No, the disloyal Adrienne apparently
told the interns that Cy Benedict, the personnel consultant Rebecca had hired, would only be her escort if he
got paid his hourly rate.

Rebecca hadn't known until she read the article.

"'The only way I'd spend one minute more than I
have to with the Iron Lady is if you paid me.'"

Those had been his words, Adrienne had told Rebecca when she had confronted her assistant. But in her mind, Rebecca could hear Cy saying it. Saying it in that honey-wrapped-in-smoke voice that he had. The voice that she couldn't get enough of.

Rebecca rolled down the windows of her SUV as her face heated. She'd called him several times asking for clarification on his reports just so she could hear that voice.

She'd seen him from a distance, but had never spoken to him face-to-face. He was a tall man with brown hair shot with silver and looked as though he spent a lot of time outdoors. He appeared vibrant and alive and very much like someone she would like to get to know.

Rebecca had thought asking him to accompany her to a business-oriented event was the perfect way to approach him. If they clicked, then great, and if they didn't, well, it was just business after all.

His brutal rejection stung. This stupid article stung. The fact that she wouldn't have been number one unless Patricia had sold her business stung.

Life just stung in general.

She had success, wealth, social stature, and striking good looks—that was a quote. From a woman, but still a quote.

But she was forty-three and manless and apparently that was what counted in the world.

So, okay. She'd deal with it. Rebecca got out of her car, slammed the door and locked it, then strode toward the pink door of the Warfield Retreat before she could change her mind.

Once inside, she slipped off her sunglasses and approached the receptionist, relieved to find a woman of about her own age exuding charm.

"Welcome to the Warfield Retreat," said the woman. Her pink-and-purple plastic name tag read Maxine. "May I have your name?"

Had she given her real name when she made the reservation? Had she truly been that stupid? Rebecca couldn't remember, but she must have done so. What if word of this got out? If anyone knew she was here, especially after that article…

Rebecca wanted to leave. Yes, she, Rebecca Ironwood, who had founded Ironwood Executive Staffing, a company with an annual gross of over fifty million dollars, wanted to back down from a challenge.

The receptionist noted her hesitation. "Our discretion is assured. And there is nothing to be ashamed of in seeking help."

"It shouldn't matter!" Rebecca burst out. "I am a successful contributing member of society and it shouldn't matter whether or not there is a man in my personal life. I shouldn't have to change myself back to a female of the dark ages just to get a man, let alone pay an exorbitant amount to do so!"

"But you are and you did," replied the implacable Maxine. "Fill out this form and I'll show you to your cabin."

Yes, she was and she had. There was the form to prove it. Rebecca dutifully filled it out and followed Maxine, meekly rolling her suitcase over the rough Italian tile in the hallway and out a side door.

Meekly. Yes, Rebecca Ironwood was doing meek and the world still spun. Did the woman even notice Rebecca's meekness? For pity's sake, she was making an effort here. She was also lugging a carryall, her makeup case, a computer satchel and another satchel bulging with papers and files. And Cy Benedict's report, a report in which he'd stated that she appeared remote and unapproachable to her employees, but she wasn't thinking about that right now.

Right now, she was thinking about a bellman, only there appeared to be no bellman. Had she complained? No. Not yet, anyway.

"You're in cabin number 13."

It figured.

"You and your roommates have been deliberately matched to form an optimum support group after you leave here."

As if Rebecca would ever blab her problems to strangers. Except this once, for which she was paying a lot of money, so she expected *them* to provide the support. But, she was being meek, so she said nothing, even though everything within her wanted to rebel. She'd spent years—decades—counseling young women not to be meek.

"As part of the Warfield method, we expect you to practice the strategies you'll learn in our workshops with your roommates, so that you get along. Remember—breathe...consider...act."

Rebecca found herself breathing right along with Maxine as the woman swiped a card in the security lock box for cabin 13 and stepped aside.

Well, now, this was okay. Very okay. Cabin, bungalow, or whatever, this was not the primitive Girl Scout camp she'd been tortured with in her youth. This was rustic chic. Lush carpets, classic neutral colors and separate bedrooms. It was the kind of place where the roof didn't leak. Things were looking up.

Still meek, and feeling like a pack mule, Rebecca wheeled her suitcase into the only unoccupied bedroom. Queen-sized bed and good lighting. Excellent.

"You have only a few minutes to get settled," Maxine said. "The morning session will begin shortly."

Rebecca let the bags fall from her shoulders onto the bed. "I thought it wasn't going to start until ten o'clock."

"It *is* nearly ten." Maxine glanced first at the clock radio on the nightstand and then at her watch.

Five minutes until ten. Rebecca must have spent more time banging her head on the steering wheel than she'd thought. "You're right." She added a smile. Smiles were good, weren't they? This woman wasn't giving her a whole lot of positive reinforcement. So why was she bothering to make any effort at all?

Because she was out of touch. Unapproachable. Cold. The Iron Lady.

And because it cost ten thousand dollars.

So the last one had the most influence. Sue her.

"The conference center is a five-minute walk from this cabin." Maxine handed her a pamphlet that unfolded into a map of the Warfield Retreat. "Head along this path and follow the signs. I'm going that way now."

Be more approachable. "Could I walk with you?" Rebecca abandoned the thought of unpacking now. She could have her clothes pressed later.

Maxine hesitated as though actually considering giving up the chance for five minutes alone with Houston's Female Business Owner of the Year. Was she nuts? Did she not know that Rebecca was a valuable contact? Rebecca's agency staffed dozens of companies and this woman was—what? A receptionist? Didn't she want a better job?

Rebecca knew for a fact that Adrienne—the whiner—had been bribed to set up just such chance encounters. It had amused Rebecca until she'd discovered that Adrienne had actually accepted one of the bribes. But since the bribe in question had been a trendy cool Fleur de Lis bag, Rebecca could hardly blame her. Especially when Adrienne, caught red-handed—or red-bagged—had insisted that the Fleur de Lis had been meant as a present for Rebecca.

Rebecca had been on the waiting list for that very bag—though in navy, not red—but she'd accepted Adrienne's gesture, met with the client, and allowed Adrienne to escape unscathed. See? She could be nice. Wasn't that being nice?

Maxine set a brisk pace along a springy mulched path through the pine trees. The grounds were manicured while still managing to preserve the "we're roughing it" tone of the retreat, Rebecca noted with approval. This showed an attention to detail she appreciated. So many people let details slide these days.

"Since you were running late, I didn't get an opportunity to show you around the cabin."

Rebecca heard the rebuke in Maxine's voice and let it pass. She had *not* been running late. She'd been distracted.

Maxine continued. "In addition to the three bedrooms, there is a living area and full kitchen as well as a common business center with a printer, fax, wireless Internet. Land lines are available in each room for secure calls."

"I'm relieved that there will be time to check in with my company," Rebecca said. "I wasn't sure of the schedule of activities here." She figured it was understood that "check in" meant several hours of work.

"We're not unrealistic. We're aware that our clients find it difficult to spend two weeks away from their work and social responsibilities."

But apparently, this realistic attitude didn't extend to living arrangements as Maxine then informed Rebecca that she and her roommates would be responsible for their own meals, cleaning and laundry. Clearly, the "rustic" part of rustic chic.

They reached the central lodge housing the conference center before Rebecca could formulate a diplomatic way of telling Maxine that she was crazy.

What kind of chintzy place was this? And was it too late to back out? What about a refund?

Cy Benedict's report sounded in her head. *Out of touch. Cold. Unrealistic expectations.*

Oh, shut up.

Maxine pulled open yet another pink door and Rebecca heard the murmur of female voices. She was instantly soothed because this was the murmur of professionals networking, not the chirpy babble of a women's club.

"I'll find your roommates and introduce you to them," Maxine said.

"Thank you," Rebecca said demurely. *Demurely.* She nearly gagged. How long could she keep this up?

She signed in at a table and slapped on a name tag, thinking this was like the countless other seminars and business conferences she'd attended. Maxine beckoned her across the room where two women stood with her. One was flawlessly made up in a way that told Rebecca she was in a business where appearances counted. The other, near her own average height, had the expensive shoulder-length, straight hair and sophisticated clothes of the very rich. "This is Cassandra Devane and Barbara Powers. You three will be roommates for the next two weeks."

In a show of the Warfield spirit, Rebecca suggested that they sit together, Barbara pointed out the spaces she'd already commandeered, and Cassandra handed her a bottle of chilled water.

Rebecca smiled her first genuine smile in days. Strategic planning. These were her kind of people.

Maxine strode, unmeekly, to the lectern in the front of the room. "Please take a seat and we'll get started."

"They call her Mad Max," Barbara whispered.

Maxine pasted a professionally pleasant smile on her face, one every woman in the room knew, and waited, undemurely, as everyone quickly took a seat in the sudden silence. Nobody wanted to waste time here.

"Hello, I'm Maxine Warfield. Welcome to the Warfield Retreat."

Maxine Warfield. Rebecca cringed. Just a receptionist. Right. At least she'd behaved herself.

"Let's get one thing straight right now—you are all successful women and have the privileges, trappings and responsibilities that come with that success. You deserve them. You've worked hard and are the target of envy and resentment from those who have no idea what it takes to get where you are and stay there. If you were men, you'd be admired and respected, but you're women. You want to be liked and you're hurt that you aren't. You're called cold, aggressive, ball-breakers—"

Rebecca wanted to know why no one was standing up yelling, "Right on, sister!" Maybe she would.

"—and it's not fair. Let's all agree on that up front. It's not fair." Maxine paused, clearly expecting something from the group.

There was polite murmured agreement while Rebecca still considered leaping to her feet with a rallying cry.

"You're here because you're women and you need the social connection. There are virtually no programs for men quite like this one. For them, being disliked or feared in business and social situations is a badge of honor. But we're wired differently, so we're going to accept that difference and then let it go and move on with our life's journey. Got it?"

"Not fair." Oh, so right. "Move on." Good advice. Rebecca exhaled, feeling inexplicably lighter and heard her sigh echoed by others. They were right and the world was wrong. Validation was good.

"During the next two weeks, you will relearn the basics of interacting with others. And when I say basics, I mean housework, grocery shopping, driving in traffic—the chores of daily life. You can call it connecting with ordinary people—but you didn't hear me say that."

Polite laughter rippled through the crowd as Rebecca thought about Cy Benedict and how he wasn't ordinary, though she'd certainly like to connect with him.

"If this group is like past groups, you're all single. By single, I mean you lack women friends as well as male lovers."

Rebecca flipped through her mental file of close friends and, even stretching the definition, came away with few names. Okay, two. And one she hadn't seen for seven years. As for male lovers, the file was empty.

"You need people in your life." Music began playing. "And when you have those people, you'll find you are much more effective in your life."

It took Rebecca a few moments to realize she was

listening to a recording of Barbra Streisand singing "People." Oh, how hokey. She suppressed a giggle, but someone started laughing and they were all lost.

It was the perfect tension breaker and when the laughter eventually quieted, Rebecca gazed at Maxine Warfield with new respect.

And, she dared to admit, hope.

CHAPTER TWO

THE TELEPHONE RANG just as Cy Benedict was leaving for lunch, a daily hour break he cherished.

Cy spent the time outdoors when he could. He packed his own lunches—usually a whole-wheat bread sandwich, a piece of fruit, an oatmeal cookie with walnuts and dried cranberries and a bottle of water. Maybe some carrots, if he was in a chew-out-his-frustration mood. Today, he had carrots. A lot of carrots.

Cy always walked during his lunch hour, always seeking green. A pocket park, an atrium, or even the strip of grass dividing sections of a parking lot would do. He walked in the rain, in the heat and in the face of pressing deadlines.

He stared at the ringing phone. And he'd walk in spite of the Iron Lady, too.

That woman had gotten under his skin as no other since...well, no other. How he could secretly admire her and want to strangle her at the same time baffled him. Maybe it wasn't strangle so much as get his hands on her throat, learn the texture of the white skin there, feel her pulse beat beneath his fingers as they curved around her neck and he drew her... Cy gritted his teeth. Enough.

He'd never even met her face-to-face, not that there

was any reason he should, but it would have been a friendly gesture on her part. It would have taken a minute of her time and would have made him feel appreciated.

And that was the reason for her employees' dissatisfaction: they didn't feel appreciated.

The phone continued to ring. It was the Ironwood woman—he knew it. And just like her to want to interrupt his lunch. He couldn't yet tell if she did it deliberately or not.

He might have taken the call and shifted his lunch a half hour or so, but today he couldn't since he'd scheduled employee meetings at one o'clock.

So, Cy left the ringing phone, shrugged his cooler strap over his shoulder bandoleer-style and headed down the stairs, completely and totally guilt-free. He even remembered to relax his jaw.

Ironwood Executive Staffing was housed in a building with both an atrium and access to a carefully landscaped common park in the industrial complex. Cy gave high marks to the developers who incorporated green space into their designs. Now, if he could only convince people like Rebecca Ironwood to encourage her employees to use it.

Early June in Houston could be sweltering or gently warm, as it was today. Cy unscrewed the cap on his water bottle and drank deeply as he strode toward one of the benches on the grounds.

He gazed into the distance, deliberately letting his eyes unfocus and rest. Even five minutes outdoors would increase employee efficiency—that and reasonable work hours. People shouldn't live to work; they should work to live.

Cy, an independent personnel consultant, worked to

afford his boat, the *Azure Dreams,* and a big job like the Ironwood evaluation would pay for a month of sailing, doing a little fishing, a little drifting and a lot of nothing.

"All you care about is that boat," his ex-wife had raged.

And by that time in their marriage, she was right. Life was easier now that he didn't have to deny it.

The problem with Rebecca Ironwood was that her work was all she cared about, but Cy didn't delude himself into thinking he could ever tell her. She had no life outside her business and forgot that her employees did.

Cy reached the circular bench surrounding the trunk of a pecan tree, brushed debris off the seat, and sat.

Peace. Quiet. Nothing but the muted traffic sounds of a large city. He was alone. There were other buildings and other businesses—maybe hundreds of people worked in this complex—and yet he was alone. He shouldn't be alone. The park should be crowded with people de-stressing and getting their blood pumping. Resting their eyes and ears and skin from fluorescent light and filtered building air—

His cell phone rang. He'd forgotten to turn it off. Too bad. He still wasn't going to answer it.

Now, where was he? Right. Lunchtime zone out. Breathe in smog-laden air, breathe out smog-laden air. Rest eyes on carpet of green St. Augustine grass, heavily manicured and mowed by workers with bags attached to the mowers to collect the clippings, and then fertilized because heaven forbid the natural decomposition should feed the—

Zoning out wasn't working.

Cy's phone rang again. It was that woman, he knew it. Rebecca Ironwood was exactly the type of person to call his private number when she couldn't reach him in the office. Yet, when he glanced at the number displayed, he didn't recognize it. Maybe his answering service had forwarded a call to him.

"Hello?"

"Cy? Rebecca Ironwood."

Ha! "It's lunchtime." She was officially "out-of-pocket" for a couple of weeks, which he approved. He never liked having the management of the company he was evaluating watching over his shoulder as he talked to the employees.

"Of course it's lunch. That's the only time I have a break."

"I don't suppose you'd consider using your break for eating lunch?" He deliberately crunched one of his baby carrots.

"The line was too long."

Cy continued to crunch unrepentantly. He had no idea where she was and he wasn't going to ask. He hoped she was on vacation. She needed one.

"I've read your report on the first phase of your evaluation. I...didn't expect..."

Cy stopped crunching and swallowed. She sounded hesitant, unsure. And was that hurt in her voice? The Iron Lady? Hurt?

"...such animosity," she managed to get out before he could say anything.

He'd been surprised, too. After considering whether he should, he told her so. "Your salaries are competitive, even slightly above average, and you have a good benefits package. The reactions I got didn't follow the usual paradigm." In fact he'd repeated the survey and it had come back worse the second time.

"Then why? Why don't they like...working for me?"

And there it was: genuine bafflement and hurt.

That was the moment Rebecca Ironwood became human to him. Cy winced. No, no. Not that. Not human. The thing of it was, Cy had been walking well across the line of political incorrectness and considering her as a sex object recently. Fantasizing, actually. Completely reprehensible, yet apparently unavoidable. But the key word was *object*. Now she was a human. A female. The object part had slipped away. He tried to get it back, but failed when he heard the catch in her breathing. It drew him in and tweaked emotions he didn't want tweaked.

Cy wasn't good at emotional detachment, so it was good that the nature of his work consisted of limited time spent at each location. So that way when, and it was usually when, he became emotionally invested in people's concerns, he had an automatic out.

He wasn't looking forward to the end of the Ironwood project and that could be a problem. He sipped some water and grappled for a professional distance.

Why don't they like working for me? That's what Rebecca had asked, but what she really meant was why don't they like *me?*

Cy concentrated on his answer. "You expect a lot of your employees, true, but you compensate them fairly in return. But there is a perception that you do not and I haven't figured out why. That misperception is one of the reasons I recommended that you spend time working at the lowest levels of your organization. Show that you're approachable. Show that you care. Show that you aren't afraid to do anything that you ask of your employees."

"Oh, for pity's sake," she snapped. "It's not like I'm a general sending troops into battle! Filing invoice copies is hardly the best use of my time."

Okay, that took care of Cy's tender feelings. The "Be the Boss for a Day" strategy, in which the boss changed places with an employee, was one of his favorites. It sounded elementary schoolish, but he'd seen it work time and time again. That was why he'd told her she should try working for herself and see how it felt. Ironic that he, a man, was preaching feelings to a woman.

"You might find that the problem is not you at all, but how your upper management interacts with the employees," he responded mildly. Professionally. And then he blew it. "I don't know why you bothered hiring me since you won't implement any of my suggestions." He heard the sulkiness in his voice and muffled anything else that might come out of his mouth with a bite of sandwich—salmon and watercress, in case she was interested, which she patently was not.

"I..." She was silent.

He chewed.

"I'm disturbing your lunch."

"Yes."

"And you're annoyed."

"Yes."

"I'm—" She broke off the apology as a car horn sounded. "Where are you?"

"On a bench under a tree in the common park."

There was silence for a moment. "And what are you having for lunch?"

Cy actually pulled the phone away from his ear and stared at it. "A sandwich." He heard the irritation in his voice and elaborated. "Salmon and watercress on whole-wheat bread. And I make my own sandwich spread. I like fresh, real food." Why had he said all that?

"Do you even make your own bread?"

"When I have time—I mean, we're talking bread machine here."

"That counts."

"And when I don't have time, I buy from the Rustic Hearth." Listen to him just chatting away like they were on a date and he wasn't being interrupted by a woman he disliked.

And, yes, was attracted to. Sure, he'd admit it. Admitting a problem was the first step in overcoming it.

"It sounds lovely, your picnic." She sounded so wistful.

Cy grabbed the water bottle before he could do something stupid like invite her on a picnic.

"I'm sorry I disturbed you. In the future, I'll try to remember not to interrupt your lunch break." And she hung up without saying goodbye or giving any indication when she'd call again.

The abruptness was typical of her. The chatting was not.

She had potential, especially if she followed his suggestions.

Cy finished his sandwich and bit into his cookie, realizing that he'd spent his lunch thinking about Rebecca Ironwood. That wasn't good. Her type of woman, with a hard shell protecting a soft interior, was his weakness. That mix of toughness and vulnerability got to him every time. It was the potential for intimacy, the challenge of getting to know a part of a woman she couldn't reveal to anyone else. He found it incredibly sexy.

And dangerous. And very inconvenient.

As sexy as he found them, these women were not for him, because he was their opposite. Soft on the outside, empathetic, a good listener. They always felt betrayed when they discovered his shell was on the inside, surrounding his heart.

EYES CLOSED, Rebecca cradled the phone. What was this, high school? She was acting as though she had some big crush on Cy Benedict. And maybe she did, but she was certainly well past the age when she couldn't help acting like it.

She wondered if he could tell. *Do you bake your own bread?* She cringed.

Oh, get over it.

Rebecca was suddenly hungry. Salmon sounded good.

BY MIDAFTERNOON, Rebecca had been through the wringer. First up was an individual session with Mad Max—Rebecca was so onboard with the nickname now—to pinpoint Rebecca's desired objectives. It had begun awkwardly, skated through embarrassment, and landed in humiliation.

Rebecca had teared up. She hated that. But after two minutes with Maxine, there she was, blubbering about whiny Adrienne and the article and Cy Benedict, who wanted to be paid to spend time in her company.

She hadn't planned to mention Cy Benedict at all.

And speaking of company, she wasn't doing so hot with personnel turnover and employee satisfaction, and how humiliating was that when she was in the staffing business and she couldn't even adequately manage the staff in her own company. *Sniff.*

Maxine began writing. "So your goal is to attract Cy Benedict?"

"No!" Did she actually think Rebecca was so desperate that she'd pay a large chunk of change and spend two weeks of her extremely valuable time here just because of a man? So she'd mentioned him a couple of…a few times. He was currently working for her. Why wouldn't she mention him?

Maxine looked up at her, but continued to write.

"I'm…I'm engaging in behaviors that my employees and…business associates find too harsh. What I believe is efficiency and professionalism, they say is cold and bitchy. Cy Benedict is a consultant I hired to discover the source of my employees' dissatisfaction. His preliminary assessment indicates that I have unrealistic expectations." Rebecca swallowed, expecting at least a nod from a fellow business owner. No sympathy was forthcoming.

She wanted sympathy, damn it. Or at least an acknowledgment that she wasn't the horrible ogre everyone seemed to think she was. "I want to know just when expecting employees to have a solid work ethic became unrealistic? I can't believe—"

"Cy Benedict insulted you. You want to prove him wrong."

"This is *not* about Cy Benedict." *Breathe. Consider. Act.* Maxine had used the words, oh, about a million times this morning. Rebecca breathed. There was an audible hitch. She considered—considered walking right out. And she acted. "He didn't insult…well, he did, but I doubt he knew he was going to be quoted in a magazine article."

They stared at each other, Maxine's gaze unblinking and Rebecca's blinking a whole lot to stem the tears. Unsuccessfully.

"Fine-tuning your interpersonal relationship skills should improve employee morale, increase productivity, and decrease turnover. Are these areas in which Cy Benedict indicated you were deficient?"

"I...yes." Rebecca's face grew warm. She was either blushing, something she'd outgrown long ago, or having a hot flash. Neither thought was pleasant.

"And after you modify your behavior, you will hire this man to assess whether or not you've removed those deficiencies?" Maxine was so clinical, so matter-of-fact. And so ruthlessly to the point.

"Yes."

Maxine drew the workshop schedule toward her. "So an acceptable outcome of our sessions would be for Cy Benedict to wish to associate with you without being paid to do so."

Obviously, nobody was fooling anybody here. Rebecca thought about protesting, but ultimately abandoned her pride. "What about my business issues?"

"Naturally, they'll improve but quantifying that improvement will take time. Winning Cy Benedict's approval is a faster way to tell if you've succeeded."

Winning his approval like he was some great prize? *The only way I'd spend one minute more than I have to with the Iron Lady is if you paid me.* The words pulsed in her brain in neon red. Cy Benedict's words, according to Adrienne.

Rebecca remembered his irritation when she'd interrupted his lunch. He so didn't want to talk with her. In fact, he wanted nothing to do with her. And, so help her, Rebecca wanted him to change his mind. That's what this was really about, and Maxine, bless her heart, hadn't been fooled. She gave the woman a wry smile. "Yes. If Cy Benedict changes his opinion of me, I'll consider this time well spent."

Picking up her pen, Maxine ticked off the workshops Rebecca should attend.

AND SO during the first week Rebecca attended workshops such as Reconnecting with the Real World, which addressed the minutiae of daily life, minutiae that Rebecca had long ago delegated to others. Her time was more efficiently employed elsewhere. Before she remembered that she was supposed to be letting go of the unfairness of it all, she harbored a bitter thought that men had wives who took care of life's little details and no one called *them* remote and out-of-touch.

She didn't have children, so she didn't have to attend Negotiating without Nannies and Participating in Neighborhood Carpools, but she actually was forced to go to a seminar on Interacting with New Parents to be told that new parents were sleep-deprived and liked to discuss their babies incessantly. Duh. For this she'd paid ten thousand dollars? Even worse, during one night of her stay, recorded sounds of a crying baby woke her up to develop her empathy with the sleep-deprived. Rebecca was more cranky than empathetic.

In fact, she was having a difficult time letting go of the unfairness of it all. She would like to hear of a single businessman going through new baby empathy training. Just one. One.

And nobody better get her started on the horrors parents of teenagers went through. Hormones. Driving lessons. The college application process, and then paying for college. For this workshop, she had to analyze her personal financial resources and imagine supporting a family of four while saving for tuition.

Rebecca was having a *very* difficult time with the unfairness thing. It was all about choices. She'd chosen to start her own business. Others had chosen to replicate themselves. She didn't see anyone empathizing with her about sliding commissions and meeting the payroll, did she?

All that week, she reacquainted herself with such apparently exalted chores as grocery shopping and scrubbing toilets. Really, was any employee going to discuss the merits of Brite and Clean versus Scum B'Gone bathroom cleaner with the CEO?

She bonded as best she could with Cassandra and Barb. They might be her kind, but her kind was not easy to live with. Nobody cooked. Nobody cleaned. And nobody had been without a personal assistant or social secretary in years. They were great at delegating—only nobody wanted to be delegated to. They each wanted to be the delegator.

Fair enough. They'd decided they would each delegate in different areas.

The second week had more interesting seminars. Rebecca particularly enjoyed the body language workshops, language analysis, and the psychology refresher. Okay, the Warfield method wasn't so bad after all. Rebecca felt very open, very approachable. She had recipes to share. She'd discovered a new bathroom cleaner. And, yes, Houston's traffic *was* bad. Meat prices *were* way too high. Children *were*...a lot of trouble. She could empathize with people who had to deal with these things.

All in all, Rebecca thought she'd done splendidly—as if there had been any doubt. Only one more hurdle—the makeover.

Rebecca's dark hair had begun going gray in her twenties and now was a striking silver. It had been her trademark look and she liked to think her hair and her name were why she was given the unoriginal nickname of Iron Lady. She'd played on her appearance, wearing only black and shades of gray with a splash of red lipstick. It had given her authority at a young age. It was perfect for her and they wouldn't dare change it.

"We're going to lose the gray," Frederick of the Frederick salon told her. "We'll still be light, but a warm blond tone."

"Blond?" Rebecca congratulated herself on not gagging. Or shrieking. "No way. I am not the blond type."

"Think silver to gold. Gold is warmer." His voice dropped seductively. "More valuable."

"Fool's gold," Rebecca grumbled.

"And the style," Frederick went on as though Rebecca had actually agreed to dye her hair blond. "Not so severe. Some feathering around the face."

"Oh, so I can be a flighty blonde." As if.

Frederick chuckled, humoring her, and picked up the scissors.

She didn't look *bad,* Rebecca thought three hours later, after she'd opened her eyes to view the horror. She didn't look like herself, though. But since herself wasn't working, she'd give this new blonder self a try. She wondered if Cy Benedict liked blondes.

Rebecca now sat in a dressing room. It was wardrobe consultation time. Even she knew that with her new hair color and makeup, she'd need less severe clothing.

At least the consultants brought the clothes to the Warfield Retreat, saving her a public outing, though their cost wasn't included in the tuition.

"Hello," a brisk woman with gray hair and a black suit said. Ha. Rebecca's old look wasn't so bad, was it?

"I'm Jennifer and I'm thinking pink for you."

And now the horror was complete. "And I'm thinking why don't I save us all a lot of time and just wear a sign that says 'marshmallow fluff'?"

Jennifer draped color swatches around Rebecca's face and shoulders. "If your authority is based solely on your appearance, then you don't truly have authority at all, do you?"

Nobody could take a joke around here. "But appearance does affect people's perception of you and your ability to do the job," Rebecca pointed out.

"Exactly, and it also affects how you perceive yourself." Jennifer wheeled in a rack of clothes and pulled out a pink jacket. "Don't worry. We're keeping the sharp, tailored lines you like, but softening the color. Try on the jacket for me."

The jacket was a pink silk tweed and as soon as she put it on, Rebecca knew she was going to buy it. It was amazing. Honestly, she was so not a pink person, but her skin just glowed. The tailored cut was fabulous and her hair...the gray had been striking but now she looked, well, pretty. Rebecca had never thought of herself as pretty. Attractive, yes. Striking, certainly. But pretty? Never.

She hated to be wrong.

Still, she had doubts. "It might be too soft. Too ladies-who-lunch."

"So bring out the jewelry. Wear hard pieces. Cuffs, collars." Jennifer shook her wrist to draw Rebecca's attention to the sculpted silver cuff she wore. "Nothing wimpy. Invest in some obviously expensive pieces if you don't have any. You've already achieved success and you don't have to look harsh and defeminize yourself to be taken seriously. The jewelry will be a subtle reminder of your status."

Okay, so maybe pink wasn't such a bad color after all.

CHAPTER THREE

IT WAS exit interview time.

"We're glad you chose to attend the Warfield Retreat. We hope you've found our strategies beneficial." Maxine Warfield slid an envelope across her desk to Rebecca. "This is your evaluation and assignment."

"I have homework?" Oh, goody. Rebecca bent the clasp and opened the manila envelope.

"You had employee relations issues on several levels."

Rebecca wondered if Cy Benedict was considered one of those levels.

"As you know, we believe experience promotes understanding and empathy. Therefore, your assignment is to spend time working for yourself."

"I beg your pardon?" Rebecca stared at Maxine Warfield, and then flipped to the last page of the report. Yes, that's what it said, all right.

"Get a job in an area where you aren't known and see what it's like working for your own company."

"You mean spy on my employees?" Rebecca felt her lip curl in distaste.

"I mean experience work conditions in your company first-hand." Maxine's gaze traveled over her. "You know, you aren't likely to be recognized right away. You have a unique opportunity should you choose to exercise it."

An Important Message from the Editors

Dear Reader,

Because you've chosen to read one of our fine novels, we'd like to say "thank you"! And, as a special way to thank you, we're offering you a choice of two more of the books you love so well, and a surprise gift to send you – absolutely FREE!

Please enjoy them with our compliments...

Pam Powers

Peel off Seal and Place Inside...

FREE GIFT
EDITOR'S SEAL
THANK YOU

What's Your Reading Pleasure...
ROMANCE? _OR_ SUSPENSE?

Do you prefer spine-tingling page turners OR heart-stirring stories about love and relationships? Tell us which books you enjoy – and you'll get 2 FREE "ROMANCE" BOOKS or 2 FREE "SUSPENSE" BOOKS with no obligation to purchase anything.

Choose "ROMANCE" and get **2 FREE BOOKS** that will fuel your imagination with intensely moving stories about life, love and relationships.

FREE!

Choose "SUSPENSE" and you'll get **2 FREE BOOKS** that will thrill you with a spine-tingling blend of suspense and mystery.

FREE!

Whichever category you select, your 2 free books have a combined cover price of $11.98 or more in the U.S. and $13.98 or more in Canada.

And remember... just for accepting the Editor's Free Gift Offer, we'll send you 2 books and a gift, ABSOLUTELY FREE!

**YOURS FREE!** We'll send you a fabulous surprise gift absolutely FREE, just for trying "Romance" or "Suspense"!

® and ™ are trademarks owned and used by the trademark owner and/or its licensee.

Order online at
www.FreeBooksandGift.com

THE EDITOR'S "THANK YOU" FREE GIFTS INCLUDE:

▶ 2 Romance OR 2 Suspense books

▶ An exciting surprise gift

YES! I have placed my Editor's "thank you" Free Gifts seal in the space provided at right. Please send me the 2 FREE books which I have selected, and my FREE Mystery Gift. I understand that I am under no obligation to purchase anything further, as explained on the back of this card.

PLACE
FREE GIFTS
SEAL
HERE

Check one:

☐ **ROMANCE**
193 MDL EE3L   393 MDL EE3X

☐ **SUSPENSE**
192 MDL EE3W   392 MDL EE4A

FIRST NAME   LAST NAME

ADDRESS

APT.#   CITY

STATE/PROV.   ZIP/POSTAL CODE

▶ DETACH AND MAIL CARD TODAY! ▶

(ED1-SS-06) © 1998 MIRA BOOKS

The Reader Service — Here's How It Works:

Accepting your 2 free books and gift places you under no obligation to buy anything. You may keep the books and gift and return the shipping statement marked "cancel." If you do not cancel, about a month later we'll send you 3 additional books and bill you just $5.24 each in the U.S., or $5.74 each in Canada, plus 25¢ shipping & handling per book and applicable taxes if any.* That's the complete price and — compared to cover prices starting from $5.99 each in the U.S. and $6.99 each in Canada — it's quite a bargain! You may cancel at any time, but if you choose to continue, every month we'll send you 3 more books, which you may either purchase at the discount price or return to us and cancel your subscription.

If offer card is missing write to: The Reader Service, 3010 Walden Ave., P.O. Box 1867, Buffalo, NY 14240-1867

BUSINESS REPLY MAIL
FIRST-CLASS MAIL   PERMIT NO. 717-003   BUFFALO, NY

POSTAGE WILL BE PAID BY ADDRESSEE

THE READER SERVICE
3010 WALDEN AVE
PO BOX 1341
BUFFALO NY 14240-8571

NO POSTAGE
NECESSARY
IF MAILED
IN THE
UNITED STATES

Rebecca opened her mouth to protest, and then closed it when a paragraph from Cy Benedict's findings whispered to her: *Employees hesitate to communicate concerns and issues to management because management has not responded empathetically in the past. Management is perceived as harshly unrealistic. Suggest regular communication meetings. Or walk a mile in your employees' shoes.*

Rebecca was pretty sure she hadn't used the word *empathy* in any of its forms for years and now she was running into it in every conversation.

So everybody wanted empathy. Touchy-feely stuff. Okay, fine. She could touch and feel with the best of them. "I'll do that," she said to Maxine. And she knew exactly where she was going to hire herself.

CY BENEDICT STARED at the new hire. She'd just been introduced to him as Becky Wood and was going to be working as a junior interview counselor.

He observed as Crystal, the counselors' assistant, showed her the ropes. Becky Wood carried herself with confidence and appeared to be familiar with employment agencies. Her clothes were stylish and of obvious quality, and he knew enough about women to recognize a good haircut when he saw one.

If he had to guess, and as long as he was making excuses to stay near the reception area he might as well, he'd say that she was a former lady-who-lunched forced back into the workplace after her marriage broke up.

She wouldn't be able to afford clothes and shoes like those on the salary a junior employment counselor was likely to make, especially at Ironwood Executive

Staffing. Ironwood was okay on the salaries, but there were no bonuses. What the company had in place was fair, but nothing to get excited about. He'd recommended a five-percent, across-the-board salary increase and an end-of-year bonus plan, but didn't expect the Iron Lady to agree.

He hadn't spoken to Rebecca Ironwood since the lunchtime phone call and it was probably for the best. There had been a few impersonal e-mails back and forth, but no hint of the vulnerable and thus extremely attractive woman who'd interrupted his lunch. And continued to interrupt his thoughts.

Enough already. He'd give Becky Wood time to settle in, and then he'd question her about her first impression. He watched her nod, her blond hair swinging forward. She tucked it behind an ear as Crystal showed her the different aptitude tests and personality evaluations the agency used.

Yeah, he'd ask for her impression. Maybe over lunch.

REBECCA WAS SWEATING. Sweating in her brand-new pink silk tweed jacket. Cy Benedict was even better-looking up close. When he'd shaken her hand, she'd felt calluses, which she'd found kind of a turn-on. That was unexpected. Then he'd smiled, his eyes crinkling with squint lines caused by the sun. A woman would run screaming to her dermatologist for a peel, but on Cy they added to the outdoorsy look he had going. Very nice. The blond streaks in his hair were one hundred percent genuine sun streaks and his aura radiated peace and serenity.

His aura. Where had that come from? Rebecca wasn't an aura-noticing type of person and certainly nobody at the Warfield Retreat had mentioned anything about auras. Still, his practically glowed.

This man's passion so clearly lay outside his day job that Rebecca wondered what—or who—claimed it and how she could find out.

She was aware that he stood by the doorway and watched as Crystal got her settled. He'd begun the personnel efficiency phase of his evaluation and Rebecca could predict the report. *New employment counselor was instructed by clerk. Recommend manager of department define and familiarize new hires with job duties.*

Rebecca was surprised, herself. She'd have to talk with Lorena Martinez, the department manager, when she was back to being herself. In the meantime, she was getting a quick, but adequate overview.

"And if you have any questions, you can ask Joanna or Tara." Crystal pointed in the direction of two other women in glass cubicles. They were currently with clients and didn't look up.

"Um," Crystal waved vaguely at her desk. "There are some people waiting…um, do you want to start now?"

Rebecca gazed at Crystal in astonishment. "You mean…interviewing job placement candidates?"

"Well…yeah."

"All on my own? Nobody is going to sit in with me for the first few times?"

"Well, Lorena said you were really experienced…."

Rebecca knew, because she'd given herself a glowing recommendation. "Okay, then." She walked around the desk, pulled open the bottom file drawer, and put her purse into it. "Give me five minutes to figure out where everything is and then send in the first client."

BECKY WOOD SLIPPED into her job as if she were born to it. Cy could tell that she was much too experienced for the junior counselor position—at least in his opinion, which had been formed from spending far too many minutes staring at her the past couple of days. He couldn't help it. She was the first woman to distract him from his preoccupation with Rebecca Ironwood in weeks.

She hadn't noticed him watching her—at least he hoped she hadn't noticed—but he'd spent an awful lot of time at the filing cabinets where he could see through the glass-walled interview room. Funny how she looked vaguely familiar.

He shrugged and wondered if Becky Wood was the sort of woman who liked impromptu walking lunches with Cajun fried turkey on corn-bread sandwiches. Good thing he'd packed enough for two today.

REBECCA BIT INTO a weird, but surprisingly good sandwich. Surprising, too, that she could actually chew and swallow.

When Cy Benedict had tapped on the door of the interview room, Rebecca had felt her heart pound as though she were a girl about to be asked to the eighth-grade dance. Part of that was wondering if Cy would, or had, recognized her yesterday. And part was just because she found him attractive.

He'd asked her to lunch. Yes, he'd shared his sacred lunch hour with her and, judging by the conversation, it was a working lunch for him.

As they walked toward one of the benches surrounding the trees, he'd asked her about her first impressions of Ironwood Executive Staffing. To Becky

Wood, it would have been idle conversation, but to Rebecca Ironwood, who had hired Cy to analyze her personnel problems, it was anything but. She still couldn't figure out if he knew who she was so she went ahead and gave her honest impression as Becky—that the orientation process could be improved. And then she'd bitten into the sandwich before she could say anything more.

Only she should be saying something, something…connecting. Something to show that she was approachable.

Breathe. Consider. Act.

Rebecca inhaled and nearly choked on a piece of the sandwich. She considered how awful that would have looked as she chewed and swallowed. And then she acted by biting into it again.

She had to think of something unrelated to business to talk about. "This is really good," she finally said. "Did you make the bread yourself?" Recipes. Warfield had said recipes were a good topic. Except maybe not with the Cy Benedicts of the world. But hadn't he told her he liked baking his own bread?

No. That's what he'd told Rebecca Ironwood. Oops.

"Yes, I did." He must not have caught the slip. "It's a bread machine recipe and I like it with ham and this Cajun turkey."

There was no "Aha! You're the evil Rebecca Ironwood. Now I'm going to have to bill you for this lunch hour." Though she exhaled, Rebecca wasn't exactly relieved because she didn't like pretending to be someone she wasn't—except it had been *his* idea in the first place and could she help it if he didn't recognize her? "Becky Wood" wasn't exactly a deep cover sort of name.

"Sandwich making is a minor hobby of mine," he offered.

She should say something. "I've never heard anyone with a sandwich hobby." Maybe something else.

"There's a Dagwood Society—you know, after the comic character with the elaborate sandwiches?"

Definitely something else. "And you're a member?" This could not be good.

"No."

"That's a relief."

He laughed. "Was I sounding a little weird?"

"You were definitely wandering too close to the line between interesting and weird."

"Isn't there an eccentric buffer zone?"

Rebecca shook her head. "Eccentrics are just weird people with money."

He grinned as he unscrewed the cap on a bottle of water, tilted back his head and drank.

Blue sky and green leaves framed his head. He looked like a commercial. And man, would Rebecca buy whatever he was selling.

"The traffic was really bad this morning, wasn't it?" Inanities. She was reduced to inanities. Boring inanities.

"Seemed typical to me." He broke off a piece of a cookie and glanced at her and then away. "So what's your story?" He popped the piece of cookie into his mouth.

Oh, great. How was she supposed to answer that? "What do you mean?"

He looked directly at her, his eyes a deep blue echoed by the sky.

She couldn't believe she'd noticed his eye color. She was acting as though she was going to run home and write about him in her diary. They were adults. She found him attractive. Dealing with it should be a no-brainer, except that she'd been humiliatingly rejected already. But that was as Rebecca and she decided she wasn't going to initiate anything as Becky because, well, because it wasn't right.

Her head hurt.

"You're too experienced for the junior position."

Uh-oh. Now her head really hurt. Was it time to 'fess up?

"I thought maybe you had been out of the job market for a few years and…maybe a divorce or empty nest…?" he prompted.

"Long-divorced. No kids." And then she added, "No boyfriend, no social life and no pets, either." Now *that* sounded attractive. "I'm a workaholic. This job is less stress."

He actually smiled. "Good for you for realizing that there are more important things in life than work."

This was the moment. She should tell him who she was right now. Right this very minute. Of course then he'd leap to his feet in horror and never come near her again.

Still, it had to be done. Except that he was smiling and his eyes were crinkling and what she actually said was, "These cookies are *fabulous*. Could I have the recipe?"

CHAPTER FOUR

IN CY'S EXPERIENCE, women were as much trouble as boats. They required constant maintenance, were expensive to take out and rocked in stormy weather. Ah, but when the sailing was smooth, they were sublime.

The thing was, Cy already had a boat, so if he also wanted a woman onboard, so to speak, she'd better be worth the trouble. He was considering whether or not Becky Wood might be worth the trouble when they entered the foyer of Ironwood Executive Staffing after their lunch. He had a meeting in another part of the building and turned to say goodbye. They stopped walking and he looked down just as she turned her face to look up.

Fortunately, or unfortunately—he couldn't decide—she stood in the foyer with the business portrait of Rebecca Ironwood in the background and for a moment, her expression, with the close-lipped smile and the lighting the way it was, was mirrored by the portrait. And that's when Cy realized he'd had lunch with Rebecca Ironwood, herself.

How about that? She'd honestly taken his advice! But before he could be too pleased with himself, he rewound as much of their conversation as he could remember, hoping he hadn't come off like a pompous ass. She didn't act ticked off, so he must have sounded okay.

Now that he knew who she was, the change in her appearance wasn't as dramatic as the change in her demeanor and attitude. This wasn't the hard-nosed businesswoman. This was the woman who'd chatted after interrupting his lunch a couple of weeks ago. He liked that woman. Then again, he didn't really know the other.

"Thanks for lunch," she said. "I wonder why more people don't go outside and use the office park? In the summer, it'll be too hot, but it sure makes a nice midday break." She gazed outside. "Maybe if there was a covered area…and a fountain? I don't know."

"It sounds like a great idea," he managed to answer.

She turned back and smiled at him again.

Cy gathered his wits and took his cue from her. She didn't want anyone to know who she was and he respected that. He murmured a goodbye and watched her walk to the interview area.

On one hand, he was glad he hadn't asked "Becky" for a date, but on the other… No. There was no other hand.

"I CAN'T BELIEVE THIS!" Crystal carried in a huge carton. "The Iron Lady wants this done in time for the training seminar tomorrow morning."

Rebecca, who was in the reception area filing the personality profile tests from the morning's interviewees—which, by the way, was one of Crystal's jobs—glanced into the box as Crystal went to get another.

The box contained the new folders Rebecca had just had redesigned and printed for the training seminars Ironwood offered to those who needed to brush up on their interviewing, word processing or office equipment

skills. She'd long ago discovered that offering employment candidates the training at a below-market cost
enabled them to get better jobs, which made her
company look good and her clients more satisfied.

The new cover folders for the course materials had
arrived before she'd left to go to Warfield. And Crystal
was only now starting to assemble them?

Even worse, Crystal appeared as though she was
going to spread them all over the reception area. Paper
everywhere wasn't going to make the best of impressions on anyone arriving for afternoon appointments.

Rebecca picked up a box and gestured with her head
as Crystal carried in more materials. "You should
use the conference room where you can spread out on
the table. I'll help you carry the stuff in." Hey, look.
Empathy.

"Leave it," Crystal said. "If I'm in the conference
room, I can't be answering the phones in here."

"Oh." Okay, she had a point. "Is this what you
usually do when you have to put together packets?"

"*Usually* the trainer who's leading the course does it."

Probably because you don't, Rebecca was thinking
when Crystal dumped her latest load of boxes onto the
floor. One fell over and a stack of buff-colored papers
spilled out, creasing when the box lid landed on them.
And they weren't just any papers; they were the special
linen-weave, sixty-pound papers that Rebecca had paid
extra for. Quality attracted quality.

"Oops." Crystal didn't sound sorry, but she had no
idea how much they'd cost. She picked up the papers
and restacked them in the box.

"You...you can't use those," Rebecca told her.
"They look bad."

"Big whoop." She gave Rebecca a look. "It's real hard for me to get all excited about a last-minute job that's going to run way past quitting time."

So you should have started earlier, the pre-Warfield Rebecca would have snapped at her. The post-Warfield Rebecca was breathing—yeah, through gritted teeth, but still breathing. She was considering—considering giving Crystal a verbal smack upside of the head. But Crystal beat her to the "acting" part.

And what acting it was. Crystal looked down and shook her head and when she looked back up, she was biting a quivering lip. "It's just...it'll take me hours and...I had something else planned this evening."

Rebecca might have felt sorry for her if she hadn't known that Crystal had had three weeks to collate the materials. Rebecca was still considering.

"I mean, come on! It's Friday night! Who heard of classes starting on a Saturday, anyway?"

Rebecca was about to explain, and possibly reveal who she was, when a familiar voice answered.

"So people who already have jobs don't have to take off work." Cy walked into the reception area, his voice causing a pleasant tingle of awareness in Rebecca. Maybe more than pleasant.

"Do you often find yourself in a time crunch, Crystal?" he asked.

"Yeah, like everyone else who works for the Iron Lady. She loves to squeeze extra work out of us."

Breathe. Consider... to hell with it. She was just going to breathe. Deeply. Acting in her current frame of mind would only lead to nasty lawsuits.

"I've been trying to get to this all week and now..."

Crystal gave a great sniff. "And now I'm not gonna be able to—" She broke off and just sniffed again.

"What?" Cy asked.

"My...little girl's dance recital. It's tonight."

Rebecca narrowed her eyes. How many times had she seen this in movies?

"When?" Cy apparently bought into it.

"Seven-thirty." Crystal glanced at Rebecca and defiantly added, "I'm a single mom."

This was one of those empathy situations she'd studied at Warfield, but all Rebecca could think about was that if going to her daughter's dance recital was so important, Crystal should have assembled the course materials before now. If she had to work late, then what about last night? What about the night before? Why was Rebecca supposed to feel empathy for somebody who couldn't manage her time? This was a consequence and she was about to let loose and tell Crystal so when Rebecca's three-thirty appointment arrived. It was probably for the best because she didn't trust herself to properly express the Warfield empathy. Or any empathy, actually.

She went to meet the client herself instead of letting poor overburdened Crystal do her job. Still, Rebecca couldn't resist commenting as she took the man back to the interview area, "You've got four hours. Better get busy."

She considered the advice very restrained. Cy Benedict no doubt considered it an unrealistic expectation.

A sulky Crystal infected everyone who had the poor luck to come into the area during the next two hours, and by five-thirty, Rebecca wanted to flee to the nearest bar and mainline margaritas, herself. Even she hated the mean old Iron Lady. That couldn't be good.

The image of Crystal stuck with her through dinner, and by six-thirty, the Warfield philosophy of empathy had taken hold of Rebecca but good. Honestly, Crystal could leave, go to her daughter's recital and come back if she wasn't finished yet. Wait. *Single mother.* Crystal was a single mother. She'd have to get a babysitter or ask the one she had now to stay late. Maybe her little girl was about to miss her recital, too.

By six forty-five, Rebecca was back in her car and headed toward the office where, yes, lights blazed from the foyer.

Crystal, moving at a languid pace that had Rebecca internally screaming, answered her knock on the glass doors. "What's up?"

"How are you doing with the course folders?"

Crystal gestured to the mess behind her. "I'll be here till midnight."

Rebecca drew a deep breath. She'd already considered and acted. "It's seven. If you leave now, you should still be able to make it."

"Huh?"

"Your daughter's dance recital."

"My...oh." Crystal blinked. "Oh, yeah."

"Hurry. Go. I'll finish these."

"But—"

"No need to thank me. Just have a good time."

"I was going to ask if you knew how to put the folders together."

"Of course." But Becky wouldn't. "It's just collating. I'll look at the ones you've already finished."

"Okay. Thanks!" Crystal gave her a smile. Not a wide smile, and not exactly a relieved smile. It took Rebecca about twenty minutes to decide that it was a satisfied smile, which was strange. At least Crystal could have gushed a little.

The folders were a mess. Rebecca prided herself on her company's presentation and here were papers just thrown in any which way. Some were missing sheets and some held duplicates. And don't get her started on the creased ones. The work was sloppy and Rebecca was horrified.

She was arranging the materials for a more efficient assembly line when a tapping on the glass doors startled her.

Cy Benedict stood in the glow of the security light. Rebecca's heart thumped.

"I didn't expect to see you here," he said when she opened the door.

He looked...delighted. That was good, wasn't it?

"Ditto." Thump. Thump. She tucked a lock of her still unfamiliar hair behind her ear. "And what are you doing here?"

He grinned and there went the crinkly eyes. "Thought I'd help Crystal. I'm a sucker for a hard-luck story."

"Sucker being the operative word here. Check out this mess." Rebecca picked up one of the folders. "Papers just shoved in, not to mention that some are missing. It makes the company look bad. I know Crystal was mad about working overtime, and clearly was being passive aggressive, but possibly missing her daughter's dance recital was her own fault for mismanaging her time. It's called consequences." Rebecca was aware that she was talking far too much.

Cy looked at her. "And yet you, out of everyone here, came to her rescue."

"Yeah, well..." Rebecca glanced away.

"Hey."

"Hey, what?"

When he didn't answer immediately, she turned back to him.

His expression of warm approval and something else made her catch her breath.

"Rebecca, I know who you are, but I'm not sure whether I'm supposed to know."

She exhaled. "Well, that's a relief. I wasn't sure whether I should tell you or not."

They exchanged smiles of equal parts relief and possibility. "You working here *was* my idea," Cy said.

"So now that you've seen through my not-so-clever disguise, what are you going to do?"

Cy picked up a folder and studied the contents. "Collate training folders with you." He grinned and held her gaze just long enough to let it slide from being politely professional to warmly personal.

And yes, something warmed within Rebecca. Something she'd better cool. "At your hourly rate?" She picked up a folder and started moving down the stacks.

His gaze hardened. "I'm off the clock here."

"Oh." She made the word sound insultingly surprised.

He blocked her way around the L-shaped work area she'd arranged.

"What just happened here?" he asked.

Rebecca wasn't the sort to play games by pretending she didn't know. "I was referring to your quote in the *Future Business Women's Journal*."

"What quote?"

Maybe he hadn't seen it yet. "You don't keep up with professional publications?"

"Not that one."

Even though her photo had been on the cover, Rebecca had discreetly removed all loose copies of the newsletter and its unflattering article from the waiting area in the foyer. She knew where the file copies were, though. Rifling through the receptionist's periodical archives, she withdrew a copy, opened it to the article about her and pointed to Adrienne's quote of Cy.

He read in silence.

Rebecca grew antsy. "So is this what you said, or not?"

"I did."

Rebecca felt an irrational disappointment. And noticed that he didn't apologize, which irritated her.

"But this makes it sound worse. Your assistant wasn't clear about whether I was being asked to attend in a professional capacity. I clarified, and since I already had weekend plans, I declined. In words to that effect."

Rebecca reread the hateful quote. "How many words?"

He squinted and looked off to the side. "Most of them."

"I see."

"So you weren't exactly my favorite person of the moment. You'd interrupted every single one of my lunches that week. I get cranky without a midday break."

"Cranky enough to call me Iron Lady?"

He gave her a one-sided grin. "Oh, come on. You like knowing people call you the Iron Lady."

"Not really."

"Sure you do."

Rebecca was nonplussed. How did he know how she felt about it?

"A name like Iron Lady makes you sound strong and

in control. A woman alone at the top needs all the edge she can get."

"Apparently, I have too much of an edge."

Cy tossed the newsletter onto the receptionist's chair and leaned against the desk. "Do you honestly care if people like you or not?"

"Of course!"

"Like or respect—which one?"

"Both!"

"One. Only one."

"Respect," she murmured reluctantly.

"Don't be ashamed—own it."

"What if I only want to rent it?"

He gave a crack of laughter.

"Does hate have to go with respect?" she asked.

"No, and that's what we're working on."

Unexpectedly, he reached out and tugged on the end of her newly layered hair. "You're changing your image. Nice start."

"I—I went to—" *A place to learn how to attract you.* Admitting that out loud would either jump-start a relationship or end it altogether, but most likely would make her look pathetic. "—a seminar on employee relations." That sounded good.

"Excellent! Which one? I'm always looking for a good one to recommend."

"Um…this one is private." She smiled. At first, she'd been going for a flirtatious smile and changed her mind at the last minute so it ended up as a fake baring of her teeth.

"Ever the competitor. Okay, I get it. You're not going to tell me." He gave a huge sigh as fake as her smile.

"Even though I'm giving up my evening to bail you out of a mess."

"You're bailing Crystal out."

"Details, details."

She laughed. "Speaking of, we're going to redo most of these. Crystal is just plain sloppy."

Cy started emptying folders and restacking the papers before she asked him to.

Rebecca finished assembling a folder the way she wanted and displayed it on the table. "You do know that I'll have to speak with Crystal about her attitude. It's affecting everyone."

Cy flipped through the pages. "The atmosphere has been shaky since you fired Adrienne. She and Crystal were buddies."

Rebecca didn't hear any rebuke in his voice, but she still wanted to let him know she was not negotiating on this point. "Adrienne betrayed me. I have to be able to trust my personal assistant."

"No arguments, but you left immediately afterward, and as far as anyone knows, you're still gone. People are nervous."

"Oh, for pity's sake." Rebecca walked down the tables and took a piece of paper from each stack. "I wish people would just do their jobs and stop with all the drama." She arranged the papers in a folder.

Cy followed right behind her. "Then I'd be out of a job."

Rebecca started on another folder. "I get the impression that you wouldn't be too torn up about that."

"Only until I ran out of money. Hurry up. You're too slow."

"I want these to be perfect."

He shook his head. "Aim for excellence, not perfection."

"But—"

"We're going for the A, not the A plus."

Rebecca stopped. "Ironwood Executive Staffing is an A-plus organization."

Cy reached around her and continued gathering the papers. "Maybe that's your problem."

Rebecca opened her mouth and heard Maxine Warfield's voice admonishing *Breathe. Consider. Act.* Was he right?

Cy moved around her again.

Had she put unreasonable pressure on her employees to meet impossible standards?

"You think?" She tapped the papers and wondered if she should cut an inch off the ones in the front so they'd cascade nicely within the folder. She reached across the desk and took the scissors out of Crystal's pencil drawer. She cut off the bottom of one of the sheets and stuck it in the front. Much better. The Ironwood logo was visible now on both pages.

"Cy, I want to—"

"No."

"You don't even know what I'm going to say."

"I've been watching you. You're fussing."

She held up the folder. "It looks so much better."

"It would look even better in color and with gold tabs. Gold would evoke quality. Be unusual. Eye-catching."

He was brilliant. Absolutely—

"I. Am. Kidding."

"You're too modest."

"This is what I'm talking about. We're already

redoing Crystal's work. Not only do you want perfection, you keep redefining what perfection is."

"People should have high standards."

"People should get things done." He gestured with his head. "While you've been playing around, I've put together four folders. You had one. And then you messed it up."

Silently, Rebecca replaced the sheet she'd cut and meekly followed Cy around the table. More of the meekness stuff. She hoped it wouldn't become a habit.

A few moments passed before she realized that he was moving faster and faster. If she didn't hurry up, he'd lap her. Rebecca forgot about making every page just so and simply got them into the folder in order. "I'm going to get paper cuts," she complained mockingly.

"Well, if you do, then don't get blood on the papers."

Rebecca just stopped and laughed. Then she laughed some more. Laughed deeply in a way she hadn't for weeks. Maybe even years. Laughed until she became aware of Cy's quizzical stare.

"No, I'm not losing it," she told him.

"Didn't think you were. Feel better?"

Rebecca finished her folder in progress. "I wasn't feeling bad before." Just, well, tense.

"I thought you looked tense."

"I did not look tense." She'd tried very hard not to look tense.

"You just looked like it had been a long time since anyone had rubbed your shoulders."

What was she supposed to say to that? Since he'd been looking down at the papers and not at her, she couldn't read his expression.

"Has it been?" he asked softly.

He could seduce her with that voice. And maybe he was. "Are you talking professionally?"

"Hmm, I was asking about enthusiastic amateurs."

"Cy, are you flirting with me?"

He looked up. "Do you want me to be?"

"I *hate hate hate* it when men do that! Don't pull your punches, either commit to making a pass or not."

"Hey, we're on your turf." He waved an arm around the foyer. "Your name is on every sheet of paper in these stacks and your huge, giant, enormous, intimidating portrait is staring at me. Give a guy a break."

"Depends—are you married?"

He gave her a shocked look. "No!"

"Aha! So you *were* flirting with me!"

The shock remained on his face. "You're good."

"Yep."

"And cocky."

"With excellent reason."

He dropped the folder, spun her around and planted his large, warm hands on her shoulders. "I am a *very* enthusiastic amateur."

Surprise held her still. His thumbs quickly found the spot above her shoulder blades that ached whenever she spent too long at her desk. He pressed and moved his thumbs in a circle as his fingers gripped the muscles just below her neck.

She hadn't expected him to do that and the tenseness she wasn't going to admit to returned.

"Relax," he whispered.

"You're kidding, right?"

He chuckled and continued to massage her shoulders.

Sooner or later, one of them would acknowledge that

Cy's shoulder massage was not exactly appropriate. It wasn't exactly inappropriate, either, since Rebecca was soaking it in rather than pulling away.

"You carry too much on these shoulders," he murmured in that voice, the voice that could convince her to let *his* shoulders carry her burdens. And no man had *ever* prompted that kind of feeling before.

Or maybe it wasn't *his* voice. Maybe it was *her* blond hair and pink suit.

"Ironwood Executive Staffing is your life."

"Pretty much," Rebecca answered. "I built this company and I enjoy running it. And I know I've helped people get better jobs than they ever expected." She reluctantly pulled away from the magic in his hands and began filling the folders. "But you're Benedict Consulting, so you know how running a business is."

"No." He gave her a faraway smile. "I don't."

"Oh." Maybe it was his father who owned the company. Or a brother. Looking down, she efficiently filled another folder while he watched her. "What?" She looked up at him.

"Know anything about boats?"

"Where did that come from?"

"Do you?"

"No."

"I have a boat. Come out with me on Sunday."

She acted before considering. Even before breathing. "Okay."

CHAPTER FIVE

"I CALL YOU for support and advice and the best you can do is tell me to carry condoms?" Rebecca exclaimed. Okay, shrieked. With a humiliating high squeak at the end. Some conference call this was turning out to be.

Cassandra laughed. "I already gave you makeup samples."

"*Fabulous* makeup samples," Barb added. "What more do you want?"

"I—I…" What did she want? "It's, well, it's been a long time and I wanted to know how—"

"*How?*" they hooted.

"How to *act!*" Rebecca raised her voice so they could hear her over their laughter.

"I don't think that's changed a whole lot over the years," Barb drawled.

Honestly, they were being no help at all. She felt like tattling to Maxine. "I'm glad you two are amused, but I'm panicking here."

"*The* Rebecca Ironwood in a panic?" Cassandra teased.

"Some support network you are."

"I know it's not easy. Believe me, I know," Cassandra said more seriously, giving Rebecca the impression she might be having her own romantic difficulties. "But try to just have fun."

"Fun? How can anything that causes this much anxiety be fun?"

"Relax." Barb, too, was full of useless suggestions.

"I'm not going to relax unless Cassandra puts Xanax in her moisturizer."

There were a few more exchanges of the "get a grip" kind. Rebecca was about to hang up when she took a chance and confessed what was really bothering her—or bothering her the most. "I don't know whether he asked me out as Rebecca or as Becky."

There was silence.

"He knows who you are?" Barb finally asked.

"Yes."

"Then he asked you out as you."

Rebecca squeezed her eyes shut. "But he didn't like me when I was me."

"He didn't know you."

"He doesn't know me now."

"I'm guessing that would be the point of going sailing with him," Cassandra said.

"Have you ever been sailing?" Barb asked.

"No."

"Wear deck shoes. That's my best advice."

"He didn't exactly say *sailing*."

"Wear deck shoes anyway."

"And we're assuming you have a fabulous bathing suit," Cassandra piped in.

"About that…" Rebecca looked at her bed, where eight new swimsuits were laid out. "Do I go for sexy?" Could she still wear a bikini? "Serviceable?"

"Sexy," they said in unison.

"You've still got it," added Cassandra.

"Yeah, but 'it' is lower than it used to be," Rebecca

grumbled. "I'll try for something in between obvious and not-trying."

"Sounds good."

What a wimpy answer. Rebecca waited, but they didn't say anything else. "I'm not feeling supported here."

"Hey, you've got waterproof makeup with sunscreen, condoms, and deck shoes," Cassandra said. "Once you decide on a suit, you'll be good to go."

"Think of it as one more step in life's journey," Barb quoted.

She did a pretty good Maxine imitation. "Would you stop with the life journey talk?"

"Well, that's what it is," Barb said. "And don't forget to report back. We'll want details."

IRONICALLY, Rebecca found that the only way she could quell her nervousness was to pretend to be Becky Wood. Rebecca was never nervous—worrying about something wasn't going to change the future—so she had no idea how to deal with it. She decided this unfamiliar case of stomach butterflies must belong to Becky Wood and Becky would have the means to handle it. Besides, if she were Becky Wood, then this really didn't count, did it?

And Becky Wood did look hot, if she did say so herself. She'd brought more than one swimsuit with her. The one she was currently wearing under her shorts and top was more of a sun-and-display suit. The other was a working suit in case she had to throw ropes or move sails or something.

Okay, it was in case she felt like being not so hot. In fact, maybe she should find someplace and just change into the thing now, she thought as her confidence slipped away.

What was it about dating past forty that made a woman have the same self-doubts about her body as a thirteen-year-old? Back then, it was all about boobs—who had 'em and how big they were. Come to think of it, that's what it was still about.

Rebecca arrived without incident at the marina at South Shore Harbour near Clear Lake just south of Houston. Where was the infamous Houston traffic when she needed it? She might need it as a conversational topic later.

She'd been surprised when Cy had told her to meet him here, since she'd been to the conference center several times before and the marina was more upscale than she'd expected for a casual outing on the water. This wasn't the place to leave a rowboat or a little sailboat. Nope, not at all, she thought as she drove past some pretty significant adult water toys. Cy must take his boating very seriously. And of course, Rebecca had absolutely no experience—a fish out of water. Ha ha.

Breathe. And it was *breathe,* not hyperventilate. *Consider* didn't mean panic, and *act* didn't mean turn the car around.

When she parked in the area Cy had reserved for her and found him waiting for her, she was glad. She really liked the guy and wanted him to like her.

He stood on the other side of the wooden guardrail, leaning his forearms against it. He wore a white T-shirt, faded, ragged-hemmed jean shorts and deck shoes that looked like a larger version of the ones she wore.

He looked hot.

He swung himself over the guardrail with an ease that told her he'd done so a zillion times before. To meet other women? No. She was not going there.

Her heart thudded and she felt like the smart but shy freshman all over again. Except she hadn't been a pink-wearing blonde when she was a freshman, so maybe this could work.

Cy opened her door, probably because she still had the steering wheel in a death grip.

"Hi."

"Hi." So far, so good.

She swiveled her legs and saw him check them out, which made her feel marginally better. She gestured to the cooler in the back seat. "I know you said I didn't have to bring anything, but I ignored you."

He frowned. "Typical." Not good. Or maybe, in spite of what she'd seen, he owned a really small boat. Maybe the cooler was too big. Had she inadvertently insulted him?

Rebecca was not in her element. She liked being in control of a situation and knowing what was expected of her. She knew nothing about boats except that they floated and some were really big and expensive and qualified as yachts and some went really fast and got blown up in James Bond movies.

"You're frowning," she said.

"I'm thinking. Thinking about whether I can put your stuff in with my stuff so we don't have to make two trips."

"Thinking is not a good look for you."

He grinned. "So you like 'em dumb and handsome?"

"That is not what I said!"

"Then what kind of man do you like?" was the next question he threw at her.

She wasn't ready for this kind of flirty talk.

He raised his eyebrows at her as he opened the back door of her car.

Oh, a challenge. Now she understood. "I like a man who's a man and who isn't afraid to let a woman be a woman." Take that.

"And I like a woman who's a woman and who isn't afraid to let a man be a man," he shot back with a grin.

Rebecca thought about what he'd said. "That doesn't sound so good, but I can't figure out exactly why."

He propped his arm on the open car door. "Because you really want the man to let the woman be a man, too."

"That doesn't sound good, either, but I *know* why. It's not true." But wasn't there an element of truth? Rebecca did not like elements of truth. "So, effectively, you don't like strong women."

"I like them fine when they realize they don't have to be in command of every situation all the time."

Since they were being so direct... "Are we talking about women in general, or me in particular?"

"Right now—you in particular."

That was blunt. "I do *not* think I have to be in charge of every situation all the time!"

He studied her. "If I'd asked you out to dinner at a nice restaurant, one of the 'in' places, what are the chances that you not only know the manager or maître d', but would have called ahead of time to make certain everything went smoothly?"

Her eyes widened. How did he... "Okay, you got me. I've done it before. So?"

"Why do you think we're here and not in a restaurant?"

"So you can be the strong smart man and I can be the blond bimbo?"

He smiled. "There's a thought, but no. So I can be in charge and you can go with the flow. Although the more I think about your version, the more I like it."

Rebecca blinked. Truly, she couldn't think of anything to say. She was in an interesting situation. Here was a man who was neither intimidated by her, nor intimidating. He was being very direct. At least she thought he was being direct. But direct about what? He *was* attracted to her, wasn't he? Except for noticing her legs—and that could just be reflex—had there been anything in his demeanor or their conversation that was in the least romantic? Uh, no.

Had she been projecting? Was this a business-only get-together? Was she obsessively overanalyzing?

Cy had turned back to the car. "So what have you got in here?" He lifted the lid on the cooler.

"Just wine and nibbles." Both red and white wines. A sauvignon blanc. Well, and a Riesling because it was sweeter. And a merlot in case he was a red drinker, and a pinot noir, which could go with fish, if they were actually having fish. And a cabernet sauvignon because…well, because it went particularly well with one of the cheeses. She had both hard and soft. And a Stilton because you never know. And with Stilton you had to have port, so she'd included a bottle of that as well.

Cy stared at the contents of the cooler. "You're very thorough."

"I like to be prepared."

"Or drunk."

"I wasn't sure if…there were other guests."

"Other guests?" Cy straightened and looked hard at her.

"I wasn't sure," Rebecca explained, though she'd been *pretty* sure.

He continued to stare at her, his expression unreadable and she really wished she could read it. She tried meeting his eyes, but darned if she could.

"Let me clarify things for you."

With one hand, he reached around to the back of her neck, drew her forward and kissed her. Planted a big one right on her mouth. No social air kiss, no peck on the cheek. No, this was a me-man-you-woman, like-it-or-leave-it sort of kiss.

There was no mistaking this kiss for anything except what it was: the kiss of a man attracted to a woman. Very attracted. To her. And since Rebecca hadn't been expecting it, she sort of gasped and Cy took full advantage, slanting his mouth over hers until he found the perfect fit. Deepening the kiss, but leaving a lot to explore later. Letting her know there *would* be a later.

You should be kissing him back, a part of her whispered.

He's got things under control and I'm going with the flow, another part of her sighed.

Rebecca was used to being the aggressor, in a way giving the men she was with permission to kiss her. It wasn't nearly as much fun, which was probably why there hadn't been all that many men. She'd even begun to wonder if something was wrong with her and had gone so far as to have some blood work done just in case her hormones had dried up or something.

What a waste of time and money when all she'd needed was to be kissed by Cy to know all was well.

His mouth was warm and firm and mobile and the man sure knew his way around a kiss.

He broke it by pulling away slowly, an effective contrast to the way he'd begun. "Any questions?"

Rebecca leaned on the open car door for support. "Yeah. Where did you learn to kiss like that?"

He smiled, a very male smile that she felt all the way to her toes. Actually, she was surprised that after that kiss she still *had* toes—that they hadn't curled up and fallen off.

"Still want to come onboard?" he asked.

And she knew exactly what he was asking. Knew that he was attracted to her and wanted to explore that attraction. Rebecca managed a smile and a wobbly salute. "Aye, aye, captain."

Still wearing that smile—and wasn't it veering just the slightest bit in the smug direction?—Cy bent toward the cooler. "We'll take the cheese and the port and this very nice sauvignon blanc here, and leave the rest in the cooler." He piled the things into her arms, snagged her satchel, and slung it over his shoulder, then took the bottles from her.

Taking the bottles was good because she might have dropped them. Cy strode off and Rebecca, once she was sure her legs were working, followed.

CHAPTER SIX

CY HOPED he could make it to the *Azure Dreams* without dropping the wine. He was on a mission and his mission was to keep Rebecca Ironwood off balance and out of her element so he could get to know the woman beneath the tough business exterior.

But after the kiss, *he* was the one caught off balance. He'd expected to enjoy kissing Rebecca. He hadn't expected to nearly lose himself in the heat of her mouth. And that was with her being stunned into immobility. A little kissing back on her part and they might still be in the parking lot. *Would* still be in the parking lot.

They walked down the pier in silence. Cy didn't speculate on what Rebecca was thinking because he was doing his own thinking. Part of him welcomed the opportunity of finding a life mate. He didn't go out of his way looking, but he certainly wasn't going to close himself off from the possibility. And, he reminded himself, Rebecca was currently only a possibility. She was more of a possibility now than before he'd kissed her, but nothing more. For now.

The other part of him, the part in charge of the shell around his heart, usually scoffed—no woman was getting through his defenses. That part had been very quiet since Cy had kissed Rebecca. By now, alarms should have sounded.

He would have chosen to ignore them, but he should have heard alarms by now.

"Where is your boat?" she asked.

"Down at the end. I should have told you we had a hike ahead of us. Sorry." He glanced at her. "I was distracted." He liked that he could be direct with her. If ever there was a woman who didn't play games, it was Rebecca Ironwood.

She peered ahead of them. "I guess we can't see it because of that big blue one. What's the name of your boat?"

"Azure Dreams."

"What a coincidence. That big blue one is named *Azure Dreams.*" She nudged him with her elbow as they approached the slip. "You might have warned me. I didn't know whether to expect a rowboat or an outboard motor or a party pontoon or…" She gestured to the boat.

"A motor yacht." He heard the pride in his own voice. Didn't care. "Sleeps six. Eight if two sleep in the salon." Cy became aware that Rebecca had stopped walking. Sure the *Azure Dreams* was a heck of a boat, but there were others bigger. Maybe none as loved. He turned back, expecting to see her staring at the boat, but she was looking at him.

"This is you, isn't it?" She waved her arm. "When I first met you, I thought here is a man who isn't married to his work. This is your passion. This is what makes your blood sing." She looked back at the boat, shaking her head in admiration. "What a beauty."

Something within him eased. She understood. They hadn't set foot onboard and she got him already. Knew who he was. Cy stared at the woman who'd bedeviled him for weeks and felt nothing but a sense of inevitability.

She glanced up at him. "I'm right, aren't I?"

He nodded. "This is where I'm me. Where I'm happy."

"And you invited me to share it with you." She drew a breath and exhaled. "I'm honored."

And he was lost. No wonder he hadn't felt any warning alarms. She'd already snuck past his defenses. Wait a minute. Rebecca hadn't snuck past his defenses; she'd stormed past them. And he didn't mind at all.

THERE WAS SOMETHING freeing about not being expected to know everything.

Rebecca looked across the flybridge to where Cy had peeled off his shirt and admitted to herself that there was something about being here on this exquisite boat. With Cy. Actually, the luxurious watercraft didn't matter to her. Cy did.

He was a mature man, still in his prime, and he made her feel like a mature woman, still in her prime. So primed that she kept her purse with her. He probably wondered why. She grinned into her wineglass and hoped he'd find out.

No doubt this was rash, impulsive, if she could call something she'd hoped for all day impulsive. But she didn't care.

There had been a seminal moment for her, back when she'd agreed to come onboard after he'd kissed her. She'd felt carefree, which was not one of her usual moods. And then when she'd understood why he'd wanted her with him today, well, that was pretty much it for her. The guy had to know that as a lure, sharing something so vital to him had no equal. Or maybe he didn't know. She loved that he took nothing for granted.

And she loved being here with him. Oh, she was a goner, vulnerable as heck. But she didn't care. She was wearing her hot suit. Admiring his back muscles. His chest. His front muscles. His shoulders. His tanned skin, which was a natural to-heck-with-it bronze despite that he still slathered it with sunblock. Except for that spot he'd missed that she was going to help him with just as soon as she trusted herself to casually approach him and not lurch forward and fling herself at him.

He'd mentioned fishing and was now setting up poles after sailing them to the middle of nowhere in the Gulf of Mexico on a glorious June day. The sky was a faded blue and drilling rigs pierced the horizon. Seagulls fluttered around them and the waves lapped hypnotically. The sun was warm and she was, dare she say it, relaxed. Mellowing into sleepiness.

Okay. Right now. Right now, she was going to sit up from this most comfortable deck lounger, sip her wine, slip her feet into the deck shoes wonderful, wonderful Barb had told her she had to have, sashay over in her hot suit—how fortuitously tremendous that she'd worn this coral-and-gold bikini that was wildly flattering, and not the thicker-strapped one-piece. Not that it wasn't just as fabulous, but fabulous in a more subtle way. Besides, a bikini was so much easier to get off.

She covered her mouth to stifle her smile and realized that she was just the slightest bit loopy and figured it had more to do with the feeling of anticipation than with the half glass of wine she'd drunk.

They'd eaten one of Cy's sandwich creations for lunch—chicken salad on whole-wheat croissants—and were going to catch fish for dinner. Honestly, Cy's galley was no smaller than the kitchen of an apartment she'd once lived in, and had granite countertops to boot. There was a master stateroom and two others each with their own bathrooms. Heads, as Cy insisted she call them. Okay, if he wanted to play captain of the high seas, she'd play first mate with him. And speaking of mating…she giggled silently again. She sipped her wine and eyed Cy as he fastened the rods in their holders in front of what he called fighting chairs.

He was one good-looking man, especially in his element as he was now.

Rebecca fit her wineglass in the recessed holder, grabbed a tube of sunblock and made her way over to Cy. "You're going to have a very oddly shaped sunburn on your back tomorrow unless you let me fix it right now."

She kinda wondered why they hadn't played the suntan lotion game yet. The one that went *you slather my back, I'll slather your front and, oops, let's not miss that spot and have you heard that UV rays could penetrate clothing?* That game. Maybe she should start.

"Did I miss a spot?" Cy glanced with disinterest over his shoulder and swatted at his back.

"Here. Let me." She squirted suntan lotion onto her palm, and then leaned around him to put the tube in a cup holder.

He stood patiently, not even noticing that she'd removed her matching coverup and was showing a fair amount of skin now. She rubbed the lotion between her palms and smoothed them over the middle of his back. Stroking, massaging, she thoroughly worked the sunblock into his skin. He felt good beneath her hands. Surely this felt good to him, too. Any minute now, he should turn and take her in his arms. Some positive reinforcement would help. At least he could flex or tremble or have an involuntary shudder as he fought overwhelming desire. Okay, that was her. But they'd been together for hours now and she was completely besotted. And he'd been watching her in that careful way men watch women they want.

The lotion was all but absorbed into his skin. She'd hoped that he would have made the first move, but in a second here, it wouldn't matter.

CY BIT THE INSIDE of his cheek and drew blood. He concentrated on the drilling rigs on the horizon to distract himself from the feel of Rebecca's hands. Any second, and she'd remove them and go back to torturing him from the lounger.

One glance—and so far, he could only stand glances—had told him she had a fabulous, womanly figure. Not girly thin, but a womanly take-me-to-bed figure.

And he wanted to, but not yet. Not so far from shore because on the chance—miniscule, but still present—that they didn't click, the long ride back would be painfully awkward.

Her touch relaxed as much as it aroused. Involuntarily, his head dropped back and her hands drew away.

"The tops of your shoulders could use more." Her voice had lowered in pitch.

He turned to tell her they were fine, because it was time to put distance between them, and he caught sight of her bending to retrieve the suntan lotion. Her suit gapped a little and his eyes were drawn to the shadowy area between her breasts. Desire shot through him, the intensity causing his breath to hitch.

Rebecca stood, the tube in her hands, and met his eyes. She'd heard that hitch. She knew what it meant.

They stood like that, swaying with the rocking of the boat. Cy waited for the first surge of desire to run its course but it only grew.

"A man doesn't look at me the way you're looking at me without something happening," she said.

"Oh, it's happening." He took the lotion out of her hand and tossed it toward the table where it landed and bounced onto one of the swivel club chairs.

"But not very fast," she muttered and he grinned.

"Hey." He took one of her hands. "We're out so far we could fish for red snapper. Do you want to? I don't want you to feel uncomfortable. Or pressured."

"I don't." She gripped his hand. "I do feel impatient."

"And nothing has to happen that you don't want to have happen."

"There isn't much I don't want to have happen."

He could feel his heart pound. "You are just shredding all my good intentions."

"I'm more interested in your bad intentions." She gave him an exasperated look. "And since there doesn't seem to be a mood to kill, I'm going to tell you that I'm disappointed that I have to make the first move."

"You didn't make the first move."

She pulled her hand away. "Excuse me? Suntan lotion?"

Slowly, he leaned down until his lips were a breath away from hers. "Excuse me? Kiss on the dock?" And he straightened, not kissing her at that moment one of the great achievements of his life. "You've been thinking about that kiss and how it made you feel. So have I. You've been enjoying the anticipation and so have I. Now, take a seat and let's catch dinner and anticipate some more. And try to remember that you're not in charge."

He could hear the angry huff in her breathing as she sat down.

He showed her how the reel worked and how everything fit into the holder. "As long as we're being honest here, I'm disappointed that you don't want to get to know me more. I don't want to be just another one of your boy toys."

She actually spluttered. "Boy toys? I do not have boy toys. Who told you that?"

"Nobody. I just wanted you to know there was more to me than my fabulous bod."

She burst out laughing. "You nut! We've talked for hours! We've talked about our failed marriages. We've talked about our businesses and schools and politics and vacations and which vodka is best. We don't like the same music and you know I don't cook."

"So what you're saying is that I don't have the bod to be a boy toy?" He hitched up his trunks.

"I did n—" She broke off, her eyes narrowing, focused on the waistband of his swim trunks. "You have no tan line."

"No."

Her eyes met his and, this time, he thought he *would* kiss her. Soon. Hard. And often.

"Show me."

They might just have cheese and crackers for dinner after all. Cy gazed at her, waiting for a little less demand, a little more pleading.

"Please," she added, understanding at last.

He stood, locked the fishing rods into place, and unknotted his swim trunks.

Her eyes widened and her lips parted.

Cy abandoned the restraint he'd fought for all day. The more they'd talked, the more he'd wanted her. They had a lot in common and, even better, their disagreements only enhanced their relationship. It was the great thing about being at this stage in their lives; they could accept their individual preferences as simply differences and not obstacles.

They could savor being in each other's company and had. But now, Cy was ready to savor on another level and he knew Rebecca was, too.

Cy hooked his thumbs in his waistband and pulled his trunks down his thighs. He was hard with wanting her, and if she had doubts about his desire before, she couldn't now.

He let her look at him, let her desire fuel his own.

"You're such a beautiful man," she breathed. "Cy…"

"Shh." He snagged the suntan lotion and stood behind her chair. "Lift your hair off your neck."

She responded without question and something about the vulnerability of her bare nape caught at him. He bent and pressed his lips to the soft skin, loving the feel and taste of her sun-warmed skin.

"You gave me goose bumps."

He smiled against her skin, knowing that he was about to make love to Rebecca Ironwood. Not have sex, but make love and he wanted her to feel the same way.

He raised his mouth and unfastened the halter strap of her swimsuit. Dribbling lotion across her shoulders, he massaged it into her skin.

"I think I have a new fantasy," she murmured. "Being massaged by a bronzed naked masseur. I can't think why that's never been one of my fantasies before." She tilted her head back against the fishing chair.

The tops of her breasts curved above the loosened top, causing Cy a few fantasies of his own.

He dribbled more lotion onto her throat. As he stroked her collarbone, she sighed and closed her eyes. He didn't want her *too* comfortable. Leaning down, he unhooked the back strap of her top and flicked the whole thing away.

Rebecca's eyes were definitely open now. But thank heaven she didn't cover her breasts because Cy had never seen anything as beautiful as a half-naked Rebecca Ironwood on the top deck of his boat against the muddy blue of the ocean.

"We're alone," he reassured her.

"I know." Releasing her hair, she leaned back in the chair, one foot propped against the railing, her hands dangling over the chair arms. "This is the first time I've sunbathed topless and I trust you won't let me burn."

"The sun isn't going to make you burn. I am."

SHE FELT gloriously free and completely unselfconscious. Being with Cy on the *Azure Dreams* was being in another world, and she was another person, a person she couldn't be otherwise.

She caught her breath when cool lotion dropped onto her chest and she moaned when Cy's hands smeared it over her breasts, the calluses on his palms tightening the peaks.

He swiveled the chair to face him, knelt and slowly, thoroughly, coated her thighs and calves and even her feet.

Warmth radiated from his touch. Heat radiated from the look in his eyes. She gripped the arms of the chair with the effort of remaining seated. "Cy?"

He stood and held out his hand. When she took it, he pulled her out of the chair and into his arms, pressing his body into hers.

His kiss was warm and possessive and, yes, he was making her burn. Still kissing him, Rebecca shimmied out of her swimsuit bottom.

Their foreheads touching, Cy looked down at her. "You are incredibly beautiful."

"You make me feel beautiful."

The smile he gave her was full of sweet intent. "Hold out your hand."

When she did, he put lotion in it and then in his. "This is one time we don't want rosy cheeks." Reaching around her, he massaged the lotion over her hips.

She did the same for him, enjoying the play of his powerful muscles and then forgetting about muscles as they bumped and rubbed and swayed against each other.

They explored each other's bodies in the afternoon sun, Cy setting a leisurely pace. There was no hurry, no pressure and plenty of time to think about what they were doing.

Plenty of time to fall in love.

At last, Rebecca knew it was time, even before Cy spoke. "The master stateroom has a king bed and a hot tub. We can go there."

And she smiled up at him. "Do we have to?"

Smiling back, he shook his head. "Later, then." Walking over to the banquette ringing the flybridge, he flipped open one of the seats, revealing storage beneath, and took out large navy-and-white beach towels which he laid across the hot leather.

"My purse."

Rebecca started for it, but Cy laced his fingers

through hers. "This is a place of many nooks and crannies." He opened a narrow drawer and she smiled.

She lay on the banquette in the late-afternoon sun, tears coming to her eyes at the way Cy looked in the light, all golden and masculine.

He settled next to her on the narrow seating and stroked her hair from her face, holding her gaze with his. "Look at me."

Rebecca wouldn't have closed her eyes for the world.

"What we have is rare. Precious," he told her. "You've touched something in me that I didn't know needed to be touched. And I hope that you—"

"Yes! I feel the same way. I've been holding a part of myself back." She placed her hands on either side of his face. "And I don't want to do that anymore."

"Never hold back. Not with me." He gave her the sweetest kiss she'd ever had in her life and nestled himself between her thighs. They came together easily and naturally, their cries mingling with those of the seagulls.

CHAPTER SEVEN

WHEN SOMETHING SEEMS too good to be true, it usually is. Not the oversized spa bathtub in the master stateroom on Cy's boat—that was good *and* true. But the way Rebecca and Cy separated their two worlds and moved between them seemed unbelievably effortless. For the next two weeks, they spent every spare moment they could on the *Azure Dreams*. And Rebecca was literally another person at Ironwood Executive Staffing.

It was romantic. It was easy. It was perfect. Except it wasn't real.

And unfortunately, Rebecca feared now was the time for a reality check.

Cy had been making remarks, casually mentioning trips on the *Azure Dreams*. And these trips involved taking off and sailing for weeks at a time, something she certainly couldn't do. He seemed to have forgotten that she ran a company.

They never discussed their situation but they were going to have to because after two weeks of working as Becky Wood and running the company on the sly, Rebecca was ready to go back to being herself. Cy had nearly finished his evaluation and was writing the final report.

Rebecca was trying not to think about "what happens

next" and enjoy the moment. But some of those moments involved Crystal.

This morning she'd been late. Thirty minutes late. And Rebecca had covered for her. Again. She was trying to be empathetic and use her Warfield training, but when Crystal sashayed in wearing the same outfit she'd worn yesterday, that was it.

Actually, that hadn't been it. Rebecca had looked up her personnel file. *That* had been it. She'd forgotten to breathe. Forgotten to consider. She only wanted to act by confronting Crystal.

She knew she looked angry. She *felt* angry.

"Thanks for covering for me." Crystal eyed her warily. "My kid wasn't feeling so hot this morning."

Rebecca gazed at her. "What's your daughter's name?"

"Um…" There was a hesitation, slight, but telling. "Tiffany."

"Do you have a picture of her?"

"No."

"You know, I never saw pictures of the dance recital."

"I, uh, haven't downloaded them from my camera yet."

Rebecca tapped the personnel employment file. "And you didn't sign Tiffany up on your insurance."

Crystal pointed. "What's that?"

"Your personnel files."

"Hey, what are you doing with those?"

"Reading them. You don't have a daughter. You lied to me."

Crystal rolled her eyes. "Okay, you caught me." She smirked. "I guess this means you aren't going to cover for me anymore."

"It means that you're fired."

"I don't *think* so. I'm not the one snooping into confidential files. So you can forget about trying to get me fired."

"Crystal, I'm Rebecca Ironwood." *And you are toast,* she wanted to add. Empathetically, of course.

She watched as Crystal's eyes shot to the portrait in the foyer and then back to Rebecca, where they narrowed.

"So you come in here spying on us and fire me for pretending I have a kid? I had a date, okay? You can't fire me for having a date."

"I'm firing you because you're frequently late and you don't adequately fulfill your job responsibilities."

"Huh?"

"You're a receptionist and you're supposed to assist the counselors. It's not that hard, Crystal."

"That's what *you* think," she grumbled. "The phones ring all the time with people whining about their interviews and asking questions and wanting to set up appointments. There's always filing and photocopying and CDs to burn for those stupid course booklets. And don't get me started on making coffee. There's never any chill time."

Who hired this woman? Crystal had expressed no remorse and hadn't apologized. "Take a few minutes to pack up your things, and then see human resources. They'll discuss your severance terms."

"Just like that." Crystal made a rude noise.

"Yes," Rebecca said. "Just like that."

REBECCA IRONWOOD WAS BACK. Word reached Cy even though he was on the other side of the building. And the word wasn't good.

She'd had a showdown with Crystal and fired her. As

an employee relations move, not so good. They hadn't discussed how she should reveal that she'd been working incognito, but this wasn't it.

That woman. Cy shook his head. She had him twisted all nine ways to Sunday. That he had a thing for her, he had no doubt. That she irritated him, he had no doubt. That he could convince her to take off with him on his boat for days at a time…now that he had doubts about.

He sought her out in her office, passing little conversational clusters along the way. He'd have to convince her to do some serious damage control.

REBECCA LOOKED UP to see Cy standing in her doorway. It was the first time they'd seen each other all day. The first time they'd been together when she was Rebecca Ironwood and definitely in charge. "You've heard."

"That you fired Crystal? Yes."

She tried to read his expression and decided that it was faintly disapproving. "And you disagree."

"As a matter of fact, yes." He leaned against the doorway, arms crossed over his chest. "You want to hear why?"

If he'd come all the way into her office and sat down to talk, maybe it would have been okay. But how many times had she seen him prop himself in the galleyway in just that position, watching her as she struggled to figure out something to do with his boat and then fixing what she'd done or showing her how to do it properly?

But this was *her* company. *Her* turf. "I'm not asking for your approval."

"And I'm not giving it. After spying on your employees, you fired a single mother, the sole support of her family, because she wouldn't work overtime on a Friday night."

"That's not true! You know it's not true."

He nodded. "But that's what the buzz is."

"Crystal lied. She doesn't have a daughter, she's incompetent, routinely late and has a bad attitude. I can't imagine how she was hired."

"She was a friend of Adrienne, your former personal assistant. Word was that no one was to complain about Crystal or Adrienne would give them a hard time."

"You're kidding." He had to be kidding.

He shook his head. "And I wish you'd told me before you revealed who you were. It could have been handled better from a PR standpoint. Now, you've got a big mess."

"So I'll deal with it."

"But there didn't have to be a problem. Rebecca, I just don't get you." He came inside her office and shut the door. "You make everything so hard for yourself. It's as though you're so used to struggling that you're suspicious when things come easy. At the beginning, you *did* have to struggle, but you can back off now." He smiled gently. "You know how."

He wasn't supposed to refer to their time on the *Azure Dreams*, but he was. "You know what it's called when a company's leader backs off? Stagnation."

"Rebecca..." He exhaled her name before quietly continuing. "Nine out of ten companies I analyze are management heavy, but not you. Your managers all report directly to you. You need an executive level in between. Let them handle the day-to-day routine. Save yourself for the important stuff."

"It's all important stuff!"

Emotion flashed across his face. She'd never seen

him angry. This might be it. He stalked across the room and propped his fists on her desk and leaned toward her. "More important than what? Having a life?"

"I like my life."

"Really." He straightened. "And the weekends?"

"I like them, too."

"And this weekend?"

Not fair. *Not fair.* "This is my first weekend back."

"I knew it," he spoke under his breath. "I knew this would happen."

"Cy, be reasonable."

"*You* be reasonable. You're functioning at max and that includes the weekends. You want to talk stagnation? This is a textbook case. You can't grow because you won't relinquish any control. Take Crystal—what were *you* doing firing her?"

"She—"

"You were suckered and your pride was hurt. *I* was suckered. As for her job performance, her supervisor should have called her in for a review. She should have been given the opportunity to improve. If she hadn't improved, *then* you talk termination. This is an *employment* agency. You, of all people, should know the drill."

He was probably right and somehow that made it worse. "I'm not going to sit here and listen to you tell me how to run my company."

"But you did hire me to evaluate your company, which I have done. I'll have my final report on your desk by the end of the business day."

And he left. Just left. She hadn't indicated the meeting was over.

Rebecca felt raw. So much for being nice. So much

for being empathetic. So much for the Warfield strategies. So much for men.

So much for love. Because, oh, yes, as if things weren't bad enough, she'd fallen in love with Cy Benedict. Knew it was happening, hadn't stopped it, and hadn't cared that she was leaving herself vulnerable. She'd seen the truck coming and hadn't even tried to step out of the road.

Rebecca stayed in her office for the rest of the day. She went to the break room to get a bottle of mango guava juice, because she felt she deserved a treat. Of course that would be the time when Cy delivered his report.

Clearly, he'd been avoiding her.

So. This was the end. And he hadn't even said goodbye. The sense of loss she felt took her breath away and she had to press her fingers to her breastbone. *Breathe. Con— breathe. Breathe again.* She couldn't consider.

She'd known Cy was too good to be true. But she could not have him thinking anyone was in charge of Ironwood Executive Staffing but her.

Rebecca stared at the hard copy of his report. She wasn't even sure she wanted to read it. But she did. She almost wished she hadn't.

On the positive side, he felt her business was well run. He'd analyzed job functions and employee hours and made lots of lovely charts that she'd examine later.

She flipped through to the observations. As he'd said, he recommended an additional executive level to increase efficiency and position the company for growth. He'd also mentioned that her female employees felt she was less responsive to them than to the males. The females felt she was not empathetic.

That word again. Rebecca gritted her teeth. She'd been empathetic with Crystal and where had it gotten her?

Cy felt her perceived lack of empathy had contributed to increased employee turnover.

She wasn't going to read the rest of it. She was going home.

CY DIDN'T EXPECT Rebecca to join him for the weekend. He figured she was feeling defensive and would have a lot to absorb in his report. But he also figured she was smart and, once she calmed down, she'd sort it all out. Besides, he had boat maintenance he'd been neglecting. He didn't leave the marina, but he sure missed having Rebecca with him. That, more than anything, brought home the depth of his feelings for her.

His love for her. Yeah, that woman had gotten to him big time, prickliness and all.

He almost phoned her, but decided to let her think about things for a day or two.

And he'd do some thinking, as well.

REBECCA ASSUMED those who studied human behavior knew all the names for the stages she went through that weekend. She'd been angry, hurt, lonely, embarrassed, angry again, defiant, resigned, whiny, and, okay, angry yet again, but she never felt the least bit empathetic. Empathy was a wasted emotion, as far as she was concerned. But if there had to be a thing call empathy, it was time someone had some empathy for *her*. She guessed that last stage would be called pouting. Actually, the last stage was the Ben & Jerry's stage.

She read Cy's report again. This time it didn't hit her quite so hard. This time, she could grudgingly accept the points he made. This time, she got chocolate ice cream on some of the pages.

On Sunday afternoon, she read the report again. On the favoritism issue—could he be right?

She was still thinking about it when he called.

"Smart man. You waited until I cooled off before you called."

He laughed. "I've missed you. It's not the same. You've ruined my *Azure Dreams*."

"You'll get over it."

"Not gonna happen. Hey. Get in your car and drive down here. Right now."

Briefly, pleasure washed over her and made her forget the ugly scene in her office. "Cy! It's Sunday night! Some of us have to work tomorrow."

"You don't have to work. You own the company. You can do whatever you want."

Pleasure sure evaporated quickly these days with her. Cy was driving home his point about how she should run her company. Rebecca closed her eyes and tried very hard to keep her temper. "It sounds like you don't take my business seriously. I hope you didn't mean it that way."

"No, of course not. It was just a whim. A thought. Speaking of which, do you have any thoughts about the report?"

"Ooo, you are living dangerously." She was trying to keep things light. Trying not to fall into patterns she'd had with men before. She loved Cy. This was different. "You make some good points. I'm going to call an employee communications meeting tomorrow and talk to them myself. I'll explain the problem with Crystal and with Adrienne and bring up some of the points you made in your report."

"I think that's very wise, Rebecca, and I know it'll be difficult for you. I'd like to be there."

Rebecca didn't know whether it was the tone of voice, which she felt was slightly patronizing, or the words he used, but what he said struck her the wrong way. "Because you don't think that I'm capable of handling a meeting with my own employees by myself?"

"Rebecca," he said on an exhale. "Don't be this way."

"But I am this way, Cy." This way wasn't working. *They* weren't working. And she'd thought this time it would be different. "Look, it was fun being your weekend mermaid, but I've got a business to run."

MAYBE HIS CRITICISM had bothered her more than she'd thought. But Rebecca was a professional and she'd get over it. Get over him.

On Monday, Rebecca swallowed her pride and called together her female management team and opened the floor for complaints. She was discussing some of the points Cy had made in his report when he walked through the door and took a seat at the conference table.

She hadn't expected to see him. She wasn't sure she wanted to see him. But there he was. He looked good. More than good. And not smug. She couldn't have handled smug.

She acknowledged him with a nod and a brief smile and decided to get the Crystal mess out of the way first thing.

She explained what had happened and then addressed the really hard stuff. "I understand that you felt that Adrienne was speaking for me and while it's true that she did on occasion, she never had the power, for lack of a better word, that you thought she had. And I regret that the atmosphere was such that no one felt she could bring the Crystal situation to my attention. And as for Adrienne, I was trying to mentor someone, not create a monster."

There was laughter and Rebecca felt the tension in the room ease. She looked around the table and noticed that the expressions had changed. Had become more open.

She drew a breath. This *breathe, consider, act* thing was becoming addictive. "It is my intention to be more approachable in the future. I want you to be able to bring me your concerns and I want to be able to bring my concerns to you. For instance, Mr. Benedict's report says that you feel I favor male employees. While it might appear that way, you should be aware that eighty percent of requests for time off come from the female staff. And the number one reason by far is to deal with child-related issues. Staff members who don't have children or provide the primary care for them feel it's unfair."

Women bond through verbal communication, she heard Maxine's voice saying. "There has to be a solution. Let's brainstorm." And she did something she'd never thought she'd do—defer to someone else. "Cy, you've probably encountered other companies with this problem. What did they do about it?"

Cy kept his smile professional, but his eyes blazed with approval. She didn't want to feel all warm and happy just because he approved, but she did. And *that* made her cranky, so she stayed quiet and listened.

"Several strategies have worked," he said. "There's the employee team method where teams are assigned tasks and hours are set within the team by the team. The job is always covered. The downside is that there are

always those who take advantage. Flextime is another
option."

"What about job sharing?" Lorena, one of the department managers, asked. "We're losing commissions
because we operate strictly business hours. We should
stay open late at least two days a week. Two people
could share a twelve-hour shift and maybe even babysit
each other's kids."

It was as though a dam had broken. The suggestions came fast and enthusiastically. Rebecca should
get cranky and then shut up and listen more often.
She'd never dreamed her management team would
encourage *more* work.

As they discussed strategies, Rebecca was aware of
Cy. He paid keen attention, offered suggestions and occasionally met her eyes across the table.

He was distracting her. She found it difficult to con-
centrate just when she needed to the most. Control of
the meeting shifted away from her. Rebecca could
stand up, walk out of the room with Cy and nobody
would miss them.

Okay, it was an exaggeration, but the thought
alarmed her. If she continued seeing him, someday
she might do that very thing—abandon her responsibilities and sail away with him. She couldn't take
that chance, and the more she saw him, the more
likely it was.

Already, the weekends weren't enough time with
him and she couldn't spare more. She was going to
have to break it off. She'd worked too hard establishing her business to give it up for lazing around on the
water. She knew herself. She'd get bored. Maybe resent-
ful. She'd take it out on Cy and they'd break up anyway,

and then she wouldn't have her company. Might as well break up now while she still had her business.

The meeting went on for two hours and when the team stopped for lunch, they were still talking excitedly. Rebecca told them Monday communication meetings would be a regular part of the schedule in the future.

As the last of the team left the room, Rebecca busied herself gathering up stray pieces of paper and cups. Cy sat at the table shaking his head.

"What?" she asked.

"Why are *you* cleaning up the conference room?"

"Because it needs to be cleaned."

"And because you usually do it."

"True, but this time it's because I'm putting off the conversation I know we're going to have."

His smile as he approached her warmed her through and through. "You shouldn't. You were great. The meeting was extraordinarily productive." He took the cups from her hands and placed them on the table. "You have a good, solid team there. Congratulations."

He leaned toward her and she knew he wanted to kiss her. She turned her cheek. "Thanks. And thank you for your help. It's been great." She swallowed. "And I'll always remember—"

"Tell me you're not breaking up with me."

She'd hoped to ease into it. "Well, Cy, I—"

He took hold of her shoulders. "Tell me."

"It isn't going—"

"And at least look me in the eye when you break my heart."

She hadn't expected it to be easy. She raised her head. "I don't want to break your heart or mine, either, but things can't continue the way they are."

"Of course they can't." He drew her to him and planted a kiss on the top of her head. Not her favorite place to be kissed, but because she was in his arms for the last time, she'd take it. "I love you, Rebecca, and I'm not going to pretend that I don't."

The matter-of-fact way he spoke brought a hard lump to her throat. "I feel the same way," she managed to say.

"Hey." He raised an eyebrow and she knew he wanted her to say the words.

"I love you, too." It was a relief to get it out in the open.

"That wasn't so hard, was it?"

"No, loving is the easy part. Making it work is the hard part."

"Maybe not. I was awake all night trying to come up with a plan and it wasn't until I listened to the brainstorming session that I figured out what we're going to do."

"Oh, you did? All by yourself?"

"This is not a power struggle between us." After a quick kiss, he released her and pulled out a chair. "Sit and let me tell you what I was thinking."

Rebecca sat. There was a time when she wouldn't have. If that wasn't love, she didn't know what was.

"Neither of us has had any success with traditional relationships, so we'll just try an untraditional one." He looked so pleased with himself.

"That's it? That's your big plan?"

"I didn't say it was a big plan. You heard what your people had to say about flextime and job sharing. We can do that, too."

"How?"

"I'm glad you asked."

"Oh, I know you are." But she smiled when she said it.

"I'll work here at Ironwood and help you establish your executive management level. Then we'll take over some of your responsibilities—I said *some*," he emphasized when she started to protest. "You can keep cleaning up conference rooms and collating training packets if you want."

She made a face at him. "It sounds good, but, Cy—"

"The point is that it'll free up your time to spend with me. Once the new management system is set up, we can take three- and four-day weekends together."

An absentee owner. He wanted her to be an absentee owner. She looked into his face and said, "No."

"No? How can you say no? It's perfect."

"It won't work."

"How do you know until you try?"

She shook her head.

He leaned back in the chair and studied her as he swiveled from side to side. She was reminded of the captain's chairs on the flybridge. And naked fishing, a new sport they'd invented. And how she didn't have any tan lines. And how good his hands felt. And how free and...she closed her eyes.

"What are you afraid of, Rebecca?"

"I'm afraid of losing..." She'd started to say "my company." She'd meant to say "my company." In the past she would have said "my company." But that was before Cy. So what she said was, "You." She drew a breath. "I'm afraid of losing you. You can't spend all your time working here and when you're at your other consulting jobs, I'll be just as busy as ever. And I'll get sucked back in—I know I will."

"I quit," he said promptly. "No more consulting jobs. You're my full-time consulting job."

"When did you quit?"

"Just now. Didn't you hear me?"

He made everything sound so simple and uncompli-
cated.

"You can't just quit."

"Sure I can." He looked smugly confident. "It's my
company, I can quit if I want to." His expression
suddenly changed. "Oh."

Oh, was right. She'd wondered when he'd find the
catch.

"I will have to ask that you hire my receptionist. I
can vouch for her." He grinned. "And I know you need
one."

Rebecca laughed. She didn't remember the last
time she'd laughed. Maybe their future *could* be just
that simple.

"So what do you say, Rebecca?"

"But your company—you could just walk away? No
regrets?" She knew *she* couldn't walk away.

"My self-esteem has never been tied up in my company."

"Unlike some people, right?" She wasn't going to
apologize. She knew of a certain boat that meant a lot
to a certain owner. "You won't have a problem with me
being your boss?"

"I'm sure there'll be excellent benefits." He gave
her a look.

She gave him one right back. "You know it."

"And as long as you understand that there's only one
captain of the *Azure Dreams*."

"I can live with that."

Cy tugged her out of her chair and onto his lap.
"Good, because I can't live without you."

EPILOGUE

One year later...

From the *Future Business Women's Journal*:

For the second year in a row, Rebecca Ironwood of Ironwood Executive Staffing was named Female Business Owner of the Year. Ironwood's company has exhibited a remarkable twenty-seven-percent growth, attributed to a job-sharing plan instituted in the past year. With its flextime and on-site day care, Ironwood has become a model for our community.

The award was accepted by Lorena Martinez, Executive Vice President, as Ms. Ironwood and her new husband, Cy Benedict, were honeymooning on his yacht in the Caribbean. We send them our best wishes.

FLIRTING WITH AN OLD FLAME
Cindi Myers

CHAPTER ONE

BARBARA POWERS STUDIED the gallery of photos on the wall behind the desk. Women accepting awards. Women in lacy wedding gowns. Women with babies, or posing with husbands and children.

Staring at a photo of an attractive couple holding an infant, longing was a physical ache in the pit of her stomach. That was what she wanted, the whole reason she was sitting here right now, in the offices of Warfield Boot Camp, her insides doing nervous backflips, as if she were thirteen years old, summoned to the principal's office, instead of thirty-five, a successful business-woman in charge of her own company.

"I ask all my alumni to send a photo they feel illus-trates what they've achieved because of their experience here at Warfield," the woman on the other side of the desk, director Maxine Warfield, said. "You'll be sending one soon, I'm sure."

"What happens if I don't?" Barb shifted her gaze from the photos to Maxine. *If I don't send a picture. If I don't find the happiness I'm looking for.*

"Then I'd have to photo-shop one. And it wouldn't be pretty. You might end up with an unfortunate moustache."

A startled laugh escaped before Barb could choke it off. She hadn't anticipated humor from the woman known around the compound as Mad Max for her drill-sergeant demeanor.

But then, what else had she expected from a place with *boot camp* in its name? Warfield, located just outside of Houston and "Dedicated to the Womanly Art of Romance," was designed to teach wealthy, powerful women how to reclaim their inner femininity, relearn relationship skills they'd lost on their way to the top, and find true love with their soul mate.

Maxine threw around a lot of words like *soul mate, inner femininity* and *personal strengths.* They made for great sound bites, quoted copiously by the gullible media.

Who was she to scoff? Barb had fallen for the lines, too. After one too many weekends spent watching *The Bachelor* reruns and crying into her cabernet, she'd signed up for the boot camp, eager to learn the secret to finding a man who'd stick with her for the long haul and not just until someone younger, prettier or more docile came along.

Ten thousand dollars and two weeks later—after enduring long days of lectures on everything from deportment to delegating, and lessons in everything from cooking to rock climbing—here she was in front of Maxine, waiting for her final evaluation before graduation. Would Mad Max give her an A for effort, or judge her a failure?

Maxine opened a file on the computer to her left and scanned it, then studied Barbara. Maxine's steel-blue eyes held little warmth, though her expression was pleasant enough. "You've applied yourself well here at Warfield," she said. "You've shown a particular aptitude in the physical activities such as the Challenge Course."

"Thank you." Let Maxine think all those hours in the gym had prepared Barbara for the physical tests of the camp. The gym hadn't hurt, but more likely growing up in the woods of East Texas and competing with an older brother in everything had made her unafraid to cross mud bogs or dangle from ropes strung high in the trees.

"Studying your test scores, I would say your weaknesses are delegating and expressing your emotions." Maxine's eyes met Barb's. "These are common problem areas for women who've risen to the top of their professions. You've had to take charge and keep your feelings hidden in order to get ahead. Unfortunately, this can make it more difficult for you to let down your guard enough to establish lasting relationships."

Barb clenched her hands into fists, the tips of her freshly manicured nails digging into her palms. Right now the emotion she was dying to express was her frustration with having her flaws analyzed so coldly. "Are you saying these two weeks haven't done me any good?" Had she wasted her time and money on a useless quest for happiness?

Maxine smiled, her face transformed by the expression. "On the contrary, I think you've come a long way, Barbara Jean."

Barb flinched at the use of a name she'd put behind her when she left her hometown of Cut and Shoot, Texas, sixteen years before. She wasn't Barbara Jean, the "hick from the sticks" as some of her college roommates had dubbed her, but Barbara Powers, CEO of Powerful Images, one of the top image consulting firms on the west coast. She'd left her old name and her old town behind and moved on to something better.

"I prefer just Barbara," she said, shifting in her chair.

Maxine's smile didn't falter. "Yes, but I think you and Barbara Jean have some unfinished business to take care of, which is why I'm giving you an assignment."

"An assignment? But the course ends tomorrow. How will I have time—?"

"This is an assignment for after graduation. Something that will force you to put the lessons you've learned here into practice right away."

"What are you talking about?"

Maxine's smile was gone now; she was back in full drill-sergeant mode. "In making yourself into a successful businesswoman, you turned your back on your past so completely you've lost touch with the woman you used to be. Your assignment is to return to your hometown for two weeks, to put aside your designer suits and day planner, to reacquaint yourself with the positive qualities of Barbara Jean that you left behind."

"Go back to Cut and Shoot?" Barb stared at Maxine. Had the woman lost her mind?

Maxine nodded. "You've come halfway across the country to Warfield. Why not travel a few more miles down the road and apply the lessons you've learned here? In fact, I wouldn't be surprised if you discover that the man you've been searching for is there waiting for you."

If Barb hadn't been so stunned, she might have laughed in Maxine's face at the thought that any dream man waited for her in Cut and Shoot. "I can't go back there," she protested. "I have a business to run."

"Which is more important, your business or your future happiness? Besides, it's been running fine while you've been here at Warfield, hasn't it?"

She nodded. Her assistant, Eveline, had assured her everything was going smoothly. Until the stockholder's meeting next month, Barb had nothing pressing to attend to.

"I cannot, of course, force you to do this," Maxine

said. "But if you refuse, I'll feel you've wasted your money and my time."

"So you think my spending two weeks in Cut and Shoot, *getting back to my roots* is the key to not spending the rest of my life ordering takeout for one?"

"I do."

She sighed. "Then I guess I have to give it a shot." If nothing else, she could try out some of the skills Warfield had taught her, away from the gossip of friends and colleagues back in San Diego.

Maxine folded her hands on her desk and nodded, a clear dismissal. "That will be all then. I'll see you at the graduation ceremony tomorrow."

Barb left the headquarters building and headed down a shaded stone path to the cluster of bungalows the campers shared. Despite its austere name, Warfield recognized the need to cater to the wealthy and pampered women who enrolled in the camp. Set in the deep woods, the bungalows were plush, with private bedrooms for each woman. The compound also had a gym and a spa. In keeping with the camp's emphasis on real-life skills, the women had to do their own cooking and housekeeping, but after a day of running obstacle courses or listening to lectures on the differences in male and female communication the women could relax in the sauna, have a manicure or pedicure or enjoy a massage.

Barbara stopped outside the beauty salon and dug her cell phone from her purse. The women had been ordered to leave them behind in their rooms each day, but Barb bet she wasn't the only one who promptly "forgot" that rule. She hit number one on her speed dial and tapped her foot, counting the rings.

Eveline answered on the third ring. "Just checking in," Barb said. "How's it going there?"

"Great. Sonja said the meeting with Reynolds Anderson went well today, and Walt signed a new contract with a software firm headquartered in Bakersfield."

"That's good. Be sure to tell him to call me if he has any questions or concerns. And Sonja's working on the Mayfield account?"

"Yes. Everything is going fine."

How could everything be fine without her there? Powerful Images was her baby. Leaving her "child" with other people for all this time was killing her. "I may have to be gone a while longer," she said. "Though if it's going to put everyone in a bind, I can cancel."

"I don't think it will be a problem. Everything's running smoothly so far. Take all the time you need."

Did Eveline have to sound so cheerful about it? "I'll have my phone with me, so don't hesitate to call. I can get the next plane back to San Diego if you need me to put out a fire."

"No fires so far. Are you having a good time on your vacation?"

"Um, it's okay. This other thing I have to take care of is family business."

"Oh. I hope everything is okay." Eveline sounded genuinely concerned.

"It's fine. I'll be in touch. Let me know if you need anything."

"Will do, boss. Don't worry."

Except that Barb couldn't help but worry. She'd spent the past ten years worrying about her business; she was halfway convinced all that worrying, that attention to every detail, was what had made her successful.

She stashed the phone again and turned onto the path leading to the bungalow she shared with two other women. She let herself in and found one of her roommates, Rebecca Ironwood, stretched out on the sofa in the living room, watching CNN. Barb tried not to stare, but it was still a shock seeing the woman who had arrived as a silver-haired executive who favored tailored black and gray suits, transformed to a blonde in a flattering pink dress. Barb guessed she should be glad Maxine hadn't ordered *her* to have a makeover as part of her graduation assignment.

Rebecca sat up and punched the remote to turn off the TV. "How did it go?" she asked.

Barb sank into the chair beside the sofa. "Not too bad. She praised some things, pointed out some weaknesses, then gave me my assignment."

Rebecca's perfectly plucked eyebrows rose. "And? What do you have to do?"

Despite the ten-year difference in their ages, Barb and Rebecca had a lot in common. They were both successful businesswomen, both native Texans—though Barb had long ago moved to San Diego while Rebecca remained in Houston. They were both driven, serious and hardworking. And they were both very lonely. Whether it was loneliness or a common background, or the experience of being thrown together these past two weeks, the two had grown close. Barb welcomed the chance to confide in her now.

"She said I needed to go back to my roots. To Cut and Shoot." She made a face. Even the mention of her hometown made her uncomfortable. Except for brief visits to her mother every other year or so, she'd managed to avoid the place. In Cut and Shoot she was Barbara Jean, the weird kid who wore homemade versions of designer clothes she'd copied from magazines, instead of jeans and T-shirts like everyone else. Barbara Jean listened to the opera on the radio and talked about going to New York or Los Angeles to live instead of memorizing the lyrics to country songs and looking forward to settling down someplace local.

"So your Mr. Right is supposed to be in Cut and Shoot, Texas?" Rebecca smiled. Obviously, she could appreciate the humor in that notion.

"Apparently so. Though from what I remember, the place is full of rednecks and cowboys. Or redneck cowboys." Barb shook her head. "Not my type at all."

"Maybe not." Rebecca leaned forward and tucked a strand of hair behind one ear. "Then again, nothing's worked out so far with your type of man. Maybe a change of scenery is a good idea."

"Hmm. I'll admit, some of those cowboys are pretty sexy." Barbara grinned. "Maybe a fling with one of them is just what I need to get ready for the real Mr. Right."

Rebecca laughed. "That's the attitude. Go for it."

"What's so funny?"

Their other roommate, Cassandra Devane, appeared in the doorway to the bathroom. Dressed in a feminine, and no doubt expensive, sundress, Cassandra was perfectly made up, even though she probably hadn't been awake an hour yet. She looked exactly like the head of a cosmetics company ought to look.

"Barb just got back from her interview with Mad Max," Rebecca explained. "Her assignment is to go back to her hometown and find Mr. Right."

Cassandra made a face. "Maxine has a thing for revisiting the past, doesn't she?" Yesterday, Cassandra had received her own assignment to find closure with her ex-husband.

"I hope Maxine doesn't decide to send me on a trip down memory lane," Rebecca said. "I have no desire to see my ex."

Barb looked at both her roommates. "This is probably going to sound strange, but I'm jealous of both of you."

"What?" Cassandra moved into the living room and sat on the sofa next to Rebecca. "Jealous why?"

"Because both of you have been married. Even if it didn't work out, for a while you had somebody. I've never even come close."

"Oh, hon, it's going to be different now." Cassandra leaned over and put her hand on Barb's. "That's what this boot camp is all about." She smiled.

"We're new women now," Rebecca added.

Barb nodded. She'd settle for the same woman with a new man.

The man, she reminded herself. The true soul mate Maxine had assured her was waiting.

CHAPTER TWO

SCOTT CADEN SHORTENED up the lead line and led the little mare around the circle pen one more time. She was skittish, but coming along. In a few more weeks she'd be a fine riding mount, one with the bloodlines to fetch top dollar.

The whine of an engine downshifting to take the curve of the highway made him look up in time to see a bright red sports car speed past. He caught a glimpse of designer sunglasses, streaming blond hair and a slim, tanned arm showing through the open window. That brief impression was alluring enough to make him turn and stare.

The car's right blinker stuttered on and the car slowed, then turned into the driveway across from his place.

"Well, well, well," he said softly. The mare's ears twitched and she rolled her eyes back to look at him. "Looks like Maggie Powers has a real interesting visitor."

The horse blew out a breath, nostrils quivering. Scott worked his way up the lead line and took hold of the bridle. "I might think Bryce had a new girlfriend, except this one looks too classy for him." Bryce Powers had been Scott's friend for going on twenty years now, but the two men definitely differed in their taste in women. Last he'd heard, Bryce was seeing a cocktail waitress from the Wildcatter Lounge, while Scott had recently parted company with a former Miss Rodeo Texas. Nice girl, but she'd spent too much time trying to remodel him into the man she thought he ought to be, instead of being happy with the man he was.

In any case, he'd been feeling the itch to have a woman in his life again.

"Maybe it's time I stopped by and said hello to Maggie, see how she's getting on," he said. Before the mare could object, he fit his foot in the stirrup and swung into the saddle.

The mare danced around and bucked a little, but she soon settled down and he turned her toward the front gate. Her shod hooves rang against the pavement as he trotted her across the road, then were silenced by the pine needles that lay thick on the shoulder and along the Powers' drive.

He could see Maggie and the blonde standing beside the red car, now parked next to the house.

"Mornin', Maggie," he called when he rode within earshot. He touched the brim of his Stetson in a salute to the older woman who raised her hand in greeting.

"Hey, Scott. Look who showed up out of the blue— Barbara Jean."

The blonde turned, mouth gaping in surprise.

Scott was startled himself. The last time he'd seen little Barbara Jean Powers, she'd been headed off to some fancy west coast university. He'd made a point of not speaking to her then, but he'd stared after her car until she was long out of sight.

Sensing his unease, the mare chose that moment to bow her back and attempt to toss him the dirt. He tightened his thighs around her and gathered in the reins, determined not to make the moment worse by landing on his ass in front of Barbara Jean.

"Are you here on business, or for a visit?" he asked,

his voice even, his face expressionless. He wanted her to think he didn't remember any of what had happened between them all those years ago.

"I'm taking a little vacation," she said, in a butter-soft voice, with just a hint of a drawl. The kind of voice that made a man hot just listening to it. A voice he hadn't forgotten.

"She's staying for two weeks," Maggie said. "I figure it's a good excuse to throw a barbecue. Tomorrow night—I expect you to be there."

"A barbecue? Mama, you shouldn't go to all that trouble." Worry lines showed faintly across her forehead. So apparently her good looks were not the result of Botox.

"Nonsense. All your friends will want to see you. Scott will be there, won't you?"

He shifted in the saddle. "I guess I could come." His gaze shifted to Barbara. "If you don't object."

"Why would I object?" Did he imagine that her cheeks turned pinker?

"Then I wouldn't miss it." He touched his hat brim again and nodded. "I'll see you both later."

He waited until he'd turned his back to them to let the smile spread across his face. So little Barbara Jean had come home for a visit. She wasn't so little anymore. And she'd even spoken to him, almost friendly-like.

The memory of just how friendly the two of them had once been made him shift in the saddle. She'd made it clear back then she had no interest in settling down with the likes of him.

But who said anything about settling down? They were both older now and, he hoped, wiser. Why not spend the next two weeks getting to know each other again?

Strictly for old times' sake.

BARBARA WATCHED Scott ride away, her eyes lingering on the way his undeniably attractive backside sat in the worn saddle. Though she wouldn't have thought it possible, he was even better looking now than he'd been eighteen years ago, when she'd made a fool of herself with him. Ironic how a few lines and a touch of silver at the temples made a man even sexier, while a woman had to fight those changes every step of the way.

"He's still single, you know."

Her mother's words interrupted her reverie. "Oh? I would have thought some local girl would have snapped him up by now." Her voice was even, but her racing heart mocked her pretended indifference.

"Oh, he's tomcatted around, of course." Maggie waved her hand, as if that was only to be expected of any man, but especially one like Scott Caden. "His last girlfriend was a former Miss Rodeo Texas—a real looker and smart, too. She did something with computers. It looked for a while like they'd tie the knot, but nothing ever came of it." She picked up one of Barb's suitcases and turned toward the house. "Let's get you settled, then you can help me call around and invite people to the party."

"That's sweet of you, Mama, but are you sure anyone will even come?" She picked up the second suitcase and followed her mom up the steps into the house that hadn't changed in thirty years. The same plaid sofa and leather La-Z-Boy chair sat in the living room. The same white-and-gold bedroom set filled the room that had been hers as a girl.

"My goodness, of course they'll come." Her mom hefted the suitcase onto the bed and turned to stare at her. "All your friends will want to catch up on old times, see what living the high life in the big city has done for you."

Barb dropped the suitcase she was carrying and sank onto the edge of the bed. "You mean they'll all want to come and gawk." She shrugged. "It's not like I was ever one of the popular kids."

Maggie clucked her tongue. "You were always a different child, with a lot of outlandish ideas. But people still liked you. And they'll want to see you now."

Maybe they'd all want to see how the weird girl with her uppity ideas had turned out. Still, there were some people she wouldn't mind seeing. "We could invite Faye Caden if she still lives here." She and Scott's sister had been friends in school.

"She does, only she's Faye Mitchell now. And Theresa Ledbetter is still here. She married a truck driver from Willis, works at the bank. And Steve Spencer and Polly Isinberg. They got married two years ago."

She was amazed at how many of her classmates had stayed in their hometown. "It'll be like a reunion," she marveled.

"And don't forget Scott. He said he'd come."

"Mmm. It was good to see him." He'd acted friendly, as if he'd forgotten the harsh words they'd exchanged the last time they spoke.

Maggie opened one of the suitcases and began taking out clothes and putting them in drawers. "To tell you the truth, at one time, I thought you'd marry Scott."

"Where would you get an idea like that?" A pinch of pain, mixed with embarrassment, tightened in Barb's chest at the memory of her last date with Scott. They'd been going out for a few months then, and she'd fallen hard for the handsome older guy who was her brother's best friend. He was the first man she'd made love with, the first man to break her heart.

When she'd told him she'd been accepted into UCLA, she'd expected him to be happy for her. Maybe even a little proud. Hadn't she spent hours talking about her hopes for the future, how she wanted to graduate with a degree and eventually open her own business? She'd thought he'd understood those dreams, but that night made her doubt he'd ever listened to her at all.

"You can't go away," he'd said, confusion and hurt clouding his dark eyes. "What about us?"

"Scott, you know I can't stay here." She put her hand on his arm, but he shook her off. "I have to go away to do all the things I want to do."

"I thought you wanted to stay here with me." He bowed his head, the muscles of his jaw bunching. "Hell, I was even going to ask you to marry me."

All the breath rushed out of her at his words. "Marry you? Scott, I'm only eighteen."

He raised his head, chin set at a stubborn angle. "We wouldn't necessarily have to get married right away. You could go to the community college for a while. Get your degree even."

"So you'd *let* me get my degree? How generous." She crossed her arms over her chest and turned away from him, not wanting him to see the tears that stung her eyes. She'd thought Scott was different from the other guys she knew. Not so old-fashioned in his thinking about the roles men and women should play. Obviously, she'd been wrong.

"Don't twist my words," he said. "I want you to be happy. But why can't you be happy with me?"

She shook her head, and struggled to force words around the knot in her throat. "I do love you, Scott. But I'll never be happy staying here. I'm sorry."

He was silent until she finally turned to look at him.

Then words exploded from him. "Go on then. Go off to the big city and act like you're too good for the rest of us. I'll find somebody else, don't you worry."

But he hadn't found anyone else, had he? And neither had she. Why was that? she wondered.

She'd come home to try to find the best parts of the girl she'd left behind and the man who could love her. That man obviously wasn't Scott Caden. Scott wanted a woman whose dreams matched his own. He was still rooted here in Cut and Shoot, and she'd seen enough of the world to know she'd made the right decision to leave.

The best she could hope for was that the two of them could be friends. Maybe reconnecting in that way with the man who'd first taught her about love would help her to find the person she was meant to spend the rest of her life with.

MAGGIE POWERS DECIDED to go all out for her barbecue. Thus, Barbara was recruited to help hang paper streamers and foil stars all around the carport, where chairs and tables had been set up for the guests.

"We lucked out with the weather," Maggie said as she spread a blue paper tablecloth on one of the picnic tables. "It's not too hot for May."

"Yes, it's been great. Like California weather."

"I doubt you get a sky like this in California."

Barb would rather be in California right now, getting ready for the stockholders' meeting next month. She'd checked in with the office that morning, but Eveline had assured her things were going "great."

It had been all she could do to keep herself from making a reservation on the next plane to San Diego, to see for herself how "great" everything was without her. But she'd been strong, reminding herself that these next two weeks could be important to her future. Maxine believed so, anyway, though Barb still had her doubts.

"There's not some special reason for this sudden visit, is there?" Maggie glanced at her daughter, worry lines forming a deep V across the bridge of her nose. "There's not some trouble with your business you haven't told me about?"

"No. The business is going great." That word again. "This was just a good time, before the stockholders' meeting next month, to take a few days to relax."

Her mother pursed her lips. "Then if it's not the business, is it trouble with a man?"

"A man? Mama, where would you get that idea?" Though Barb supposed her mother wasn't too far off the mark. The trouble wasn't a man, but rather, the lack of one.

Maggie shrugged. "If you'd just split up with a man, it stands to reason you might want to get away for a while."

"It isn't trouble with a man. I've been too busy working to have time for any serious relationship." She manufactured a smile. "Can't I come visit my mom if I want to?"

"Of course you can." Maggie finished spreading the last tablecloth. "I'm happy to see you any time. And it's nice to see you taking time off for yourself. You work too hard."

"I enjoy my work."

"Whatever the reason, I'm glad you're here."

Maggie went into the house and Barb returned to hanging crepe paper, thinking about her mother's words. True, Barb put in long hours at work sometimes, but Powerful Images was a labor of love. Part of being a successful entrepreneur was taking the time to be personally involved with every aspect of the business.

Your test scores show one of your weaknesses is delegating. Maxine's voice echoed in Barb's head. She hunched her shoulders guiltily. So maybe she had a *little* trouble allowing others to take charge. She could work on that.

Just as she could work on some of the other things Maxine had emphasized, like dating skills and communicating with men. At least in Cut and Shoot, no one she knew professionally would see her if she flubbed flirting or struck out at seduction.

Of course, first she'd have to find some suitable man to practice on. Except for Scott Caden, she didn't know any unattached men close to her age.

Scott would be a terrific candidate for a practice fling, except he was the kind of man who was used to calling all the shots. If something wasn't his idea to begin with, he wasn't interested.

You could make him interested. Maxine's voice again—or was it Barb's subconscious nudging her?

Could she do it? Could she seduce Scott Caden and sharpen her relationship skills with him? If she *did* reignite that old flame, was she wise enough this time around to keep from getting burned?

CHAPTER THREE

SCOTT LEANED against one of the posts that supported the carport and watched Barb. Since arriving at the barbecue, he hadn't been able to take his eyes off her. While most of the folks here were dressed in jeans and cotton shirts, she was wearing a soft, full-skirted dress and red leather boots. The effect was feminine and sexy as hell.

He watched as she smiled and said something to Dan Patrick. Dan the Man, as he was known in the ads for his car dealership, laughed and put a hand on Barb's shoulder. Scott's fingers tightened around his glass.

"What are you looking so sour about?" Bryce came to stand beside him.

He jerked his gaze away from Barb and faced his friend. "Guess I'm feeling like a fifth wheel, watching everybody paired off."

"Give it two more weeks and you'll have another gorgeous girlfriend on your arm. I've never known you to go without for long."

Scott frowned. "You make me sound like a real player."

"Nah. I just know women. They can never resist that Scott Caden charm." He clapped his hand on Scott's shoulder. "So what do you think of Barbara Jean? She looks pretty good for a city gal, doesn't she?"

"She's all right." He downed the last of his drink, his eyes following as she and Dan made their way to the buffet table. "Though what she'd see in a guy like him, I'll never know."

"If you don't like it, then maybe you ought to say something to her." Bryce was grinning, as if he knew something Scott didn't.

He set down his glass. "Maybe I will." And then maybe he'd ask her out himself. Show her a Texas man knew a few things those California boys hadn't even dreamed up yet.

BARB TRIED to remember everything she'd learned in the Flirting 101 class at boot camp. *Tilt your head slightly. Make eye contact and hold for at least ten seconds. Mimic his posture to show interest.* Though the movements didn't come naturally to her, they had the desired effect on Dan, who focused solely on her.

He was good-looking, wearing a western-cut suit instead of jeans and a T-shirt like most of the men here. That's probably why she'd picked him out of the crowd. She'd always preferred men in suits. She'd discovered he owned a car dealership, so they'd talked about business. He was a little touchy-feely—putting his hand on her shoulder when they'd only just met—but she reminded herself that Maxine had advised to let go of some of her natural reserve to encourage physical and emotional intimacy. Not that she was ready to jump in the sack with Dan, but there was nothing wrong with a friendly pat on the shoulder, was there?

He leaned close, so close she could smell beer on his breath. "You're beautiful, you know that?" he said.

She smiled, and waited for the thrill these words should bring. What woman didn't like to be told she was beautiful? But she felt nothing. Had she been out of the relationship game so long she couldn't even respond to a compliment? She was going to need more practice than she'd thought.

She was almost grateful when a familiar face interrupted them. "Barb, it's been ages." Faye Caden enveloped her in a hug, then stepped back, smiling.

"Uh, I'll just go freshen our drinks," Dan said. Barb couldn't decide if he was being polite, giving her time to catch up with an old friend, or if he was afraid of an estrogen overload.

"You look fantastic," Faye said. "California must agree with you."

"It does," Barb said. "You look great yourself. What have you been up to?"

"Tom and I have two boys now, and let me tell you, they're a handful." Faye looked over her shoulder, to where her husband, Tom Mitchell, stood by the barbecue pit. As if feeling her gaze on him, he looked up and smiled.

The love in that simple look made Barb's stomach clench with envy. That was what she wanted—the reason she was willing to put herself through so much trouble and expense. Having a man look at her that way would make it all worthwhile.

"Scott told me he saw you yesterday. Said you were driving a hot red sports car."

"It's only a rental," she said.

"It suits you, though." Scott joined them, stepping between the women, his shoulder almost touching Barb's.

She was immediately aware of the warmth of his body, the way the simple white cotton shirt stretched across his shoulders, the obvious masculinity of his presence. "Hello, Scott," she said, taking a step to the side, to put a little distance between them. For some reason, she was having trouble breathing with him standing so close.

"Having a good time?" he asked.

The mocking note in his voice irritated her. "Yes. Why wouldn't I be?"

"I thought maybe a barbecue was a little tame for a California girl like you. You didn't look too thrilled with the idea yesterday."

"I didn't want Mama to go to a lot of trouble." She looked around the carport, at the men and women milling around. "It's good to see old friends," she said, and meant the words. She had more friends here than she'd remembered, and she'd been touched by how they'd welcomed her back.

"Is Dan Patrick an old friend?" he asked.

"Dan Patrick? The man I was just talking to?" Something in his tone made her wary.

"How could he be?" Faye said. "Dan only moved to town three years ago."

"That's right." Scott's gaze burned into her, and the lines around his eyes deepened as he frowned. "So that means he must be a new friend. A very good one from the way you two were carrying on."

Barb's face was hot, and she had a hard time keeping her voice down when she spoke. "What is your problem? Not that it's any of your business, but Dan and I were talking."

"You were flirting. Very lovey-dovey. Maybe you don't know Dan the Man is married. And he has a sorry reputation with women. I'd have thought all those years in the big city would have taught you to be more careful. Or maybe you don't care about that sort of thing."

"Scott!" Faye glared at her brother.

Barb's eyes stung, and she blinked rapidly, refusing to let a tear fall. He made an innocent flirtation seem like some sort of cheap seduction. As if she herself was cheap, just because she wasn't the simple country girl he'd once wanted her to be. Obviously, he didn't like the grown-up version of her any better. "When I want your opinion on something, I'll ask for it," she said, her voice cold. Then she whirled and headed for the house. She wasn't going to let him see how much he'd hurt her. Or how much it angered her that words from him still mattered.

"WHATEVER IT IS you're drinking, you'd better quit." Faye glared at Scott. "You're acting like a jerk."

He felt like a jerk, but he wasn't about to admit it to his sister. "You saw how she was coming on to Dan. I just thought I'd warn her about his reputation."

"They were talking! And you didn't warn her. You lectured her." She shook her head. *"Men!"*

Women! he thought, but had sense enough to keep his mouth shut as his sister stalked off. He looked toward the house, where Barb had retreated. Faye was right. He'd been a fool. But he didn't have to stay one.

He climbed the steps to the back door and knocked. After a moment, the door opened and Barb peered out. She looked less than thrilled to see him. "Was there something else you needed to say?" she asked.

"Yeah. Can you forgive me for being so stupid?"

She blinked, and some of the tension went out of her face. "Is that an apology?"

"Yeah." He glanced over his shoulder, at the crowd under the carport. "Could I come in? So we can talk?"

She stepped back and held the door open. As he moved past her, he caught the scent of her perfume— feminine and floral.

"I shouldn't have said all that stuff about you and Dan," he said.

"Then why did you say it?" There was genuine curiosity behind her anger.

He rubbed the back of his neck, trying to come up with an answer that didn't make him sound crazy or desperate. *Because the thought of that lowlife with his hands on you made me see red* didn't seem appropriate. "I guess...I don't like the guy much, and I like you, so I was trying to warn you about him, but instead I stuck my foot in my mouth and made things worse."

"You like me?"

The surprise in her voice made him feel like a bigger heel than ever. "Yeah. I mean, I know we had a rough patch there before you left home, but I was hoping, now that we're both adults, we could be friends."

Her smile made him feel warm all over. "I'd like that," she said.

"So...you have any plans while you're here?"

"Not really. Just to relax. Have some fun."

"Want to go horseback riding with me tomorrow? I've got a couple of saddle horses that could use the exercise."

She hesitated, then nodded. "Okay. I'd like that. But I warn you, I haven't ridden in a while."

He smiled, and adopted his best good-old-boy drawl. "I always heard riding was like sex. Once you're back in the saddle, the rest just comes naturally."

"Is that so?" Her gaze was full of more heat than anything she'd directed at Dan the Man. "Guess we'll find out, won't we?"

"IT'S NOT A DATE, Mother," Barb said, as she applied a second coat of mascara—a parting gift from Cassandra—and tried to ignore the nervous flutter in her stomach. "Scott needed someone to help exercise a horse and I thought I'd enjoy the ride."

Maggie snorted. "The man has hired help. He asked you to go riding because he wanted to spend time with you. Alone."

Barb couldn't help but laugh at the ominous way her mother said the last word. "You make it sound like he's trying to lure me away somewhere to ravish me."

"I can think of worse ways to spend a beautiful morning like this."

Barb slipped a pair of silver hoops onto her ears and tweaked the stubborn lock of hair that insisted on trying to curl under her chin. Then she turned to face her mother. "How do I look?"

Maggie inspected the red silk blouse, jeans and red boots Barb was wearing. "That blouse is a little fancy for riding. I've got a red cotton shirt you can wear instead. It won't look so out of place."

Out of place. *Like I feel,* she thought as she followed her mom to the front closet and accepted the shirt. This wasn't her world anymore, so why was she even trying to fit in?

She squared her shoulders and pushed the thought away. So what if she wasn't really at home here anymore? She could have a good time visiting. And enjoy a morning in the company of a handsome man, even if he wasn't the man she was looking for.

He met her at the end of her driveway, leading a pair of matched chestnut geldings. "This is Rebel," he said, smoothing his hand down the nose of one of the horses. "The one I'm riding is Brazos."

"They're beautiful." She smoothed the neck of her mount, smiling at the warm velvet feel of the animal. Concentrating on the horse kept her from staring too long at the man beside her. Dressed in well-worn jeans, a soft green snap-button shirt and a leather vest, he looked straight out of a Ralph Lauren ad. Only more...real.

"You'll need a leg up," he said. Before she could protest, he'd dropped to one knee in the dirt beside her and shaped his hands into a step. Feeling awkward and self-conscious, she fit her foot into his hand and reached for the saddle horn. He lifted her effortlessly and the next thing she knew, she was in the saddle.

He mounted Brazos and nodded to her. "You look right at home there. You remember how to do this?"

She gathered the reins in one hand and nudged the horse forward with her knees. "I'll be fine." He might see her as a pampered city girl, but she hadn't entirely forgotten her roots.

"Thought we'd take a tour of my place," he said. "I need to check the back pastures, see if they're still muddy after all the rain we had a couple weeks ago."

She followed him across the road and through the gate to his ranch. At first she forced herself to focus on her horse and the surrounding scenery. But as the rhythm of riding came back to her, she decided the scenery she most wanted to see was the man in front of her. All her years in the city couldn't take away her appreciation of a good-looking cowboy in the saddle. Broad shoulders, narrow waist, faded denim fitted across muscular thighs and a butt no desk jockey could manage added up to a very pleasant package indeed.

She was almost sorry when the path they were on widened and she was able to ride up beside him. "Everything looks wonderful," she said. "Looks like you're doing a terrific job with the ranch."

"Things are going pretty good." He gestured toward a barn roof in the distance. "The breeding mares and their new foals are over there. I've got six new foals this year, and they're already sold. These horses we're riding will likely have buyers in another couple of weeks."

"How do you handle it all by yourself?"

"I have help looking after the horses, and a bookkeeper who does most of the paperwork, but it keeps me busy." He glanced at her. "I'm to the point where to grow any more, I need a larger place."

"Does that mean you're thinking about relocating?" Why did that question make her heart race?

"Maybe. I've looked at a couple of places in Washington County, and one up in the Panhandle. None of them were quite right."

She looked around them, at the hundred-year-old live oaks at the far end of the pasture, and the weathered outbuildings that had been built by Scott's grandfather. "I'd think it would be hard to let go of a place your family has owned for generations."

"Oh, I'd still keep this place. I'd just expand the operation on other land. Hire someone to look after it for me, maybe."

"That's tough, too. Giving up complete control." She'd spent a lot of sleepless nights before making the decision to take her company public last year. And these weeks away from the day-to-day operations of the office were killing her.

"What about you?" Scott's question pulled her back to the present. "Maggie tells me you have your own company."

She nodded. "Powerful Images. We went public last year and so far things have been going well."

"So what exactly is it that you do?"

"We specialize in helping businesses develop a distinct identity in the marketplace, an image that will readily identify them in people's minds."

"You mean, like logos and slogans and things like that?"

"That's part of it. We also help them with things like mission statements. A code of conduct for their employees and executives. Ways they can contribute to and be a part of their communities. Even product development, if that's necessary so that they become known for what they stand for and how they do business as much as for what they manufacture or sell."

"So it's a lot more than just dressing up a hog to fetch a good price at market?"

Coming from someone else, she might have found the assessment insulting. But the smile tugging at the corners of his mouth and the hint of laughter in his eyes let her know he was teasing her. "It's a lot more than dressing up a hog." She lifted her chin and allowed herself to look a little smug. "And I'm very good at it."

He gave her a long look, the not-quite-smile still on his lips. "I'll bet you are good," he said after a while. "You've certainly changed your own image. I'll bet nobody out in San Diego would ever guess you grew up in a little house out in the woods in Cut and Shoot."

His tone was less gentle now, or maybe it was just her own sensitivity to what she perceived to be criticism. It was true, almost no one she worked with knew about her past. "The subject doesn't come up much," she said. "I don't see that it matters."

"Maybe it doesn't." He bent down to slide the latch on a gate and swing it open. When they'd both passed through and he'd closed it behind them, he said, "I guess with your company doing so well, you're worth the big bucks."

The frankness of the remark startled her, but then, Scott never had been one to beat around the bush. It was one of the things she admired about him. "Does that bother you?" she asked. A lot of men couldn't handle the idea that she made more than they did.

"The idea is a little intimidating." He glanced at her and grinned. "But the reality is, it's hard to be intimidated by someone you knew when she didn't have any front teeth."

Laughter burst from her at the memory of the first summer they'd moved to Cut and Shoot. She'd recently lost both her front teeth and the new ones were slow to grow in. "You called me Gappy," she said.

He laughed. "Really, I thought you were cute as a bug. But it would have ruined my image to say so."

When was the last time she'd laughed this way? With a man? Maybe all those relaxation exercises Maxine had made them practice were paying off at last.

They passed through another gate and began riding alongside a creek. Water frothed almost even with the banks, and the horses' hooves made sucking sounds as they plodded through the mud. The air smelled rich and fertile, and the heat of the sun on her back told her summer was almost here.

"We'll stop up here, clean some of the mud off the horses," he said and nodded toward a rise up ahead.

They dismounted beside a windmill and a watering trough. While the horses drank, Scott inspected their feet. He pulled out a pocketknife and scraped away the mud that had built up on their shoes. "This wet clay is thick as gumbo," he said.

She watched, fascinated by the sure, easy way he worked. He looked strong and confident, masculine in a way only a man perfectly at home in his environment can be. The rush of desire that swept through her unnerved her, and she turned away. Leave it to her hormones to choose now to get all excited. After all, what was the point? She wanted to find someone she could have a future with, and that someone certainly wasn't Scott.

Thoughts of a cold shower weren't far from her mind when a clot of chilly mud sailed off Scott's knife and landed, splat! on her thigh. She squealed and jumped back, laughing.

"Damn, I'm sorry." He pulled out a handkerchief and scrubbed at the stain.

She choked off her laughter, her skin burning where he touched her. So much for cooling things off between them. "It's all right, really," she said, backing away. "It'll wash out."

"You sure? Those jeans probably cost more than my whole outfit." He looked up from where he was still bent over her thigh and for a moment she forgot how to breathe.

His eyes were earth-brown, with little flecks of gold in them, and black lashes most women would envy. But it wasn't the eyes themselves so much as the expression in them that moved her. He looked as though he wanted nothing better at that moment than to pull her down onto the ground beside him and do incredible things to her body. She swallowed hard, shaken by how much she wanted that, too.

He reached for her again and she managed to stumble back. Things were definitely happening too fast here. Why hadn't that boot camp offered lessons on what to do in situations like this?

He straightened and put away the knife and the handkerchief. "Feel up to a little race?" he asked, his tone casual, as if nothing out of the ordinary had just passed between them.

She was so pumped with adrenaline, she felt up to

almost anything. Especially anything that involved running away from him. "Sure. Where to?"

"Back to the house. I thought I'd fix us some lunch."

Here was where she should beg off, plead business to take care of or some other pressing engagement. *Don't be too eager,* Maxine had admonished. *Don't be afraid to be a little mysterious.* Not to mention Barb could use some time to collect her thoughts and control her hormones. But she found herself smiling at him and practically purring her answer. "That sounds great. I'm starved."

CHAPTER FOUR

LUNCH WAS A BAD IDEA, Scott thought as he dug his heels into the gelding's side and set off toward the house. If he had any sense at all, he'd have said *goodbye, have a great time, see you next time you're in town.* He had no business at all getting involved with a woman like Barbara Jean Powers. A woman who made her living whipping people into a certain image. A woman who insisted on always doing things *her* way.

But what man in the throes of lust ever could make sensible decisions? Wiping that mud off Barb's thigh, he'd become aware of her as a very warm, attractive woman. And he'd wanted her. Bad. Riding hell-for-leather across the ranch wasn't likely to change that any.

Which meant lunch was a bad idea. But unable to withdraw the offer he would have to get through it without slipping up and letting her know how he felt, and thus making a fool of himself when she turned him down cold. Ms. Barbara Powers, CEO of Powerful Images, might go horseback riding with a cowboy with dirt under his nails, but he doubted she'd lower herself enough to take the kind of ride he had in mind.

While Barb freshened up, he set about grilling burgers and heating French fries. He wasn't a gourmet cook, but he could handle himself in the kitchen. That impressed women, right? Aw hell, why was he trying to impress her anyway?

Because you want to get her in the sack, the brutally honest part of his brain reminded him. Call him a crass male, but that was what motivated a lot of men's behavior around women, wasn't it? Sex with Barb definitely wasn't an unappealing idea, except that he'd never been the love-'em-and-leave-'em type. If he invited her into his bed, it would mean starting something he wasn't sure he knew how to finish.

"You've got a gorgeous place here." She breezed into the kitchen, all smiles. A damp spot on the leg of her jeans was the only evidence of their muddy mishap. "A step above the average bachelor pad," she said, admiring a string of ceramic chili peppers that hung by the light switch.

"I can't take credit for it. My last girlfriend did most of the decorating." He frowned as he checked the fries. "Part of her ongoing effort to improve me and my house."

"You should be flattered she cared so much." She sat at the kitchen table.

"People shouldn't try to change other people." He snatched a toasted bun from the oven and topped it with a freshly grilled patty, added fries, and set it in front of her. "They should accept them as they are."

"But sometimes people need to change." She smeared mustard onto her burger. "They even want to change. How else to explain all the self-help books on the bestseller lists?"

He sat down across from her. "Yeah, well, some folks aren't ever satisfied with themselves, or anyone else."

"So you're saying you're perfect?" She grinned.

He returned the smile, some of his prickliness fading.

"What? You don't think I am?" He struck a body-builder pose, biceps pumped.

They both started laughing then, and had a hard time stopping. He began to relax. Maybe he and Barb could be just friends. It was nice to have someone to talk to about something besides horses and business. Someone who wasn't afraid to challenge him. It wasn't something he was used to, but he kind of liked it, coming from her.

It reminded him of when they were dating. Even then, she'd had strong opinions about things, though he'd never realized how strong until she told him she was leaving.

He shrugged off the memory and for the next hour, they chatted about everything from the difference between Texas and California to their mutual love of mystery novels. She had a nice laugh, and a voice he didn't think he'd ever get tired of listening to.

He was disappointed when she pushed her plate aside and laid her napkin beside it. "I'd better get going," she said. "Can you believe it's after two?"

How did it get to be that late? She stood and he rose also. "You don't have to rush off," he said.

"I need to check in with my office," she said. "Besides, I'm sure you have lots of work to do."

"I always have work to do. But it's not every day I get to visit with an old friend." *Especially one who's beautiful and sexy and smart.*

She smiled. "It has been fun, hasn't it?"

"More fun than you expected, right?" He laughed at the surprised look on her face. "Hey, after I put my foot in my mouth last night at the barbecue, I'm lucky you're even speaking to me."

"You always have said exactly what you thought."

"And it's gotten me in trouble more times than I care to remember. Thanks for not holding it against me."

"Sure. Life's too short and all that."

He walked her to the door, reluctant for this new rapport between them to end. "Have dinner with me tomorrow night," he said.

Her smile faltered and her cheeks turned a shade pinker. "I don't know…"

"Come on. If I know you, you're bored to tears over there at your mom's. A night out would do you good."

She nodded. "I could use a break from *Golden Girls* reruns."

"Then it's a date. I'll pick you up about six-thirty?"

"Sure."

She still looked a little stunned by the invitation. He grinned. He liked the idea that he could unsettle her. The sophisticated California executive hadn't completely replaced the simple country girl after all. Together, the two made for a damned intriguing woman. One he wanted to get to know better.

Much better.

BACK AT HER MOTHER'S HOUSE, Barb splashed cold water on her face and stared at her reflection in the mirror. What had she gotten herself into, agreeing to have dinner with Scott? Yes, he was fun to be with and sinfully sexy, but he was also a rancher who'd lived in the same house all his life, a man who'd made it clear he saw no need to change anything about himself or his lifestyle. She, on the other hand, had a life she enjoyed on the west coast, a business she loved, and no intention of ever moving back to Cut and Shoot, Texas.

Part of creating successful relationships, whether in business or in your personal life, is learning to compromise. Maxine's words from one of her lectures came back to Barb, like a nudge from the pitchfork-carrying angel she imagined to be her conscience. Lately, the angel had borne more than a passing resemblance to Warfield's proprietress.

"Yeah, well women shouldn't be the ones always making the compromises," she muttered, turning away from the mirror.

Scott was a man who saw things one way. His way. Once upon a time, he'd decided she should stay in Cut and Shoot, go to the local community college, settle down and be a rancher's wife. All the things she'd wanted didn't matter to him.

All his talk today about people (meaning his exgirlfriend and other women) accepting other people (him) as they were told her he was as stubborn as ever.

Still, Scott was the first man to ask her out in over a year. She shouldn't pass up the opportunity to practice some of the new techniques she'd learned at the camp. If they worked on Scott, she could be confident they'd work when Mr. Right finally made an appearance. Knowing what he was like ahead of time might even make it easier to avoid walking away with bruised feelings.

And if she failed, no one who knew her as a sophisticated, successful businesswoman would ever have to know.

SCOTT WAS NOT a man who obsessed over his appearance. Jeans and a clean shirt were good enough for any occasion, as far as he was concerned. But before his dinner with Barb, he found himself spending more time than usual in front of the mirror, combing and recombing his hair. He changed his shirt three times, and got out the shoe polish and buffed his boots a second time.

"This is what I get for asking a rich, city girl out," he

muttered as he pulled on the boots. "Keep this up I'll turn into a damn metrosexual."

He decided the effort was worth it, however, when he saw her eyes light up as she opened her door. "You look great," she said.

"Thanks. You look pretty hot yourself." Not an adjective he'd normally use with a *friend* but *hot* was the only way to describe the blue silk tank top that emphasized her ivory-white shoulders and the tantalizing hint of cleavage at the neckline, not to mention the simple black skirt that stopped a few inches above her knees. He'd always been a leg man, and already his brain was busy resurrecting fantasies featuring Barb's legs wrapped around him.

"Where are we going?" she asked when they were settled into his truck.

"There's a new steak house on the north side of town I really like."

Her mouth did one of those puckery things women do when they don't like something. "You don't like steak?" he asked.

"No, that's fine," she said, without a lot of enthusiasm. The smile that followed was a tad too bright. "If you like it, I'm sure it'll be great."

He frowned and concentrated on driving. It was the kind of thing a lot of women said, but not what he'd expected from Barb. If she didn't like steak, she should speak up. Then they could have a satisfying discussion about California finicky eaters versus the genuine Texan's love of beef.

At the restaurant, the hostess led them to a table in a secluded nook in a back corner. "Very cozy," he said, holding her chair for her and doing his best to not appear obvious about looking down the neck of her shirt.

"Yes, it's very nice."

A waitress arrived. "Would you care for a cocktail or some wine?" she asked.

"Some wine would be nice," Barb said. "I mean, if that's all right with you." She looked at him.

"Wine is fine." He closed the wine list and handed it to her. "You probably know more about this stuff than I do. You order."

"Oh. All right." She opened the leather folder and scanned the selections. "We'll have the Ravenswood Old Vine Zinfandel. The 2002, not the 2003."

"I'm impressed," he said when the waitress left.

She shrugged. "I have a couple of wineries for clients, so I've learned about the product as part of my work." She opened the menu and studied it like an accountant scrutinizing a ledger.

"See anything that looks good?" he asked.

"Hmm."

He wanted to point out this wasn't an answer, but decided to wait. He always debated better on a full stomach. Besides, he didn't want her angry with him before the evening had even begun.

The waiter arrived to take their orders. "I'll have the house salad with oil and vinegar dressing on the side." Barb frowned at the menu. "Is the fish fresh? Not frozen."

"Yes, ma'am."

"Then I'll have the snapper. Grilled, no butter, a wedge of lemon. Broccoli instead of the squash. Steamed crisp. No butter." Their server scribbled these instructions on his pad while Scott shifted in his seat. He'd always said he liked a woman who knew what she wanted, but this was taking things a little far.

"And for you, sir?" The server turned to him.

"Rib eye. Medium rare. Everything on the potato, ranch dressing on the salad."

"Got it." The waiter took their menus. "I'll be right back with your salads."

When they were alone again, Scott gave her a long look.

"What?" She fussed with her napkin, shaking it out and smoothing it in her lap.

"If you didn't want steak, we could have gone somewhere else."

"This is fine. I'm sure the fish will be delicious."

The waitress returned with the wine. She uncorked it at the table and presented the cork to Barb, who glanced at it and nodded. She poured a small amount in each of their glasses. Barb sipped hers and nodded again. "That's very nice. Thank you."

He cautiously sipped from his own glass. "It's good," he agreed. "But I'm not sure I'd know the difference between this and Uncle Seth's homemade blackberry wine." A notorious bootlegger and local character, Uncle Seth was a Cut and Shoot institution.

"Except that everybody knows Uncle Seth mixes his wine with Everclear to give it a kick."

They both laughed. "You have some experience with that, do you?" he asked.

She nodded. "Junior prom, my date and I stopped by Uncle Seth's for a bottle. An hour later I was sick as a dog all over my dress." Her face flushed at the memory. "I was mortified."

"A bunch of us went on a hunting trip a couple of years back, down in South Texas. One of the guys brought along a jug of Uncle Seth's special. Sometime after midnight they tell me I was on my knees in front of the hunting cabin, howling at the moon."

She choked back laughter and dabbed at the corners of her eyes with her napkin. "Oh my. I promise this wine won't have you howling."

"That's good. I want to remember everything about this night." Their eyes met, surprise in hers heating to a look of interest. *Tonight I think we should finish what we started eighteen years ago,* he silently told her.

She put one hand to her throat, then looked away and reached for her glass again. "I forgot to ask yesterday. How are your parents doing?"

"They're fine. Enjoying retirement. My dad's even learning to play golf, of all things."

"Your dad? The man who wore a long-sleeved shirt and starched jeans every day of his life? I can't imagine him in golf clothes."

"I can't, either, but I hear it's true."

The waitress delivered their salads, bringing the conversation to a momentary halt. That was fine with him. He enjoyed watching Barb, admiring the way the light glinted off her piled-up hair, the way her long, slender fingers looked holding the fork. Studying her like this was a kind of foreplay, his eyes wandering where he hoped his hands would later.

"So, um, tell me about yourself. Do you have any hobbies? Play any sports?"

He stared at her. They'd spent most of the day together yesterday and he hadn't mentioned hobbies or sports. Why ask about them now? It was almost as if she was reading from some kind of script. "My work keeps me pretty busy. I already told you I hunt some. What about you? What are your hobbies?"

She pushed her broccoli around with her fork. "Oh, I don't really have any. Work keeps me busy, too."

So much for the interesting conversation he'd been

anticipating since yesterday. He wasn't ready to give up yet, though. "I guess you noticed a lot of changes around town since you were last here. When was that—two years ago?"

"Three." She toyed with a piece of parsley garnish. "Mom always enjoys coming to California, so I try to fly her out once a year or so."

"And you don't enjoy coming back to Texas," he said.

Her expression grew troubled. "It's not that I don't like it here. I just…" She shrugged. "I'm more comfortable in California. I don't feel like I fit in here."

"Even when you were a girl, you always talked about going away. You had all these big dreams." He'd been naive enough at the time to think he could talk her out of those dreams. He lifted his glass of wine in a toast. "And now you've made them all come true."

"Not all of them." Her expression relaxed and she tilted her head to one side and curved her lips in a slight smile. "What about your dreams? Are they coming true?"

He realized she was flirting with him. Not that that was bad, but she'd never struck him as the flirtatious type. "Making the ranch a success has certainly always been a dream of mine. I told you yesterday I'm thinking of expanding." He had other dreams, of a wife and family. But this wasn't the time or place to talk of those.

Their meal arrived and he attempted to get the conversation back to a more interesting level, with mixed results. He caught glimpses of the Barb he'd seen yesterday— vibrant, opinionated, bossy even. Then in midsentence she would change to a flirtatious, demure, even shallow woman. When the waitress had removed their plates, he leaned toward her and asked, "Is something wrong?"

"No. Why would you think something's wrong?"

"You're acting…strange."

She flushed. "I am?"

"Yes. One minute you're fine and the next you're... you're channeling Dream Date Barbie or something."

Laughter burst from her, which she tried to cover by coughing into her napkin. "I—I'm just nervous, I guess."

Now this was intriguing. "Why are you nervous?"

She carefully lined up her empty wineglass next to her folded napkin. "I'm not sure what's going on here. Are we dating or are we just two old friends out for dinner?"

"I asked you out on a date. Do you want to keep it 'just two old friends'?"

Her eyes met his, sea-green, but troubled. "I don't know."

"Are you willing to stick around with me a little longer and find out?"

She hesitated, then nodded. "All right."

"Then let's get out of here. I've got something I want to show you."

CHAPTER FIVE

"WHERE ARE WE GOING?" Barb watched out the windshield as Scott turned his truck onto the highway that looped around the west side of town.

"You haven't figured that out?" He glanced at her, his expression revealing nothing. "Things have changed a lot around here, but I'd have thought you'd still recognize this route."

They passed an auto parts place and a convenience store, then the road to the small airport. Past the lumberyard, he put on his blinker and turned left onto a narrower road, lined with trees. Barb's heart sped up. "We're going to the lake," she said.

The sights they passed were more and more familiar, as if change had come slower to this part of town. The sign for Izzy's Tavern loomed ahead, orange neon glowing over a gravel lot filled with pickup trucks and old cars. The Taco Hut still squatted beside the road, paint seemingly not one bit more weathered in eighteen years time. Watching it all, she was a teenager again, the same giddy excitement and desperate longing churning her stomach. She felt almost overwhelmed not just by physical desire, but also by an aching to be accepted for herself, just as she was. Barbara Jean, the weird kid, who wanted someone—this man—to think she wasn't so weird after all.

He drove to an even narrower dirt road that ended in a cul-de-sac. He parked at the end and switched off the engine. In front of them, the wall of dark pines parted to reveal the glint of moonlight on water. He rolled down his window and the warm air brought the scent of wet sand and the sound of waves slapping against the buoy that bobbed just offshore.

"Do you remember this place?" he asked.

She nodded. "I remember." When she was in high school, this was known as Make Out Point. Maybe it still was. It was where Scott had brought her the night they first made love.

He slid from behind the steering wheel, closer to her. She turned to him, eyes wide. "What are you going to do?"

"I'm going to do what I've been wanting to do since I first laid eyes on you in your mama's driveway the other day."

The angel with the pitchfork protested they should talk about this first, but her body ignored this advice and closed her eyes and leaned toward him, eighteen years of memories and desire distilled into this one moment.

He kissed her with the same confidence and skill he used with his horses. His lips covered hers with the sureness of a man who knows exactly what he's doing and where he belongs. Barb responded as if only minutes had passed since they'd last been together this way. Her body shifted to shape more comfortably to his, her arms reached up to encircle his neck.

For a man she thought of as appealingly rough around the edges, he had incredibly sensuous lips. They were soft and warm, and the pressure of them against her mouth sent heat along every nerve ending.

He tasted of mint, and she realized he must have slipped a breath mint. Did that mean he'd been planning this all along? The thought made her bolder. She opened her mouth more and darted her tongue between his teeth.

He tightened his hold on her, and plunged his tongue into her mouth, an erotic, intimate gesture that seemed to say there wasn't a part of her he didn't want to explore.

He tucked his hand beneath her thighs and lifted her, until she was sitting in his lap, the hard ridge at the fly of his jeans pressed against her hip. When had a man so openly wanted her, as much as she wanted him? She clutched his shoulders, thrilling at the hard muscle that bunched with every move. He smoothed his hand down her back, along her waist, then up to cup her breast.

When he squeezed her, she couldn't hold back a moan, and she felt his lips curve into a smile against hers. "We've been waiting eighteen years to touch each other this way," he whispered, and slid his hand beneath the silk of her top, and began fumbling with the front clasp of her bra.

Her body ached for release, and every fantasy she'd ever had that involved this man whirled through her fevered brain. But the pitchfork-wielding angel chose that moment to prod her, reminding her the smartest decisions aren't always made in the throes of passion.

Somehow she slid her hands from his shoulders to his chest, and pushed against him. "W-wait a minute," she gasped, struggling to pull back.

His hand stilled, and he raised his head to look at her. "You okay?" he asked, concern edging out the lust that had darkened his eyes.

She nodded and swallowed, trying to find her voice. "Everything's just happening a little fast." She held his gaze, pleading for understanding. "I just...I don't think I'm ready for this," she said.

His jaw tensed, and the lines around his mouth

whitened, as if he were struggling against words, or feelings, or…something. He let out a deep breath, then nodded, and slid her off his lap. "Sorry," he muttered. "I didn't mean to come on like some horny teenager."

"It's all right." Maybe nostalgia had gotten the best of both of them. "I felt it, too. It's just…" She struggled for the right words.

"I'll take you home." He turned the key too far and the engine screamed, until he backed off and put the truck in gear.

She barely had time to fasten her seat belt before he whipped the truck around in a Y-turn. They hit the main road, tires squealing, and she clung to the armrest, trying to keep her balance. "Please slow down," she gasped.

"Sorry." He immediately slowed to a more reasonable speed. "There I go, behaving like a jerk again." He glanced at her. "Guess you just bring out the best in me."

His dejected look struck her as comical, and she bit back a laugh. "You're not a jerk," she said. "You're just not a man who hides his feelings. It's refreshing, really."

"Don't tell anyone. They'll take away my membership in the Macho Cowboys club."

She let the laughter escape now. "Don't worry. No one's going to mistake you for some new-age, sensitive guy. I just meant that you don't worry a lot about what people think of you. If you're mad, everybody knows it. And if you're passionate, you show that, too." She smoothed her skirt over her knees, hoping the darkness hid her blush. "I'm flattered. And it would have been very easy for me to have kept on with what we were doing back there, but I—I need more time."

"Sure. You're right. I understand."

Did he? She didn't see how he could. On one level, everything was simple. He wanted her. She wanted him.

She'd even joked about having a fling while she was here. But in her mind she'd envisioned some handsome stranger. Not her mother's neighbor, who'd known her when she was "Gappy" and who had broken her heart when she was a girl.

She'd wanted sex without the messy emotions, but with Scott that didn't seem possible. They had too much history to make for an easy future.

They were both silent for the remainder of the ride home. At her mother's house, he insisted on walking her to the door. "I'll call you tomorrow," he said. "See how you're doing."

She started to protest that wasn't necessary, then nodded. The truth was, she'd like to talk to him again. She wanted them to remain friends. "Good night," she said, and stood on tiptoe to kiss his cheek, breathing in the warm, male scent of him, smiling at the thrill even that gave her.

The evening hadn't ended as badly as it might have. They were still talking to each other, and she'd learned that she was still a desirable woman. That kind of ego boost made the time worthwhile, if nothing else.

As for the rest of it, she still had a week and a half to sort out all those feelings. She'd head back to California a wiser woman, if not a happier one.

AFTER HE DROPPED Barb off at her house, Scott drove past his own driveway, and out onto the highway. He was too restless to turn in just yet.

What the hell had happened there, at the lake? He'd started out wanting to kiss her, to satisfy his curiosity and see where this attraction between them might lead. He hadn't expected to end up trying to get her clothes off in less than ten minutes. Even as a horny teenager he'd had more finesse than that.

But when their lips had met and it was as if the past eighteen years had never happened. Or as if he'd spent all that time waiting for her to return. Everything about the moment had felt so right, so…familiar. Not like a usual first kiss, where half your brain is wondering if she likes what you're doing, if she's feeling what you're feeling, if you should put your hand there, or move it over here.

Maybe to his body, Barb was familiar. After all, the first time he'd ever looked at her as more than his best friend's kid sister, at the rodeo grounds just after her seventeenth birthday, he'd felt a connection that went beyond lust.

Once she was on his radar, he couldn't stop thinking about her. He'd had to resist the urge to whoop and holler when she agreed to go out with him, and he'd spent the next week alternating between feverish fantasies of her and admonitions to himself to play it cool.

He'd promised himself he wouldn't even kiss her on their first date. After all, he was twenty-three. A man. At seventeen, she was barely legal. That promise had held until after dinner, when she'd surprised him by throwing her arms around him and planting her lips on his.

After that, kissing her had been the most natural thing in the world. One kiss led to another and by the end of the summer they'd progressed from heavy petting in the front seat of his pickup truck to making love in that same truck…and in the barn loft, the back pasture and anyplace they could steal a moment away.

He'd been with women before, of course. Even fancied himself in love with a few. But once he'd kissed Barbara Jean he knew he'd only been fooled by a poor substitute for love. The two of them had the real thing.

So though she kept talking about going away to school and having adventures in exotic, faraway places, he'd dismissed all the talk as fantasy. When it came down to it, he'd been sure she'd do the right thing and stay with him. After a few years, they'd get married. He hadn't said as much, but if pressed, he would have admitted he pictured the two of them living happily ever after.

And in the end, those thoughts had been a fairy tale of his own making. Barb's dreams of a different kind of life were more important to her than his promise of love. Staying home with a simple cowboy like him wasn't good enough for a girl who'd always wanted more.

The girl had grown into a beautiful, successful woman, one who still would never settle for less than she thought she deserved. And he was still a simple cowboy, older but not necessarily wiser. All his old feelings for her had resurfaced, as fresh and confusing as ever. What was he going to do about Barb? Should he keep trying to get her into his bed, enjoy what promised to be some of the most mind-blowing sex of his life, then say "Thanks, it's been fun," when she headed back to California?

He'd never been one for a relationship that casual. Considering how much a single kiss from Barb had shaken him, did he have any hope of coming out of this as anything less than a basket case when it was time for her to leave?

A BUSINESS COLLEAGUE HAD once told Barb she was the most sensible woman he'd met, because she had the ability to evaluate a situation without emotion and make the decision that would most benefit everyone involved. At the time, she'd accepted this assessment as a compliment, but the boot camp experience had made her see a lot of things differently. Was emotional detachment really such a good thing? Maybe Scott's approach, to say and do what you wanted and to hell with everything else, was a healthier method.

The morning after their dinner date, she sat at the student desk in her old bedroom and opened to a blank page in her planner. Brainstorming on paper was her favorite problem-solving technique. If it worked at the office, why couldn't it help her now?

The first step was to write down what she knew about the situation.

First, she wanted to sleep with Scott. Her body still hummed with desire for him and no amount of cold showers or self-gratification were likely to ease that ache anytime soon.

Second, she was going back to California in ten days. Which could be seen as a plus or a minus, depending on the point of view.

Third, she was scared. Of what, she wasn't sure. Of being hurt. Of making a mistake.

The next step was to try to take an outsider's view of the situation. She knew what Rebecca and Cassandra would tell her, "Go for it!"

Next, she asked herself what Maxine would say. On one hand, they'd all attended a lecture on not letting hormones get the best of common sense. Yet the next day the topic had been embracing your own sexuality.

Maxine was a woman, and despite her outwardly cool nature, she'd shown signs of warmth and a sense of humor. She would no doubt appreciate what a sexy, good-looking hunk of man Scott Caden was.

So, one vote from Maxine in the go for it column.

As for the fear, Maxine was a big believer in confronting fear—a popular topic of everything from the Ropes course to classes on the rewards of taking emotional risk.

Sex with Scott would definitely be an emotional risk. An opportunity to practice some of the lessons Barbara had learned? Another vote in the yes column.

What else? She studied all she'd written so far. Then jotted down Abstinence times twenty months—the length of time since she'd had sex. Maybe that was one of the reasons she'd lit up like a firecracker last night. Easing some of that tension would be a good thing, right? When she did meet her Mr. Right, she'd be able to assess him more sensibly, without raging hormones getting in the way.

Right. Another yes vote, then.

The angel nagged that she was getting good at rationalization, but Barb told her to go take a hike and reached for the telephone, before she lost her nerve.

"Hello?" Scott answered on the fifth ring, sounding grumpy. Had he decided to sleep in and she'd awakened him, or did he not like being interrupted when he was working?

"Scott, it's Barb."

"Hey." She could almost hear his smile. "How you doing? I was going to call you, remember?"

"I know. Guess I couldn't wait. I wanted to thank you for dinner last night, and apologize for cutting the evening short."

"You don't have anything to apologize about. I was the one out of line."

"I thought maybe we could try again tonight. I'd like to fix dinner for you."

"That'd be great. Uh, will Maggie be there, too?"

She laughed at the ill-disguised disappointment in his voice. Just what she wanted, her mother as chaperone. "I was thinking maybe I could bring dinner to your house."

"That sounds good." Definite enthusiasm this time.

"But don't bring anything too healthy. No tofu and sprouts."

She laughed. "I promise you'll like what I bring."

"I imagine I'd like almost anything you came up with." His voice dropped into the sexy drawl guaranteed to send heat curling through her.

"I'll see you about seven," she said.

"I'll be looking forward to it."

She hung up the phone and stared at it, then glanced at the clock. Only ten hours and twenty minutes to plan a menu, buy groceries and make herself beautiful for what might prove to be the most erotic night of her life.

CHAPTER SIX

BARB STRUGGLED up Scott's driveway juggling a hot casserole dish and two totebags full of accompaniments. She told herself she should have taken the car, but it seemed foolish to drive the equivalent of one city block to deliver dinner. Still, halfway up the drive she was praying she wouldn't turn an ankle in her high heels, or end up dumping the hot casserole all over herself.

He must have been watching for her, because he came out onto the porch to help her carry everything in. "Why didn't you call me? I'd have come over and helped you bring all this," he said as she followed him into his kitchen.

"Then you would have had to listen to my mom give me a dozen embarrassing last-minute instructions." Her cheeks warmed at the memory. Her mother had actually told her "Don't forget to practice safe sex," along with directions for reheating the casserole.

He laughed. "Think she would have asked me if my intentions were honorable?"

"I'd have been disappointed if you'd said yes." She busied herself unpacking the dinner, afraid to look and see what kind of reaction that zinger had earned her.

He played it cool, and helped her set everything out on the counter. "What's on the menu?" he asked, lifting the lid on the casserole dish.

"Chicken with artichoke hearts and mushrooms and wild rice."

"Never had it."

"It's good and healthy."

He made a face. "No tofu or sprouts?"

"None." She pushed him back toward the dining room. "Why don't you go set the table? I'll take care of the food."

Twenty minutes later, when she carried the casserole into the dining room, she saw he'd set the table with gleaming china and silverware. A pair of candles in crystal holders glowed at the center of the table, an open bottle of wine next to them.

"That smells good," he said, taking the dish from her and setting it on a trivet on the table.

"I'll get the rest," she said.

"No, you sit down." He pushed her toward a chair. "I'll get everything else."

She started to protest that she was supposed to be in charge of dinner, then decided to sit back and sip some wine instead. Wasn't she supposed to practice giving up control of everything? Maybe she could get used to being waited on—by the right person.

He brought the salad, bread and steamed broccoli, then took his place across from her. "It looks and smells delicious," he said.

During the meal, she didn't worry about flirting or conversational technique. Instead, she sat back and enjoyed watching him. He raved about the food, and ate with enthusiasm, leading her to thoughts of other appetites.

"This stuff is really good," he said, spooning a second helping onto his plate.

"You sound surprised."

"I'm impressed that you can run your own business and cook, too."

She allowed herself a mysterious smile. "I'm a woman of many talents."

His gaze met hers briefly before he returned his attention to his plate. "So I'm learning."

When the meal was done, he insisted she remain seated while he took care of the dishes. "Just put them in the sink," she said. "We'll wash them later."

"I won't argue with you there." He stood and began stacking plates. "Why don't I meet you in the living room in a few minutes?"

While he was busy in the kitchen, she went into the living room, where more candles burned. Give the man an A for setting a romantic mood. Now if they could find their way back to the mood they were in last night....

"Have I told you how good you look in that dress?" He came up behind her and put his hands on her waist.

"This old thing?" She smiled down at the white rayon halter dress, which she had, in fact, bought that very afternoon.

"Sexy." He kissed her bare shoulder, the touch of his lips making her knees weak.

"Maybe we should sit down." She managed to move toward the black leather sofa.

He sat beside her, elbows on his knees, his eyes studying her. "What now?" he asked.

"What do you mean, what now?"

"Do we play cards, or talk, or...?"

"Or?" She fought back a smile.

"I guess what I'm asking is, how honorable are *your* intentions?"

She leaned toward him, and put a hand on his knee, the smile let loose now. "Not very," she said, as her lips touched his.

He stilled, one hand wrapped around her wrist. "I

have to know. How far do you want to take this? After what happened last night—"

"I want to take it all the way." She looked into his eyes, at the desire there that reflected her own longing. "Last night was too amazing not to see how far we can run with these feelings."

His response was to gather her in his arms and pull her tightly against his chest, while his lips and tongue enslaved her mouth.

He stole her breath and all coherent thought with his long, slow, lingering kisses, until her lips tingled and every other nerve yearned for its turn to feel him. While his lips worked their magic, his hands were busy as well, undoing the fastening at the back of her neck and folding down the fabric to reveal her naked breasts.

He broke contact at last and leaned back, smiling. "You're beautiful," he breathed.

She was shy suddenly, like a teenage girl, and resisted the urge to cover herself again. "Do you think we'll be better at this now than when we were younger?" she asked.

"We were pretty good back then." He smoothed his hand along her arm, then bent and kissed her bare shoulder. "I like to think I've learned a few things in the time between." He reached out to cup her breast.

She gasped at the brush of his callused palms across her sensitive nipples, and arched toward him. "I've had dreams like this," she breathed.

"Me, too," he whispered, and bent to take her in his mouth. The lips and tongue that had tantalized her mouth now made love to her breasts.

She writhed against him and dug her nails into his shoulders. "Scott, please!" she gasped.

He raised his head. "Is something wrong? Am I hurting you?"

She shook her head. "You're not hurting me. It's just…it's been a while. And…I want you so much."

"You don't know how much I want you." He stood and before she could protest, he'd gathered her into his arms.

"What are you doing?" she squealed, as he whirled around and headed out of the room.

"We should do this right." He nudged open a door at one end of the hall.

She had a sense of soft colors—browns and blues. A neatly made bed, simple dark furniture. And candles, glowing on the bedside table and reflecting in the mirror over the dresser. "You had this planned," she said, as he laid her on the folded-back covers.

"I was hoping," he said. "I didn't sleep much last night, thinking about you."

"I didn't sleep much, either."

"Then we'd better be careful. We might just nod off."

She reached up and undid the top button of his shirt. "Not a chance."

"You're right. Not a chance." He knelt on the bed beside her and kissed the side of her neck while she fumbled with his buttons, her hands made clumsy by the waves of desire shuddering through her every time he touched her. But the two halves of his shirt finally parted, and she pushed it over his shoulders, momentarily pinning his arms.

"Now I have you where I want you," she teased, and bent to sweep her tongue across the flat nipple almost hidden by the soft mat of hair. She pressed her hands against the defined muscle of his chest, and smoothed her palms up to his shoulders, reveling in the feel of him, his raw masculinity.

The shirt tore as he reached for her, the fine cotton shredding to rags as his arms wrapped around her. "Now it's my turn to beg," he said, his mouth buried in her hair, which hung loose around her shoulders. "I don't know how much longer I can wait to be in you."

"I don't want to wait anymore. We've already waited eighteen years."

They finished undressing quickly then, and she slid beneath the covers while he opened a drawer on the bedside table. "Do you want to play twenty questions about our pasts or just use this?" he asked, holding up a condom packet.

"No questions," she said. "This is fine for now." Already she was chilled, missing his warmth.

She watched while he sheathed himself, the simple act imbued with eroticism. Had he ever touched himself, thinking of her, the way she had pleasured herself with thoughts of him?

He lay down beside her, and gathered her close, one leg draping across her hip, holding her there. As if she would ever try to flee him. There was nothing she wanted more at this moment than to be here with him. To feel him touching her, to see in his eyes how much he wanted her.

They kissed, letting the tension build within them anew, feeling the naked length of their bodies pressed close together, but not yet close enough. He kissed her throat, along her collarbone, down to her breasts. When he suckled again at her nipples, she moaned, the throbbing between her legs building almost to the point of pain. "Scott," she whispered, her voice urgent.

She didn't need to say more. He rolled her onto her back and knelt between her legs. With one hand on her hip, the other reached between her thighs, and slid two fingers into her. She moaned and bucked against him. He grinned. "Just making sure you were ready."

Her answer was another moan, which he cut off by sinking into her.

The sensation of him filling her was pure pleasure in itself. Then he began to move, retreating and charging forward again, establishing a rhythm she was quick to follow. She cradled him with her knees, wrapped her fingers around his biceps and stared up into his eyes.

His eyes were open, looking at her with need and wonder, and a tenderness that made her half afraid she'd burst into tears. The joy she felt moved her as much as the physical sensation of almost fulfilled desire. This was what she'd craved for so long, this connection to a man, both physically and emotionally.

Her climax rocketed through her, a keening cry tearing from her as she surrendered to the sensation of soaring free from her body. She closed her eyes and arched against the bed, dimly aware of the added tension in his own body, and the stronger thrusts as he found his own release.

He collapsed against her, his head on her chest, his weight still supported by his arms braced on either side of her. She gathered him close and rolled them to their sides, and stroked his sweat-dampened back. Neither of them spoke, as if a spell had been cast over them, too fragile to risk words.

Only later, whether minutes or hours she couldn't tell, did she gently move away from him and climb out of bed, intending to use the bathroom. His hand shot out and captured her wrist. "Stay," he said, his voice rough, his eyes still closed.

She brushed the hair back from his face, and he opened his eyes to look up at her. "All right," she said, smiling. "I'll stay. For a while."

SCOTT WOKE LATE the next morning to sun streaming through the open blinds and an unfamiliar—and not particularly pleasant—aroma filling the room. He sat up and raked a hand through his hair, looking around. Rumpled sheets and a silky white dress hanging from the bedpost confirmed that last night hadn't been merely an erotic dream.

He sniffed and wrinkled his nose. Something smelled...scorched.

Heart pounding, he shoved back the covers and leaped from the bed. The smoke alarm began to shriek, and as he rounded the corner into the living room, he saw smoke pouring from the kitchen. "Barb!" he shouted, and raced toward the fire.

He found her at the sink, coughing and running water into a blackened pan, from which billowed clouds of acrid steam. He raced around opening windows, then reached up and jerked the cover off and the batteries out of the smoke alarm, silencing it. "What happened?" he demanded.

She shut off the water and waved away the last of the smoke. "I was trying to cook breakfast and the bacon caught on fire."

He walked over to survey the blackened mess in the pan. "I'd say that's burned all right."

She began to laugh, still half-choking on the smoke. "What's so funny?" he asked.

"You!" She hugged her arms around her waist and continued to laugh. "You're naked."

He looked down and realized he hadn't stopped to grab pants. "I was in a hurry. I thought the house was on fire."

"No, just me ruining breakfast." She picked up a dish

towel and began wiping water from the counter. "I have a confession to make. I'm not at all domestic."

"You're being too hard on yourself." He circled her waist with his arm and pulled her close. She was wearing one of his shirts, sleeves rolled to her elbows, and apparently nothing else. "Dinner last night was great."

"My mother made that dinner." Her eyes met his and she started laughing again. "I'm sorry. I was trying to impress you."

"I'm impressed all right." He nuzzled her neck. "And it wasn't your cooking that did it."

"You're still naked." She shimmied against him.

"And you're not." He began unbuttoning the shirt. "We'd better do something about that."

"Mmm. What if I'm hungry?"

"I'll take you out to breakfast. Later."

"Mmm."

THEY FINALLY MADE IT to breakfast at ten o'clock, and then reluctantly parted company. Scott had to meet some buyers, and Barb was anxious to call her office. "The new client from Bakersfield, Mr. Simmons, had some concerns about the ideas that Walt drew up for him, so they're meeting again today," Eveline said.

"Fax everything to me and let me look it over," Barb said. "Maybe I can make some suggestions."

"I hate to intrude on your visit with your family," Eveline said.

"Don't be ridiculous. Send them over." She flipped through the phone book and found a local place that would accept faxes, then headed to town. She should have known Walt was too new to handle a client on his own. She shouldn't have left him with so much pressure.

He needed more mentoring. If he failed with this client, it would be her fault.

The faxes weren't ready by the time she made it to town, so she walked down the street to a coffee shop. Her head was still fuzzy from lack of sleep the night before. A cup of espresso would help her wake up.

She was paying for her purchase when the door of the coffee shop swung open and Faye walked in. "Hey, girl, it's good to see you." Faye enveloped her in a hug.

"It's good to see you, too. Do you have time for a cup of coffee?"

"You bet. Find us a table and I'll join you in a minute."

A few moments later, Faye sat across from Barb with a mug of chai tea. She wasted no time getting to the nitty-gritty. "I heard you and Scott had a late breakfast together at the Corral," she said, grinning. "So are you two a couple now?"

Barb looked at her. "You heard that already?"

"It's a small town. News travels fast. So how about it? Is something going on with you and my big brother?"

She stared into her coffee cup, as if espresso beans might tell the future as well as tea leaves. "I don't know." She glanced at Faye again. "Can I ask you some questions?"

Faye's expression sobered. "Sure. Fire away."

"How did you and Tom meet?"

Faye blinked. "Um, we met at a Rotary Club dance. He was new in town and he asked me to dance."

"How long were you dating before you knew he was the one?"

"Not too long." Her smile was dreamy. "Maybe a month? Maybe sooner than that. I can't explain it. He made me feel…like no one had ever made me feel before. Like when I was with him everything was so…so right." She leaned toward Barb. "Why? Are you in love with Scott?"

Barb shook her head. "I don't know. I— Look, if I tell you something, will you promise not to tell another soul? Especially Scott?"

Faye nodded. "I promise."

Barb wrapped both hands around her coffee cup, and struggled to come up with the right words. "Before I came to visit this time, I was in the Woodlands, at a kind of camp. For executive women. It's kind of like…like a boot camp. Two weeks of learning about yourself and how to relate better to other people. Men and women, but I went there hoping to figure out why I haven't been able to have a lasting relationship with a man."

"And did you learn that?"

"I don't know. I learned some things about myself. Things I didn't necessarily like. And maybe some things that will help me relate better to men." She rubbed her thumb along the rim of the cup. "But I'm afraid of making a mistake that will leave me even more unhappy."

Faye reached out and covered Barb's hand with her own. "Don't be afraid. I think when you come right down to it, love isn't that complicated. You just have to follow your heart."

"I don't know." Barb wished she could have that kind of faith. "I think it takes more than love to make a successful marriage these days."

"You still haven't told me whether or not you're in love with Scott."

"I don't know. I mean, the two of us are so different. We live in different parts of the country."

"But is any of that really important?"

Was it? "I don't know. Maybe some of it is. To me."

Faye patted her hand. "You're a smart woman. One

of the smartest women I know. But sometimes you think too much. Don't make this harder than it has to be."

"Then what am I supposed to do?"

Faye shrugged. "You've got, what? Over a week left here? Take things one day at a time, and see what happens."

"You make it sound so simple."

"Not simple. But not so complicated, either." She stood and gathered up her purse. "I will tell you one secret about Scott, though."

"What's that?"

"I think he's tired of being alone. He's ready to settle down."

"Then why didn't he settle down with Miss Rodeo, or whoever she was?"

"Because my bro is a romantic at heart. All those cowboys are. And Tina, nice as she was, wasn't the one he really wanted. When he finds that woman, nothing in the world is going to stop him from having her."

"How do you know that?"

"That's the way he is. When he wants something, whether it's a horse or a piece of land or a woman, he gets it." She laughed. "Take it as a warning. If Scott decides he's really, truly, in love with you, you don't stand a chance."

CHAPTER SEVEN

FAYE'S WORDS FRIGHTENED Barb. On one hand, what woman didn't want to be pursued wholeheartedly by a man? But on the other hand, what if these feelings between them didn't last? What if they both made big changes in their lives, and then ended up miserable?

She'd never enter a business contract without having a good idea of what the outcome of her dealings with the other person would be. The thought of approaching love with any less thought for self-preservation frightened her. If she never risked her money with impulsiveness, why risk her future happiness on something that might only be the result of overactive hormones?

She was even prepared to refuse to see him for a day or two, to give her emotions time to cool down. But he called her that evening, and at the sound of his voice her body overruled her brain, and she found herself agreeing to go riding with him again the next day. That night she dreamed of Maxine, lecturing her on the importance of calculated risks, and woke up with a headache.

By the time she met Scott to go horseback riding, she was determined to tell him how confused she was feeling. But she hadn't counted on the effect seeing him again would have on her. It was as if every nerve in her body jumped for joy in anticipation of a repeat of the previous day's loving. "Hey, beautiful," he said, and pulled her close in a bone-melting kiss.

"Hey." She managed to smile and slip away, though every part of her was crying out to stay in his arms. "It's a gorgeous day for a ride, isn't it?" Though the days were gradually growing warmer, the intense heat of summer hadn't yet set in, and a mild breeze made for perfect riding weather.

"I can think of a ride I'd like to take with you." His eyes sparked with devilment.

She laughed and fit her foot in the stirrup of her mount. "Come on, give me a boost."

He spent the first few minutes of the ride describing his meeting with the buyer the previous afternoon. "One of these city fellows whose daughter wants a horse. I gave him the usual spiel about how much work and money is involved in owning one, but he didn't want to hear it. All he wanted to know was how much to write the check for."

"So what did you do?" she asked.

"I told him if he let me meet his daughter, talk to her and convince myself she'd take good care of the animal, then I'd sell it to him. Otherwise, I'd just as soon keep it."

She imagined Scott laying down the law for the "city fellow" with the fat checkbook. "What did he say?"

Scott chuckled. "I thought for a minute there I was going to have to call an ambulance. He turned red and all but jumped up and down, demanding I sell him a horse." He shook his head. "I can't say the man knows much about how to handle people. You don't order someone like me to do anything I don't want to do."

Some people might call Scott stubborn; she saw him as being strong in his principles. An admirable quality, but not always one that was easy to live with. "You'll find another buyer for the horse," she said.

"Of course I will. It's a good horse. And it'll go to some place where I know it'll be taken care of." He glanced at her. "Here I've been rattling on and haven't hardly given you a chance to get a word in edgewise. What have you been up to?"

She shrugged. "Not much. Trying to put out fires long-distance at work."

"Something wrong?"

She shook her head. "Not really." She'd reviewed Walt's plans for the Bakersfield company and made a few suggestions she thought the client would like. The rest was out of her hands. "It's hard, though, not being right there to oversee things."

"You'll handle it. You've always been so determined. One of the things I've always liked about you."

"Really?" The praise warmed her, but it also reminded her of the conversation she'd intended to have with him. "I have to confess, I'm a little nervous," she said. "Things are happening so fast with us."

"Some people might say we were taking our own sweet time, waiting eighteen years to get together again."

"A lot has happened in eighteen years. In some ways, we hardly know each other." What she did know scared her: Scott was a man rooted to this land, while her focus lay half a country away. Making love hadn't changed any of that.

He glanced at her. "What do you want to know about me? I'm forty-one years old. I own this ranch. I raise horses for a living. I like steak and beer and country music. And I like you."

It was an innocent statement, but the heat in his eyes when he said it made her heart flutter wildly. She swallowed and gripped the reins more tightly. "Fine, but what do you know about me?"

"You're thirty-five. You've worked your butt off to build a successful business where you tell people how to develop the right image to succeed. You live in California and you like vegetables more than I do. You probably can't stand country music, but you're too polite to admit it. You came back home after being gone for years for a reason I can't figure out, but I think it might have to do with you working too hard and maybe wanting to feel at home somewhere again."

She blinked at this astute assessment. "I've never really felt at home in Cut and Shoot."

"That's what you tell yourself, but you're having a good time since you've been here, aren't you?"

"Yes. At least, I've felt more relaxed this time. Mama and I haven't argued as much." Maybe because she'd been spending more time with Scott, but also because the boot camp had helped her accept that she didn't always have to convince others that she was right. They were entitled to their own point of view, too. "I'm remembering more of the good things about growing up here," she admitted. "Friends like Faye, and fun things, like riding horses."

"You ever ride in California?"

She shook her head. "But there's a stable not far from my house. When I get back, I'll have to visit them."

He looked away, and nudged his horse forward. "Let's ride back here a little ways. There's something you should see."

They turned down a rutted lane and made their way along a fence line to another gate. It opened onto a field carpeted with pink-and-white blossoms, as if someone had scattered carloads of blooms in every direction. "It's amazing!" she said, looking first at it, then at him.

He grinned. "I cleared this two summers ago. Once

the trees were gone, the flowers took over. I never graze it until it's gone to seed, and every year they come back thicker than ever."

She shook her head, feeling as if he'd just presented her with armfuls of blooms. And in a way, he had. "Faye told me you were a romantic. She's right."

He swung down off his horse and began leading it through the field. She dismounted and followed him. "Have you been talking to my sister about me?" he asked.

"I ran into her in the coffee shop yesterday. She said word was all over town that we'd had breakfast together."

He wrapped the reins around his hand. "It's amazing what passes for entertainment in a small town."

"Does the gossip bother you?"

He laughed. "Considering all the men who are probably eating their hearts out with envy, I'd say you're doing a lot for my reputation."

She stopped. "You think people are jealous that you might have hooked up with weird Barbara Jean from California?"

He dropped the reins and took her by the shoulders, smoothing his hands down her bare arms. "I think they're jealous I've hooked up with Barb Powers, the woman who had enough guts to go off and live her dreams. She's got a successful business and money in the bank, and she's grown up more beautiful than ever."

He kissed her, and she couldn't help but kiss him back. When she was in his arms, all her worries about the future seemed silly. All that mattered was how wonderful it felt to be with him.

"I want to make love to you," he said, his voice husky with need. "Now. Right here."

The last time she'd done something so daring had been with him. How was it he had this ability to make her want to take that kind of risk? She nodded, and began to unfasten his shirt.

They undressed each other, and he spread his clothes for them to lie on, though the grass and flowers provided a warm, soft carpet. They knelt, facing each other, their eyes locked. Here in the open, she had never felt more intimate. Or more exposed. The sun warmed her bare skin, and the flowers tickled the backs of her calves. "I feel like there's a spotlight on every flaw." She glanced down at her pale thighs, her voice shaky.

"Then don't look at yourself directly." He put his hand under her chin and tipped her head up. "Look at your reflection in my eyes. Because when I look at you, you're perfect."

He lay back, pulling her on top of him. She straddled his thighs, and braced her hands on his chest. His erection rose up between them, insistent. "Did you bring a condom?" she asked.

He reached for his pants and took a packet from his pocket. "So you *did* bring me out here to have your way with me," she teased.

"I notice you're fighting me off." He handed her the packet and she tore it open, then grinned at him.

"You look like you're up to something," he said.

"Maybe I am." Feeling a little self-conscious, she popped the condom in her mouth, then slid down the length of his body. She'd seen this in a movie once, but she'd never actually tried it herself....

When her lips closed around him, he sighed, the single sound sending an extra jolt of heat and wetness between her legs. She manipulated the condom with her tongue, managing to adjust it over the head, then beginning the slow, gentle slide down his shaft, fitting the latex over him with her teeth. "Yeah," he grunted, and propped himself up on his elbows to watch.

When she completed the task, she had all of him in her mouth, the hot, hard length of him pulsing against her tongue.

"You're incredible," he said, one hand buried in her hair, caressing her.

Careful not to dislodge the condom, she straightened and grinned at him. "What now?" she teased.

"Come up here." He motioned her forward.

She crawled up his body, until her breasts were even with his mouth. He held her there, lavishing attention on first one, then the other, until her vision blurred, and she moaned and writhed against him.

When he released her, she rose and positioned herself over his shaft. Her earlier self-consciousness had given way to an overpowering need to feel him in her.

She impaled herself on him in one smooth movement, driving him deeply into her, gasping at the exquisite sensation of heat and pressure. He grasped her hips with one hand, and used the other to fondle her clit, guiding her into a rhythm, beginning slowly, then building, until they were moving together in a swift, pounding frenzy.

She came hard, the climax rolling through her like breakers slamming against a pier. His hands on her hips urged her to keep moving, and she did, until he came also, bucking against her, his breath expelled in harsh gasps.

She lay on top of him for a long while after that, his arms holding her tightly to him. She closed her eyes and breathed in the perfume of flowers and sex, the faint scent of male sweat mixed with damp earth and sun-warmed grass.

She thought they both might have dozed, before one

of the horses wandered over and began cropping grass close to their heads, the great teeth ripping clumps of flowers from the earth, sounding like a monster tearing up the field.

Scott sat up, taking her with him. "I guess we'd better get dressed and get back," he said.

She nodded. "I guess so." That was the trouble with moments like these. Real life always intruded on the magic.

They dressed then mounted up again and rode in easy silence for a while.

"Do you ever think about moving back here?" he asked.

The question stunned her, so much so that at first she couldn't find the breath to speak. "Here?" she finally gasped.

"Well, to Houston. Seems like there'd be a lot of business for you there."

Yes, there was business in Houston. But her home—where she felt comfortable and competent—was on the west coast now. "Why do you ask?"

"Can't you guess?" He glanced at her, deep lines around his eyes. "I'd like to keep seeing you. To give us a chance. You can't deny we've stirred up some pretty powerful feelings. I'd like to see where they lead."

She swallowed hard. She could feel that pull, too, of wanting them to go on and on together. But the thought of coming back here, to try to put down roots where she'd never felt any, was terrifying, as if he'd suggested she stroll through quicksand. One wrong step and she could be pulled under. "I—I don't know what to say."

"Think about it. You might see it's not such a bad idea."

She nodded automatically, and managed to hold herself together through the rest of the ride and through helping him take care of the horses. They parted with a friendly kiss, and then she walked across the street and down her mother's driveway, resisting the urge to run as hard and fast as she could, as if she could outrun the panic that lurked on the edge of conscious thought.

CHAPTER EIGHT

BARB PACED back and forth across her bedroom, the old wooden floors creaking with every step. *I'd like to keep seeing you...move back to Houston...* She took deep breaths, trying to control her mounting panic. Finally, she snatched up her cell phone and punched in Maxine's number.

"Warfield, this is Maxine." The sound of the clipped, professional voice had an immediate calming effect. Barb stopped pacing and sat on the end of the bed.

"It's Barb Powers. I've run into a situation here and need a little advice."

"How can I help?" She pictured Maxine at her desk, surrounded by the photos of her successful alumni, her expression serene. Non-judgmental.

"I've met someone. Someone I dated a long time ago. Things have gotten serious pretty fast...."

"Yes, you've only been there a week." Barb thought Maxine chuckled. "You did strike me as someone who didn't like to waste time. Do you think you're in love?"

"After a week? How could I be?" But what else to call these feelings that gave her no peace?

"You said you knew him before. Sometimes emotions lie dormant, waiting for the right moment to surface. It's happened before."

"Maybe." She wet her dry lips. "The thing is, he's asking me to stay here. To see where all this leads."

"And you don't want to do that."

"I *can't* do that. My business—my *life* is in California."

"And this man refuses to leave Texas."

"I'd never ask him to leave. He has a ranch here. A ranch his family has owned for several generations. And he's not the kind of man to compromise."

"Everyone will compromise, given the right motivation."

Barb recognized another of Maxine's oft-repeated sayings. "He told me he thinks people should accept other people for who they are and not try to change them."

"Yet he wants to change you from a Californian to a Texan."

"I think he sees me as a Texan who forgot her roots. He thinks he's doing me a *favor* by suggesting I move back here."

"Then why don't you do it?"

She blinked. "What? I told you, my business—"

"Businesses can be moved."

She put a hand over her stomach, as if she could squeeze out the cold knot forming there. "Maxine, I don't belong here," she said. "I never have. When I was a kid, I was always an outsider. The weird girl with crazy dreams."

"Obviously, this man doesn't see you that way."

But when I'm here, I still see myself *that way.* "Maxine, do I have to give up everything else I've ever wanted in order to have love?" She held her breath, waiting for the answer.

"You don't have to give up everything, but you might have to give up something. You're the only one who can decide what that something is."

Barb tried to hide her disappointment. She'd hoped Maxine would have some clear-cut advice that would help Barb make the right decision, not more talk about choices.

"I have to go now," Maxine said. "I have a class to teach. Think about the things I've said, and the things you learned here at Warfield. I'm confident you're equipped to make the right decision."

Barb didn't feel confident at all. In fact, sitting here in her childhood bedroom, it was all too easy to recall the insecurities and uncertainty she'd struggled with growing up. Back then, she'd been certain that once she got far enough away from Cut and Shoot, she'd never have to feel that way again.

How wrong she'd been! She gripped the phone until her knuckles whitened, and tried once more to make sense of her warring feelings. This was supposed to be so simple. She and Scott would have a good time, then she'd go back to her normal life and use the lessons she'd learned to find a man who was a good fit for her. Someone who shared her interests. Someone who wouldn't expect her to change.

Instead, she'd fallen in love with Scott—a set-in-his-ways cowboy. Maybe Scott wouldn't want her to give up her business or become the perfect rancher's wife, but there'd be subtle pressure from others—her mother, and people in town—who wouldn't understand why a woman would want anything more than a home and maybe a partnership in her husband's business.

Thinking about it all made her stomach hurt. She took a few deep breaths. She needed to focus on something else for a while, give herself time to gain some perspective.

She pulled out her cell phone and hit one on her speed dial. "Powerful Images, this is Eveline, may I help you?"

"Eveline, it's Barb. How are things going there?"

"Everything's fine. Are you having a good time on your vacation?"

Not right now, she thought. "I'm fine. Listen, how did Walt's meeting with Mr. Simmons go?"

"Oh, it went great. Mr. Simmons loved all the ideas. His lawyer is looking over the agreement right now."

"Don't let him debate the decision too long. Walt should call him first thing in the morning."

"Would you like to talk to him? I can see if he's in his office."

"No, that won't be necessary. Would you give me Mr. Simmons's number?"

"Oh, uh, sure." She heard the soft click of computer keys as Eveline called up the database. "Are you going to call him?"

"I'll just say hello, let him know how glad we are he's going to be doing business with us." A call from the owner would impress him. It would be just the thing to seal the deal.

"Here it is." Eveline rattled off the number. "Oh," she added. "Don Richelieu called. He wants to set up a meeting as soon as you're back in town. What should I tell him?"

"Schedule him for next Monday."

"But I thought you were going to be gone another week."

"I've changed my mind. Three weeks is long enough to be away." What had she been thinking, leaving her business so long? Her employees and her clients needed her to be there. "I'll call you when I've confirmed my reservation. Goodbye."

She hung up with Eveline and prepared to call Walt's new client. What a relief to be able to focus on work, and forget about messy emotions for a while. Work was something she knew she was good at. Everything else was a lot harder to handle.

SCOTT KNEW he shouldn't have said anything to Barb about moving back to Texas. If the tables had been turned and she'd tried to talk him into going to California, he'd have balked, too. But he hadn't been thinking straight in those moments after making love. Maybe his blood hadn't worked its way north to his brain yet, or maybe he'd been so caught up in how good it felt to be with her, how right, that he hadn't taken into account she might not feel the same way.

He was in love with Barb. Truth be told, maybe he'd never really stopped loving her, though he'd done his best to forget about her. This time he'd fallen hard and fast and what felt like forever. He was scared and elated and half-crazy over it, but he'd never been more certain of his feelings for a woman. The idea that she might not feel the same way hurt.

He told himself he could deal with this. He'd take it slow. Give her time to own up to feelings he was sure she had. When he looked into her eyes, he saw the same kind of wonder and passion he felt. All he had to do was wait for her to be ready to admit it.

So he wasn't prepared when she pulled her car up beside the corral where he was working the next morning and rolled down the window. One glance at the suitcases piled in the back seat made his stomach knot. In a flash, he was twenty-three again, watching her drive out of his life the first time.

"Where you headed, beautiful?" he asked, faking a smile, trying to keep his voice casual.

"There's been an emergency at work. I have to get back."

"You're leaving?" The idea deflected off his brain, refusing to sink in.

"I have to." Dark glasses hid her eyes, but the tightness around her mouth told him she wasn't happy. About leaving, or about him?

He gripped the edge of the car door and leaned in toward her. "Call me when you get in. I've got an auction I have to be at next week, but maybe after that I can fly out to see you."

"No." She put her hand over his. "I've had a wonderful time with you this week. It's been…amazing. But I think we'd better leave it at that."

"What do you mean?" He stared at her, anger and confusion warring. "Just, 'so long, it's been great knowing you.'" How could she do this to him a second time? How could he have been so naive as to let it happen?

"I don't mean it like that. It's just…" She looked around, as if she expected to find the right words written across the side of the barn.

"Just what?"

"Look, I'm not the kind of woman you need. I'm not the simple country girl or the perfect cowboy's companion, or anything like that. I don't want to live in a small town—especially this small town—ever again. And I don't want to move my business or sell it or anything like that. I'm good at what I do. I'm proud of it. I believe I'm really helping people. If I try to leave all that behind—even for a man I love—I'll be losing a big part of myself."

"Nobody said you had to leave it behind. I just thought—"

She patted his hand. "I know. But it's better this way. I'm sorry."

She started to press the button to roll up the window, but he reached in and grabbed her wrist, stopping her.

"You said what we had was special and amazing and a lot of other words, but all I want to know is, do you love me?"

"Yes." She swallowed, and spoke again, her voice stronger. "I do love you, Scott. But I don't think that's enough. Not to trust our whole future to." She looked down at his hand on her wrist. "I have to go or I'll miss my plane."

He wanted to tell her to hell with her plane. He wanted to drag her from the car and spend the next few days or weeks or however long it took convincing her they belonged together. But all he did was release her and step back. "Have a safe trip," he said, words he'd have muttered to any stranger.

She rolled up the window, turned the car around and drove away. He swayed on his feet, a sense of *déjà vu* rocking him off balance. Eighteen years ago, Barb had accused him of ignoring her dreams, of only thinking of what *he* wanted.

There was truth in those words still. But he wasn't the same man he'd been eighteen years ago. Barb's dreams were important to him now, too. If only he'd found a way to show her that before he'd let her drive out of his life a second time.

He pressed his forehead against one of the solid timbers forming the corral, feeling the splintering wood against his skin, smelling the acrid odor of sun-warmed creosote. His eyes stung and a bitter taste filled his mouth. He supposed if he could cry or rage he might have an easier time of it, but that wasn't his way. He'd just stand here awhile, letting the pain batter him, taking it until he could straighten and go on again.

EVELINE MET BARB at the airport. "You really didn't have to interrupt your vacation," she said as she followed her boss from the baggage carousel toward the parking garage. "Everything's been running smoothly while you were away."

"I didn't want to take a chance. Besides, it was time for me to come home." Barb tried a smile. "Didn't you miss me?"

"Of course." But Eveline didn't return the smile. "Are you all right? Your eyes are all red."

"Airplanes are so dry. It irritates my contacts." The half hour she'd spent locked in the lavatory, weeping, had nothing to do with it. She knew she was doing the right thing, getting away from Scott, but that didn't make it hurt any less.

When they arrived at the office, she was surprised to find Walt waiting for her. "Hello, Walt. Is there something you needed?" she asked.

He followed her to her desk, his expression grim. Odd, he was usually a happy, outgoing guy. One of the reasons customers loved him. "Mr. Simmons told me you called him yesterday," he said.

"Yes. I wanted to make sure he was happy with the plan you presented him."

"I'm sorry you feel you have to double-check my work like that. I thought by this time you trusted me to handle a client on my own."

She looked at him, taken aback. "I do trust you, Walt, I merely wanted to—"

"You wanted to make sure things were done your way."

She blinked. "What did you say?"

He shook his head. "Frankly, I was amazed when you said you were going to be away a month. I thought maybe it was a sign that you were finally putting faith in your employees. That you were beginning to see you couldn't do everything now that the company has grown larger. Obviously I was wrong." He laid an envelope in front of her.

"What is this?"

"It's my resignation." He turned to leave.

"Resig— Walt, wait!"

But he'd already left. She sank to her chair and took a deep breath. The way to approach problems in business was to think rationally. Break them down into components. Obviously, Walt was insulted that she'd called his client without consulting him first. She could see how that might look like a lack of confidence in him on her part. But she hadn't intended it that way at all.

Powerful Images was her company. Her name was on it, for goodness' sake. She had a right to stay involved, to make sure everything was handled properly.

Things were done your way. The impact of the words pressed her back against the chair. Walt made her sound like some sort of control freak. *I don't want to live in a small town… I don't want to move my business or sell it or anything like that…* The words she'd said to Scott came back to her. I, I, I—never thinking about what *he* might want. What anyone else might want. Thinking like that might inconvenience her. It might mean she'd have to bend, when she'd spent so many years fighting to realize her vision of the life she wanted.

But what kind of life was that, if it left you alone, and even your employees didn't like you?

For the first time Maxine's words about compromise really hit home. Before, Barb had heard them as a call for *other* people to compromise—Scott, her employees, whoever was being too stubborn to let her have her way. With a heavy heart, she realized how much her own refusal to give in on anything had damaged her.

She picked up the folder at the corner of the desk, the

one labeled Stockholders' Meeting. It contained notes for the presentation she was going to make to the stockholders in two weeks.

She'd said Powerful Images was her company, but the truth was, it now belonged as much to the stockholders as it did her. She had to please them now, as well as herself.

Eveline knocked on the door. "Can I get you something, Ms. Powers? Coffee, or tea?"

"No." She stood. "I—I'm not feeling very well after all. I think I'll go home and lie down."

And think about what being a success really meant, and the changes she needed to make.

CHAPTER NINE

Two weeks later

BARB BREEZED INTO the office. "Good morning, Eveline."

Her assistant looked up, smiling. "Did you have a nice ride?"

Barb deposited her riding helmet on the bookshelf and sat down to take off her boots. "It was great. Just the thing I needed to clear my head before the meeting." Since she'd discovered the stable two miles from her house she'd been riding several mornings a week. The exercise and fresh air were great stress relievers.

"Is everything set up for the stockholders' meeting?" she asked.

"Carmen is printing the agendas now. The caterer will be here at one with the refreshments for afterward."

"Great." That left plenty of time for her to shower and change and go over the notes for her presentation.

"Ms. Powers?" A handsome young man stopped at her office door. "You wanted to see me?"

"Yes, Walt. How did the meeting with Mr. Simmons go?" It had taken an abject apology and the promise of a big raise to convince Walt to withdraw his resignation, but it had been worth it. The man was a great asset to the company; she wouldn't forget that again.

"Great. He loved your suggestions."

"They were your ideas. I just tweaked them a little."
She pulled off the second riding boot and set it beside
the first. "You're from Houston, aren't you?"

"Me and my wife both. Our families are still there."

"I'm curious. How did you end up on the west coast?"

"I went to college here. She came for a job." He
shrugged.

"Do you ever think about moving back there?"

He laughed. "All the time. This is great, but...Hous-
ton is home, you know?"

She nodded. "I'm from the Houston area myself."

"No kidding. Guess we can have our own little Texas
contingent out here."

"You'll be at the stockholders' meeting this afternoon?"

"In the front row, heckling you." He gave her two
thumbs up.

She laughed and stood. "Thanks for the warning."
She turned to Eveline. "I'm going to get cleaned up
now. Anything I need to address before then?"

"The mail is on your desk. I don't think there's
anything urgent there, though."

She leaned over and sorted through the pile of letters
and junk mail on the blotter. One heavy cream-colored
envelope caught her eye. She flipped it over and read
the engraved address on the back flap. Ms. Maxine
Warfield.

Smiling, she slit open the envelope and pulled out a
monogrammed note card.

I believe your stockholders' meeting is today. I
hope the event is a great success for you. I have a
spot on my wall reserved for your photograph. I
hope you will send one soon. I would be curious

as well to know how things worked out on your
visit to Cut and Shoot.
Regards,
Maxine Warfield.

Barb tucked the card back inside the envelope and
slipped it in her desk drawer, then headed for the private
bathroom attached to her office. What had she learned
on her trip back home?

She'd learned that in her drive to make her vision of
a perfect life, she'd gotten in the habit of trampling over
people, of discounting their opinions and ways of doing
things if they didn't agree with her own.

She'd learned the value of relaxing and delegating.

She'd learned what it was to love a man in spite of,
and even because of, his differences—how someone
else's strengths could make up for your own weaknesses.

And she'd learned how the wrong actions, and the
wrong words, could separate you from the one you most
wanted to be with.

She stripped off her clothes and stepped into the
shower, closing her eyes as she leaned into the spray and
thought of Scott. Though they hadn't spoken since she'd
run out on him two weeks ago, she still loved him as
much as ever. She wasn't sure what to do about it, but
he was one of the loose ends in her life that needed
taking care of. As soon as she worked up the nerve, she
was going to call him. He might tell her to go jump in
a lake—she wouldn't blame him if he did. But she
needed that chance to find out if they'd said everything
they needed to say to each other.

"I WANT TO WELCOME YOU all here to the first annual
stockholders' meeting of Powerful Images." Barb

steadied herself behind the podium and addressed the auditorium full of people. Easily two hundred people were gathered here today. She'd addressed larger crowds before, but none that mattered more to her personally. "By purchasing stock in this company," she continued, "you've all made a powerful statement of faith in the future of this business.

"Today, I'd like to share with you some of my plans for the future of Powerful Images. Plans that will help the company to grow and continue to prosper, while strengthening our position in the marketplace."

She waited for the applause to die down, then continued, "As you may know, I started Powerful Images ten years ago as a one-woman company located in a small storefront in downtown San Diego. Since then, I've always been closely involved in every aspect of the company. Deciding to go public with the firm last year was an important and, I'll admit, personally difficult decision for me. I think any of you out there who have started your own businesses will agree. It's difficult to give up control of our babies."

Several people in the front row—including Walt and Eveline—smiled and nodded encouragingly. She glanced at her notes, then pressed the button to start the PowerPoint presentation. A slide showing a group of teen girls appeared.

"One of the things I often tell my clients is that they need to think about the image they present to their community. How they're perceived in their own neighborhood can have an effect on their image with their clients as well. Though Powerful Images has always been involved in our community, contributing to local charities and things like that, I've pledged to become even more involved in those efforts.

"To that end, I'm beginning a mentoring program for teen girls, to help them strengthen their own self-image and learn skills that will help them grow to be outstanding adults."

More scattered applause. She smiled. Some of the stockholders were probably wondering what charity work had to do with the bottom line.

"On the business front, I have some exciting announcements. First of all, while I will always be involved in Powerful Images, I want to take full advantage of the great talent pool we have here at the company. And in the coming year, I'm going to strive to bring in new talent as well. I'd like to announce a couple of key promotions.

"First of all, Ms. Eveline Walker has been my assistant and right-hand woman for the past six years. She knows every bit as much about the business as I do, and while I was away for a few weeks earlier this year, she proved extremely capable of overseeing operations here. I'm pleased to announce that I'm appointing Ms. Walker Account Manager in the San Diego office."

Eveline's smile could have lit the whole room. When Barb met Eveline's gaze, she was surprised to feel her throat tighten. Why hadn't she rewarded Eveline for all her hard work sooner?

Barb cleared her throat and addressed the meeting again. "I'm also appointing Walt Bradley as vice president of operations in Houston, Texas." She clicked to a PowerPoint slide showing Texas's largest city. "That's right. As of next month, Powerful Images is going national."

Hearty applause and whistles greeted this news. Barb motioned for Walt and Eveline to stand. When the room had quieted again, Barb held up a bound booklet. "You'll each receive one of these on the way out, with information about our new Houston location and a business plan for the coming year. It should answer any questions you may have. I believe that's all we have at this time. You're welcome to join us for coffee and refreshments in the next room."

As the meeting convened, Walt and Eveline joined her on the podium. "I don't know what to say," Eveline said. "Thank you."

"Human resources has all the information on your compensation package," Barb said, embracing her assistant. "I hope you'll be pleased." She looked Eveline in the eye. "You've done a great job. I'm sorry I haven't said that more often."

"So that's what was up with all the questions about Houston." Walt shook her hand.

"I wasn't sure if I should surprise you this way, but I didn't want to leak the news about the Houston office early. I hope you'll agree to the transfer."

"Agree? My wife will be thrilled. And I've been wanting to get back to Texas."

"I'm counting on you to do a great job for me there. We'll meet tomorrow and go over all the particulars. I'm looking forward to hearing your ideas."

"If I'm handling accounts in the San Diego office and Walt is in Houston, what will you do?" Eveline asked.

"I'll be traveling back and forth between the two offices," she said. "Plus, I plan to take some more time for myself."

"You deserve it," Eveline said. "You've worked really hard."

"Pardon me, but could I interrupt?"

For a moment, Barb thought her ears were playing tricks on her. That voice was so familiar.... But when she turned, there was Scott.

Minus his cowboy hat and dressed in a tailored suit, he was more handsome than ever. Only his polished ostrich skin boots betrayed his origins. "Scott! What are you doing here?"

He glanced around the room. "I came to the stockholders' meeting." He held up a prospectus. "As of two weeks ago, I own stock in your company."

"Two weeks?" She held on to the side of the podium, afraid her legs might not support her much longer. She really wanted to hold on to him, but was afraid he might not welcome the embrace. She searched his face, for some clue to his emotions, but he revealed nothing.

"Is there somewhere we can talk?" he asked. "In private?"

"Yes, of course. My office." She led the way through the crowd to a side door, then along a corridor to her office. She was dimly aware of others glancing in her direction, expressions ranging from curiosity to concern on their faces.

She opened the door to her office and headed toward her desk, then stopped and sat in one of the chairs in front of it, motioning for him to take the other. "It's good to see you," she said.

"You look good." He pulled the chair a little closer to her and sat. "You've been out in the sun a little, looks like."

"Oh. I've been riding a few times a week. I found a stable near here."

He nodded and looked around the room. "Nice office."

It wasn't like him to beat around the bush like this. "Scott, why are you here?" she asked.

His eyes met hers, dark and dangerous, at least to her peace of mind. "I'm thinking of buying a ranch in the area. I heard of a really nice one for sale."

"You are?" She took a deep breath, trying to slow her racing heart. "That would be great."

"So you're opening an office in Houston?"

"Yes, I..." She smoothed her hands down her thighs. "I thought about what you said and I saw I was being silly to dismiss the idea outright. I guess I was just...scared."

"Scared?" He frowned. "You never act like you're afraid of anything."

"Then you found me out. It was just an act." She managed to look at him again, emboldened by the gentle look in his eyes. "I thought compromise meant I had to give up something I loved. But I'm learning it means I can have that much more of the things that matter to me."

"I did a lot of thinking after you left," he said. "I used to get mad at people when they tried to talk me into doing something in a different way. I didn't see any need to change. But then I realized how much being with you had already changed me."

"It did? How?"

He took her hand and rubbed his thumb across her knuckles. She held her breath, waiting for him to speak. "You said something when you left, that I wanted a country girl. That's not true. I don't care what you do for a living. In fact, I'm proud of the way you've stood on your own two feet and built your own company and all. And I don't care where you live. Texas or California or Timbuktu." His eyes met hers. "I just want you. I love you and that's changed everything about me."

"I know just how you feel." She touched his cheek with her free hand. "I love you, too. I've been trying to figure out a way to ask you to try again. To give me— to give *us*—another chance."

"Marry me," he said. "How's that for taking chances?"

She caught her breath, heart pounding, afraid to believe her ears. "What did you say?"

"Marry me." He squeezed her hand. "We've waited over eighteen years to be together. I don't want to wait anymore."

It was a big risk. A huge one. But one she wanted to take more than anything. "I will marry you."

They kissed, a searing, sweet kiss that brought tears to her eyes. Happy tears this time. If he hadn't been holding her, she might have floated right out of her chair. She opened her eyes and smiled at him. "We can live on your new ranch."

"When we're in Texas we can stay at the old one. And you can decorate it any way you like."

She laughed. "What if I want flowers and lace?"

He made a face. "If it gets to be too much, I'll put a recliner and a TV in the barn."

"You won't have to put a recliner in the barn. And I promise not to try to change you. Too much."

"I've heard marriage changes people anyway."

"Love changes people. But only in the best ways."

They were still kissing when Eveline found them later. "I'm sorry to interrupt," she said, her cheeks flushing pink. "There's a man here from the paper. He'd like a picture."

Barb smiled and took Scott's hand. "Send him in. He can take a picture of me with my fiancé." She'd have a copy made to send to Maxine...along with an invitation to the wedding.

Everything you love about romance...
and more!

Please turn the page for Signature Select™
Bonus Features.

BOOTCAMP

BONUS
FEATURES
INSIDE

Deleted Scene from
Kiss and Make Up
by Leslie Kelly

*This "dinner" scene was cute and let me explore
Wyatt's relationship with his sister, Jackie.
Unfortunately, it didn't add to the story and only
distracted attention from the hero and heroine. So,*
4   *though I utilized a few tidbits that I liked in other
parts of the story, the bulk of it had to hit the
proverbial cutting room floor.*

TO HIS GREAT SURPRISE, his sister pulled off a nice
dinner. Considering Jackie had set off his fire
alarm every time she'd tried to cook something
last summer when she'd lived with him, Wyatt
was impressed. "They teaching cooking classes
at Boston University now?" he asked as he
pushed his plate away and leaned back in his
chair.

Jackie shoved a forkful of spaghetti into her
mouth and mumbled something.

Wyatt couldn't help laughing. "What's Ms. Devane going to think about our table manners?"

"Considering Ms. Devane just sopped up the last of her marinara sauce with her bread," Cassie said, "she's going to think they're just fine."

Her eyes were sparkling, her lips quirked in a smile. And Wyatt was simply unable to resist smiling back.

If someone had told him one week ago that he'd enjoy an evening in Cassandra Devane's company—in his own home—he would have thought they'd been smoking something other than a cigarette. But it had happened. She was here. And it was...okay.

Better than okay.

The three of them sat at his dining room table, with Jackie at one end and Wyatt on the other. His sister had insisted on playing hostess to the nth degree, meaning Cassie was seated at Wyatt's right hand. Very close to him. Close enough that he could occasionally feel the brush of her leg against his own under the table. Which might not have been good for his sanity, but was so wickedly enticing that he couldn't bring himself to care.

He was also unable to resist leaning toward Cassie. "You have tomato sauce on your chin," he said as he carefully wiped it away with his napkin.

She turned, her blue eyes widening as she watched him. He was close enough to note the redness of her lips from the wine she'd just sipped. "Thanks."

Jackie, Miss No-Sense-Of-Timing Sister, interrupted. "I am a big fat liar. Cassie made dinner."

Wyatt immediately pulled back and gaped at his sister. Jackie's face flushed pink, and beside him, Cassie groaned.

"Just in case, you know, you were thinking Cassie couldn't cook or something," Jackie said. She nibbled her lip. "Sorry. She was trying to make me look good."

Beside him, Cassie was clearing her throat and shaking her head at Jackie. Wyatt suddenly figured out what was going on: his little sister was trying to set him up with his own ex-wife! The irony couldn't have escaped Cassie, either, because she suddenly dug into her salad, picking out the cucumbers.

He sat still, watching her, flooded with an unexpected barrage of memories. Cassie had never liked cucumbers. Just like he'd never liked olives. The two of them used to do an automatic salad dance whenever they'd gone out to eat, dumping anything they wouldn't eat into each other's servings. Glancing down, Wyatt couldn't prevent a sharp stab of sadness when he saw the lonely black olives in his bowl...and the cukes in hers.

They'd lost something. Not just their marriage, not just their passion. No. They'd also lost their friendship...that automatic connection.

It was almost too much to stand. So he changed the subject. "Have you pulled your chemistry grade up yet?" he asked Jackie.

Good tactic. His sister immediately went on the defensive, distracting Wyatt from his painful memories. "I'm not going to be a scientist. Why do I have to get As and Bs in chemistry?"

Wyatt raised a brow. "Maybe because you can't graduate if you end up with a D?"

"Seems to me I know someone who flunked chemistry in college," Cassie mumbled into her wineglass. A quick glance over confirmed the laughter dancing in her eyes.

"I repeated it," he said quickly.

Cassie smirked. "Wow, and pulled it all the way up to a C. I guess science isn't exactly the Reston family 'thing.'"

"Nope. We're creative types." Wyatt hoped Jackie hadn't been reading too much into the conversation. She had to be wondering how Cassie knew so much about him.

He should have known better. Jackie had zoned in on only one part of the conversation. "You *flunked?* You big phony, and you have the nerve to give me crap about a D?"

He shot Cassie a glare. "Mouth."

She shrugged. "Just leveling out the playing field. It's a womanly art, you know." A secretive smile told him she was talking about more than the field between him and his little sister. But he didn't have a chance to ask her what.

"Talk about double standards," Jackie muttered.

He thought about that, wondering if he had been too tough on his sister. If so, it was only because he wanted the best for her...wanted her to get a top-notch education and make the most out of every chance she got. So she wouldn't have to struggle—to fight so hard for everything she wanted. As Wyatt had.

Still, maybe she was right. He hadn't been fair to her. Jackie was no longer his pesky eight-year-old sister, who'd cried when he'd left home to go away to college. "Okay," he said, "I'm going to keep my mouth shut. You pull the grade up enough to graduate and I won't say another word about how much you'll regret not knowing the classifications of beryllium and krypton."

"Alkaline metal and noble gas," Cassie immediately murmured.

Wyatt and Jackie both stared at her, jaws open.

"What? Who doesn't know that?" She sounded defensive.

"Me," Jackie said with a frown. "Heck, I thought krypton was just made up for comic books."

Wyatt chuckled. "Me, too."

"Cretins," Cassie said with a shake of her head. "Some of us actually paid attention in science."

"Maybe *one* of us," Jackie said, giving Wyatt a conspiratorial look.

"Yeah, maybe one." He nodded at Jackie, telling his sister everything was okay between them. And somehow it was. Cassie's presence had helped Wyatt see his relationship with Jackie through new eyes. More impartial ones. "Just try to get through this semester, okay?"

His sister's huge, lopsided smile told him she would do her best. "Deal."

Cy's Cajun-Fried Turkey and Corn Bread Sandwich
by Heather MacAllister

*In Sugar and Spikes, Cy makes exotic sandwiches,
one of which is Cajun-fried turkey on corn bread.
If you're ever lucky enough to come across one of
these sandwiches, abandon all diets and eat it. It's*
10 *food for the gods.*

    *First of all, understand that we're not talking
about a supersized bucket of extra-crispy breaded
pieces here. We're talking about dunking an entire
turkey into a vat of boiling oil. Gallons of boiling oil—
peanut oil, to be precise. (If you are allergic to peanuts,
substitute another oil.) There are commercial cookers
sold for just this purpose, but purists will fashion
something out of an abandoned oil drum. We do not
need to be purists.*

    *Once you acquire a turkey fryer, for heaven's
sake read the directions and follow the safety
instructions. When we fry turkeys, the cooker is
parked on level ground—that's a patch of bare dirt
far away from houses, decks, fences and anything
overhanging, including tree branches. We corral all*

pets and children and the cooker is monitored at all times by a sober adult with a fire extinguisher within reach. This is hot oil we're talking about. If it can fry a turkey, it can fry you.

Now it's time for a party! Call it a Turkey-Fry Open House. The cookers hold about four or five gallons of peanut oil, which is pricey, so it makes sense to fry more than one turkey at a time. Find out who among your friends and neighbors wants to fry a turkey and schedule cooking times. Ideally, you should heat up the oil and fry the birds one after the other. It only takes about thirty-five to forty minutes per turkey.

Hint: To determine how much oil you need, fill the cooker with water and lower a turkey into it (an unseasoned turkey—you don't want to wash away the seasoning). Add water until the level is one to two inches above the turkey. Remove the turkey and measure the water level. That's how much oil you'll need. Pour out the water and dry cooker *thoroughly*. Remember: water and oil don't mix.

Now the best part—preparing the turkey. You need to buy a fresh, never-frozen, ten–twelve pound turkey. No bigger than twelve pounds, or the oil will slosh over the sides and possibly catch the cooker on fire, turning it into a vertical flamethrower. Not good.

And this is where we part company with the traditional Thanksgiving stuffed bird. You're going to

make (or buy—but where's the fun in that?)
marinade that you will inject into the bird. You'll
need a syringe that they sell for just this purpose.
Here's my Cajun marinade recipe...

CAJUN MARINADE

2 tbsp Lea & Perrins Worcestershire sauce
5/8 cup apple cider
3/4 cup honey
1 bottle dark beer
1 tbsp Old Bay seasoning
1 tbsp allspice
1 tbsp onion powder
1/2 cup Creole seasoning, such as Tony Chachere's
1 tsp oregano
1 tsp thyme
1/4 tsp cayenne pepper
1/4 tsp ground cloves

Grind all the dry ingredients with a mortar
and pestle and mix with the wet ingredients, or
add all the ingredients to a blender and liquefy for
several minutes. Make sure there are no lumps or
the injector will clog.

Fill the syringe with the marinade and inject
into the turkey. You might not use all the
marinade, so pour some into another container
to avoid contaminating it. Move the needle

around as you inject to get the marinade into all parts of the turkey. Don't forget the legs, wings and thighs. Also be careful not to poke clear through the breast and inject into the cavity. That just makes a mess.

After you've finished, let the bird sit for an hour before frying. For best results, it should be room temperature prior to cooking.

Heat the oil to 350° F, or follow the directions on the cooker. When the oil is ready, wipe the turkey dry and tie the legs together, and either put the whole thing into a fry basket and dunk, or use a large hook to dip the turkey directly into the hot oil. Gradually lower the bird to avoid having the oil boil over. It takes about 3 minutes per pound to cook. Internal temperature should reach 170° F in the breast and 180° F in the thigh. If the turkey floats, it's way too done.

Caution: Even though I wipe the bird dry, some marinade always leaks out, so there will be splattering as the turkey is lowered into the hot oil. And *never* use a frozen bird. Sometimes, the fresh ones will have ice chunks inside. Remove these or the oil will splatter a lot.

Surprisingly, the turkey isn't oily or greasy. The deep frying seals the outside, leaving the skin crisp, and the meat moist and tender. Ideally, the bird should rest for about thirty minutes before carving, but you'll have to guard it.

And now for the bread part of the sandwich. This is a bread machine recipe:

YEAST CORN BREAD

1 1/4 cups milk
1 tsp Tabasco
3 1/4 cups bread flour
1 cup cornmeal
1 tsp allspice
3/4 cup grated sharp cheddar cheese
1 1/2 tsp salt
3 tbsp sugar
1 1/2 tsp bread-machine yeast
3/4 cup corn, cooked, drained and cooled

Add everything but the corn in the order recommended by your bread machine.

Notes: Set your bread machine for a basic white-bread cycle. This will be a short, dense loaf. The corn is added at the end of the kneading cycle. Machines usually alert you for late additions. Don't use a delay timer or a "rapid" cycle to bake the bread.

And that's it, because I'm not going to tell you how to make a sandwich. To tell the truth, I rarely get that far. There's usually a crowd in the kitchen waiting for hot bread and hot turkey. I cut and slice; they grab and eat. After that, I cook another turkey because that's the only way I'll get leftovers.

Enjoy!

Cut and Shoot Kaleidoscope
by Cindi Myers

When I tell people I grew up in Cut and Shoot, Texas, they invariably ask, "Is that a real place?"

Yes, Cut and Shoot is a real place, one I called home between the ages of fourteen and nineteen. My mother lived there until her death in 2004, and my brother still lives there. So I'll always think of Cut and Shoot as my hometown.

The next question everyone asks, after learning that it is, indeed, a real town, is, "How did it get a name like that?" Stories vary, but they all agree that the name evolved at the time of a local feud, probably around 1912. According to various sources, the feud was over (a) the design of a new steeple for the town's only church, (b) who would preach at the church or (c) conflicting land claims among church members. Seems folks took their side of the argument seriously and there may or may not have been violence involved. In any case, Cut and Shoot had a reputation as a rowdy place.

When I was a girl, the neighboring county seat of Conroe was "dry"—meaning no alcohol could be sold in the city limits. Cut and Shoot was in the "wet" part of the county, where liquor could be sold. So thirsty patrons flocked to the bars and taverns lining State Highway 105 in Cut and Shoot. As if to balance out the proliferation of bars, the church population had also increased by this time, so that there was roughly one church for every bar.

In addition to all the churches and bars, Cut and Shoot boasted a log town hall, a volunteer fire department, an elementary school, a little red post office and a combination convenience store/pool hall where I spent one summer learning to play pool. (Unbeknownst to my mother, who would have been horrified to learn her teenage daughter was hanging out in the local "joint"—though the most harmful thing I was exposed to there was the occasional secondhand smoke from other pool players.)

Cut and Shoot had miles of red-dirt roads where we rode our bicycles. In winter, the air smelled like pine smoke and damp leaves. In summer, the tang of creosote from the plant where they made railroad ties stung our eyes and noses. At night, the gas flares from the Conroe oil fields glowed orange above the towering pines.

We'd gather in a neighbor's yard to play a combination of tag and hide-and-seek in the dark, crouching in the shadows, then darting into the pinkish glow of the mercury-vapor yard light. When it was time to go home, we'd walk down the middle of the empty road, the asphalt still warm against our bare feet from the heat of the day.

In addition to yours truly, Cut and Shoot is the hometown of boxer Roy Harris and Miss America 1983, Debra Sue Maffett. Roy Harris was a boxing sensation in the 1950s. In 1958 he fought heavyweight champ Floyd Patterson at Wrigley Field in a match that captured the attention of the entire country. He lost that match, but went on to win a string of heavyweight bouts, until he was defeated later that year in Houston by the great Sonny Liston.

Debra Sue Maffett represented California in the Miss America pageant, but she was a graduate of my alma mater, Sam Houston State University, and had close enough ties to Cut and Shoot that for years there was a billboard at the city limits with her smiling photo and the words Welcome To Cut And Shoot, Home Of Miss America Debra Sue Maffett. She went on to become an award-winning broadcaster.

For years the city-limits sign announced the population of Cut and Shoot as 400. A check on the Internet tells me that number has grown to

1,158. When I visit now, I don't see many familiar faces. The creosote plant and the gas flares are gone, as is the billboard with Debra Sue Maffett's smiling face.

But Roy Harris is still there. He runs a boxing camp and was the Montgomery County clerk for many years prior to his retirement. The bars and churches are still there, too, and the log town hall. Pickup trucks still outnumber cars, and tourists still stop to have their picture taken in front of the city-limits sign.

And my memories are still here. Like my heroine, Barbara, I was a restless child, anxious to leave home and get out into the big, exciting world. I knew there was so much out there, waiting for me, and nothing could hold me back. On a hot summer's night, when I stand on my mother's front porch and close my eyes, I can still smell pine and creosote, and I can still hear a child's voice calling from her hiding place in the shadows, "Ready or not, here I come!"

Flirting 101
by Cindi Myers

Flirt\vi **1 a:** to behave amorously without serious intent **b:** to show superficial or casual interest or liking

Oh sure, Webster's makes it sound so simple and even unimportant. But we all know flirting can be the beginning of something bigger. Flirt with that cute guy at the party and months or years later, you could be walking down the aisle to your own happily-ever-after.

Or not.

Maybe you just want to flirt to have fun. An innocent flirtation, as they say. Whatever your intent, here are a few tips to help you hone your flirting technique.

1. Body language counts. Studies by social scientists have shown that 55 percent of first impressions are based on appearance and body language, 38 percent on your style of speaking and only 7 percent on what you actually say.

2. Make eye contact. Eye contact indicates interest. So, if you see a person who interests you, make eye contact and hold it for about a second. More than that and you may come across as rude, or send the wrong message.

Caution: women need to be especially careful here. Studies have shown that men often mistake too large a show of interest as a sexual invitation. (You were surprised to learn this, right?)

3. Get a little closer. In terms of personal space, people tend to treat a distance of four–twelve feet as a social zone where they are comfortable with casual acquaintances, business associates or even strangers. From eighteen inches to four feet is for more intimate relationships. If you move in close and someone looks uncomfortable, back away. But if they seem accepting of allowing you into their "intimate" zone, don't be afraid to move in.

4. Do as I do. Copying the posture and gestures of the object of your affection is one way to establish closeness. Obviously, you don't want to be aping them in an exaggerated way, but if you tilt your head when they tilt theirs, etc., it can lead them to feel you are like-minded and in harmony with them.

5. Reach out and touch someone. Touching is a very intimate gesture and its acceptability depends on the culture and the social setting. In general, men shouldn't make the first move. A woman can show interest in a man by lightly touching his shoulder. A light touch on the hand is even more intimate.

6. Say something. Forget about crafting a clever line. Studies have shown that innocuous comments on the weather, the setting, the occasion, etc., are just as, or even more, effective than clever lines.

7. Take your turn. Flirtatious conversation is like a tennis game, with the conversational ball lobbed back and forth. We've all been trapped with social bores who monopolize the conversation. Don't be that person.

8. Conversational turnoffs: Being overly negative. Talking only about yourself. Making only the most banal comments. Being overly personal or crude. Lack of enthusiasm.

9. Conversational turn-ons: Includes compliments, humor, playful teasing.

10. Practice makes perfect. So smile at your waiter. Make eye contact with the hunk on the train. Joke with the guy who sells you new tires. Flirting can be a fun hobby and who knows...it might even lead to something more.

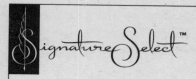
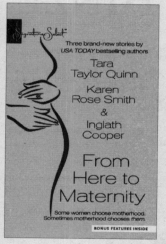

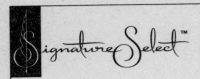

With these women, being single never means being alone

Lauren, a divorced empty nester, has tricked her editor into thinking she is a twentysomething girl living the single life. As research for her successful column, she hits the bars, bistros, concerts and lingerie shops with her close friends. When her job requires her to make a live television appearance, can she keep her true identity a secret?

The Single Life
by Liz Wood

HARLEQUIN®

Next™

COMING NEXT MONTH

Signature Select Collection
FROM HERE TO MATERNITY by Tara Taylor Quinn,
Karen Rose Smith, Inglath Cooper
Some women choose motherhood. Sometimes motherhood
chooses *them*. Enjoy this heartwarming anthology—just in time
for Mother's Day!

Signature Select Saga
HOT CHOCOLATE ON A COLD DAY by Roz Denny Fox
Despite their high-maintenance families and high-risk jobs, Megan
Benton and Sterling Dodge find plenty of ways to stay warm during
the blustery month of March.

Signature Select Miniseries
A LITTLE BIT NAUGHTY by Janelle Denison
Two sisters find blazing chemistry with the two least likely men of
all in TEMPTED and NAUGHTY—two sizzling page-turning novels
that are editorially connected.

Signature Select Spotlight
HER PERFECT LIFE by Vicki Hinze
Katie Slater's life is perfect. She's a wife, mother of two and a pilot
in the United States Air Force. But then she's shot down by the enemy,
left for dead by a man she trusted and taken as a prisoner of war in
Iraq. Now, six years later, she's back home...only home isn't there
anymore...and her perfect life has become a total mystery.

Signature Select Showcase
SWANSEA DYNASTY by Fayrene Preston
Built on the beautiful, windswept shore of Maine, the great house
of SwanSea was built by Edward Deverell as a monument to himself,
his accomplishments and his family dynasty. Now, more than one
hundred years later, the secrets of past and present converge as his
descendants deal with promises, danger and passion.